Long Ride to Limbo

by

Kit Prate

Long Ride to Limbo

Published by *Western Trail Blazer*
ISBN: 1456330233
EAN-13: 9781456330231

Edited and Produced by Rebecca J. Vickery
Cover Art and Production Consultation by Laura Shinn

Long Ride to Limbo is a work of fiction. Though some actual towns, cities, and locations may be mentioned, they are used in a fictitious manner and the events and occurrences were invented in the mind and imagination of the author. Similarities of characters or names used within to any persons past, present, or future are coincidental.

Praises for *Long Ride to Limbo*

"Kit Prate is my favorite living western writer... I've read *Long Ride to Limbo*, and it's one of the best western adventures I've ever read. A good, old-fashioned story but written in a very contemporary, breezy style, with characters that come galloping right off the page!" — *Peter Brandvold*

"Kit Prate tells a taut, action filled story and tells it well. I highly recommend *Long Ride to Limbo* for any fan of the western novel." — *Frank Roderus, two time Winner, WWA's Spur Award*

Other Titles by Kit Prate

Miss Annie
Kill Crazy
Widow
Bound for Texas

Dedication

This is for James Stacy,
whose remarkable portrayal of Johnny Madrid
on the TV show, *Lancer,* remains indelibly etched
on the hearts of his many fans. And
also to Antigoni, for being there.

Visit James at www.jamesstacy.com

FOR GOLD, GOD, AND GLORY...

Hernando Cortez had lived his life. The glory had been his. God watched over his deathbed and the gold...its secret soon to be buried with him.

CHICAGO: 1893

Ten years ago, Reese Sullivan rode away from his wife, Vanessa, and young son, Trey. His reasons were strong. And his own.

Vanessa used her beauty and cleverness to land kind, generous Wes Underwood. Now he is dead. Ambushed and robbed. With a cold irony, she has come to Detective Reese Sullivan to hunt down the killers.

Now an angry and bitter son will ride with the father he hates to avenge the death of the father he loved—and something more; to reclaim what was taken from his stepfather's body—the key to a vast and fabled treasure.

They will embark on a perilous journey that will pit father and son against unseen enemies, natural disaster, and each other—while back home the women they love face an unimagined danger at the terrifying end of the

LONG RIDE

TO

LIMBO

Prologue

Spain, 1547

The old man was dying. He lay on a narrow cot in the small tower room of his Seville *palacio,* his once powerful frame emaciated by the same jungle fever that had plagued him body and mind in his robust prime. Still conscious, he was aware of the clutch of robed men who stood in a grim circle at the foot of his bed. A faint, sardonic smile touched his lips as he listened to the prayers that came each time he took a feeble breath. The droning incantations of the priests were filled with promises of forgiveness and pledges of life eternal in some vast realm beyond the firmament; in that place they called the Kingdom of God.

Spain's God, the failing *conquistador* mused: a stern God, according to these pious saints, a God that demanded a price for his pardon. Gold offered up as penance for a man's many sins. He laughed, the throaty cackle ending in a wet cough that rattled deep in his chest, his eyes brightening as the monks scrambled to his side. His body had betrayed him, but his mind had not. He knew what these holy men wanted, what it was they were really seeking. It was not the state of his mortal soul that concerned them, but what they thought he would give to buy that soul out of Purgatory and into their God's heaven.

These priests were no different than the others who had tormented him during his long illness. His weak-willed daughters and the covetous whelps he had sired by his Castilian whore— they wanted his treasure. *They wanted to know the secrets that would lead them to his treasure.*

Amused at the irony—even he had been unable to re-find his hidden plunder—Cortez felt the need to laugh again, but this time the sound did not come. There was only silence; silence and the soft northwestern wind that brought the scent of the sea to him. Through the narrow, open window beside his bed, he could see the setting sun, and he turned his head to receive its warmth. The bright yellow ball that hung on the western horizon like some great gold medallion mocked him, as cold and as distant as the jungle fortune he had lost. He stared at it for a long, long time. The men who attended him now knew nothing of God, he mused bitterly. He knew. He had seen the living god in New Spain, and had slain him. *Montezuma*; God-king of the Aztecs, one deity above a hundred nameless others.

Like the cursed frog. Even now, Cortez could see it. The crouching, golden idol that had marked and guarded the entrance to a sacred well deep in the jungle beyond Tenochtitlan. It was an ugly thing, staring at him from atop its pedestal with wide, unseeing eyes. And yet, he had felt it watching, stoically observing the carnage as his soldiers slaughtered the temple priests who had conspired to hide and withhold Montezuma's richest treasures. Fourteen long dead and buried Aztec holy men, not unlike the fourteen shrouded zealots who now stood around his bed. The Aztecs had prayed, too.

Their gods had listened.

Gasping, Cortez suddenly rose up from his cot, his right hand uplifted as if gripping a sword poised to strike out at some unseen enemy. Once more, the stench of human blood filled his nostrils, and he heard the screams. And from a dark corner of his tortured mind, the elusive golden frog returned.

The great amphibian rose up from the damp earth where he had buried it, its unblinking eyes still hooded with the blood of the slain Indians. Like some gargantuan hunchback, it tottered upright on webbed hind feet and lumbered toward him, as tall as a man, its long tongue flicking in and out, in and out, in search of an unholy meal.

Cortez screamed. *"El rana! El rana de oro!"* The frog! The gold frog!" He sensed himself being drawn by the beast, the creature's long tongue curling around his neck to pull him deep into darkness, the stifling sweet smell of the long dead priests reaching out to engulf him.

The frog swallowed. Hernan Cortez was dead. Once more, Montezuma's gods had defeated him.

Chapter One

Arizona Territory,
Spring, 1893

A lone female condor made another full circle above the abandoned Southern Pacific water stop just north of Yuma, its four foot wings lifting, with effortless grace, to catch the updraft of hot air from the desert floor. Gaunt and hungry from its constant hunt for food for its newly hatched chicks, the big bird scanned the cluster of wind-worn buildings with a keen hunter's eyes, an instinct for impending death drawing the creature in a tighter spiral as it silently glided closer and closer toward the parched ground. And then, its quarry sighted, the vulture began her ominous wait, and danced slowly on the warm, spring winds.

Trey Underwood stood hatless beneath the high-noon sun, unaware of the big bird that circled noiselessly in the bright sky above him. Eighteen, standing a hair above six feet in flat-heeled walking shoes and wearing a twill suit that had been tailored to fit his lean build; he looked out of place in contrast to the dilapidated buildings at his back.

The young man's hands were knotted behind his head, his fingers laced together just above the collar of his white shirt. Sweat rolled down his neck to be dammed by his cramped thumbs, the loss of water intensified by a hot sun that burned into the thick mass of dark hair lying in wet curls on his forehead and above his ears. A gut-tearing frustration turned the perspiration cold as it streamed down his back, and he tensed in an effort to suppress the shudder that threatened to course through his long frame.

Trey was not alone. Four men stood before him. To his right and directly behind, the black apparition of a fifth man loomed as a bloated twin to his own slim silhouette. The distinctive image of a short-barreled Sharps carbine seemed to grow from the fingers of the dark specter at his back, the business end of the rifle mere inches from the nape of his shadow's neck.

Grim reality made the cold steel seem even closer, as if the tip of the barrel were actually touching his flesh. Trey stood stock still, his blue eyes becoming the color of smoke as he read the anguish on his father's bloodied face. Two men held a drooping Wes Underwood between them, the third *desperado* breathing hard as he stepped back to survey the effects of his grim handiwork. "It's no use, *patron*," the big man panted, lifting a gloved fist wet with blood and spittle. "The *abogado* ain't going' to talk."

The dark silhouette at Trey's right seemed to shift. The Sharps, however, never wavered. "You must be losing your touch, *hombre*." The man's voice was muffled by the cloth that obscured his mouth. "Or perhaps you've forgotten everything your mother's people taught you." There was a brief silence, and then the cold flash of sun against honed steel as a Bowie knife sliced through the air. The blade was buried to the haft between the grinning Chato Mendoza's feet, and he bent to pick it up.

Helpless, Trey watched as one of the outlaws used a free hand to grab a fistful of Underwood's hair. The Mexican jerked the man's head up and back, a soft laughter sounding as he watched his companion trace a crude half-circle with his forefinger across Wes Underwood's white throat. A dull, red ridge appeared in the finger's wake, the width of the man's ragged fingernail. "*Aqui, compadre*," he directed. He nodded at the place he had marked. "Cut him here."

Mendoza stood before Wes Underwood, relishing the man's torment and taking his time, as if really considering the other's suggestion. He held the knife between his flat, callused palms, the tip of the blade resting against the cushion of flesh beneath his rigid, right forefinger, another sudden burst of blue-white light flashing against the polished blade when he used his thumbs to rotate the knife a single time. The glowing rectangle of reflected sunlight crawled up Underwood's exposed throat and across his pale face, Mendoza sadistically focusing the cold fire on the attorney's eyes and keeping it there.

The voice at Trey's back sounded again. "I saw him cut a woman once, Underwood." There was a mesmerizing quality to the man's soft voice, the words slightly accented but precise. "One quick slice and he opened her up like a suckling pig. She was trying to stuff her intestines back in when he dumped a bottle of *tequila* in her belly, and still alive when he set it on fire.

"It's not a pretty way to die, lawyer. And it takes a long, long time."

Mendoza was laughing again, softly, something obscene in his joy at being reminded of past pleasures. Momentarily panicked, Wes Underwood began to bargain for his life. With the grinning giant that stood before him, and now -- even more urgently -- with the ominous figure that stood behind Trey's back. "For God's sake, man!" he pleaded. "I can't tell you what I don't know!" It was a lie, poorly told in a brief moment of throat-drying fear, a man's desperate attempt to hold on to a fortune in gold he was sure existed; a treasure that bound him with dreams of wealth so great that he was willing to die for it. Even now.

Suddenly, Mendoza stopped laughing. There was the subtle sound of steel slicing through starched cotton. "For God's sake..." Underwood screamed.

Trey Underwood watched as the knife ripped through his father's white shirt just to the right of the buttons. From the belt upwards, in the blade's wake, a narrow rivulet of blood appeared, bright red and spreading. Instinctively, as much as the rough hands on his arms would allow, the older man backed away from the pain. He stared down at his taut belly, aware that he had been cut, his knees going weak, and then tensing as he realized the wound was only deep enough to draw blood. He swallowed, mentally cursing the dryness in his mouth that made his tongue feel thick and unmanageable, his keen attorney's mind working. He was no good to them dead, and that thought consoled him and gave him courage. He pulled himself erect, his posture changing as his spine straightened. "Kill me," he breathed, "and you'll never find it. You won't even know where to begin to look..." A grim smile pulled at the corners of his mouth. For the first time during the long hours since his captivity, Wes Underwood felt in control.

There was a long moment of tense silence, followed by the sound of a single, whispered curse. The next words came more distinctly. "Again, Chato. Cut him again."

Instantly, a second stream of crimson appeared against Underwood's white shirt as the big outlaw did as he was told. Gritting his teeth, the attorney steeled himself against the sting of his own sweat as it mingled with the blood. The defiance gave way to a quiet anger. He had searched too long and too hard for the secrets that would lead him to Cortez' hoard to give it up now. He shook his head, the words coming in a hoarse whisper filled with a mocking contempt. "Go to hell."

Trey Underwood stared at his father in confused disbelief, in awe of what he was seeing and hearing. What he presumed in the beginning to be nothing more than a botched robbery attempt suddenly took on a new perspective, one he did not comprehend. Nothing made any sense, and there was no logic in the things that had happened. *Were still happening.* His gaze shifted to the two red tears in his father's shirt. "Give them what they want, Father," he murmured. When he saw the stubborn refusal in the man's eyes, he tried again. "Please."

Wes Underwood shook his head, as much at his son as the men who held them prisoner. "You don't understand, Trey," he began. There was nothing patronizing in this tone or his words, only something akin to apology, as if he were simply trying to make amends for their current troubles. "I..." He never had the chance to finish.

Impatient, the man at Trey's back spoke one more, cutting him off. "Chato. Again." For the third time, the lumbering half-breed did as he was told. He played a sinister game at first, touching the end of his blade to the tip of Wes Underwood's nose, deftly letting go of the knife and catching it in one swift move. This time, the keen edge of the Bowie was turned downward, and he began his upward cut with the broader tip of the dulled point.

Trey Underwood could stand it no longer. He heard the blade as it tore into his father's shirt, and saw a sudden spurt of dark, blue-red blood, the flow faster and more profuse than before. Rage—the mind crippling inner anger he had always fought to control—swept him, and he swore. "Bastards! *You bastard sons of bitches!!*"

The young man moved with the agile grace of a trained athlete. In one swift move, he swung back and out with his right arm, ignoring the pain as his elbow collided with the barrel of the Sharps carbine still aimed at the base of his skull. Head down, he dove across the narrow strip of sand separating him from his father.

He knew at once the terrible agony of an impetuous and foolish mistake. Midair, he attempted to shift his weight, and failed. His left shoulder slammed into Chato Mendoza's legs just behind the man's knees.

There was a sound; a muted blending of several sounds into one agonizing chorus of shared pain as Mendoza's knees buckled and the man suddenly lurched forward. Wes Underwood's whispered *Trey*, and the half-breed's startled *o-oo-oof*; Trey Underwood's own involuntary groan as his head snapped sideways and back from the force of impact and the long tendons in his neck stretched tight at the base of his skull and across his shoulders.

The distinct noise of steel slicing into cloth and flesh, an ominous thud sounding as the flat, rawhide bound haft slammed against Wes Underwood's bottom left rib, the blade penetrating his gut.

And then silence.

Caught off guard, the two outlaws who held Wes Underwood between them grappled with the sudden shifting of the man's weight. Their fingers grabbed at his sleeve as he sagged heavily and pitched forward, prayer-like, onto his knees. A quick surge of adrenaline stiffened his back, his eyes widening in shock as he clutched at the source of the pain that burned at his flesh, and his hands closed around the knife.

"My God, Trey," he rasped. Disbelief marred the older man's smooth forehead, deep lines forming as his dark eyes focused on the growing circle of blood spilling over his fingers and onto the ground. "*My God...*"

In agony, a tormented Trey Underwood watched as his father attempted to pull the blade free. It was like a dream, a slow moving nightmare that was abruptly resurrected from a haunted childhood. He shook his head in a vain attempt to drive the dark, familiar vision away. The remembered dream faded, but the reality of what was happening refused to be purged from his sight, and he watched as his sire's blood-slick hands slipped impotently across the leather-covered haft. "Dad..."

With great effort, Wes Underwood lifted his head. He stared at his son for a time, his eyes dimming as he struggled to stop the flow of blood that poured from the wound in his stomach. His mouth opened and closed, his lips forming distinct words that had no sound. *Tell your mother...* Then, shaking his head in denial of what was to come, he raised his hands, the palms crimson and wet. Reaching out, he fell forward, one hand grasping at some unseen thing just beyond his reach, the other brushing gently across Trey's cheek.

Outraged—angry at his own stupidity—Trey Underwood swore, a long stream of vile obscenities echoing across the desert floor as he struggled to regain his feet. Fists clenched, he turned, and felt the air beside his head swept aside in a blaze of white fire. Pain ripped at his left temple, the deafening roar of the Sharps coming a split second after the small puff of gray smoke. The noise died as quickly as it came, and the young man felt himself lifted up off his feet. Unhearing, he hung suspended for what seemed a long time, drifting in a strange limbo between the heavens and the earth, and then descended swiftly into his own private Hell. He hit the ground like a child's puppet cut loose from its string.

Unable to move, Trey felt himself being searched. Rough hands dug at the pockets of his trousers and his shirt, the same hands turned him over onto his stomach as the crude probing continued. Sound still eluded him, the voices of the men who frisked him distant incoherent rumblings that echoed and re-echoed deep within his throbbing head. He lay still, aware only of the sensation of being touched without being able to respond. Finally, they were finished with him, and there was only a minute degree of pain when a square-toed boot slammed repeatedly into his side just below his kidneys.

The dull thudding stopped, then resumed from a different place as a half-dozen shod horses were kicked into a run dangerously close to his head. Trey felt the earth beneath his belly rumble until the sound faded, and another quickly took its place. A peculiar odor reached out to him then, his sense of smell heightened by his dulled senses of sight and sound, and he felt a faint flutter across his cheek. There was a cool serenity beneath the dark shadow that spread across his face and upper body, and for a moment he welcomed the respite from the sun.

Until the big condor crooked its neck and bent low to seek out his breath, and he smelled the putrid odor of something dead deep within her throat.

Sure of an easy meal, the vulture tore at Trey's bloodied cheek with its sharp beak, narrowly missing his eye. He cried out, the primeval instinct for survival filling him with renewed strength as he struggled to raise up on his hands and knees. Balancing himself on one arm, he swung out at the big bird, lashing out hard at her naked head. Twice he came away with a handful of feathers from her massive breast, both times knowing the pain of her sharp talons across his forearm as she fought back.

A final, vicious peck caught Trey just above his ear. He fell, his arms akimbo as he sprawled face-forward onto the hot sand. Cautiously, the hen circled him, cocking her head at the sound of his breathing. And then, using her wide wings for balance, she hopped away, this time in search of a less troublesome prey.

Semi-conscious, only partially aware of what was happening, Trey Underwood lay still and silent. Somewhere behind and beside him, he heard the hollow *thunk, thunk* as the big bird feasted, the noise a hypnotic tattoo as rhythmic as a muffled drum. Weak from the loss of blood and sick from the heat, the young man was lulled into a deep, fitful slumber. The noise of the vulture's feasting continued. *None of this is real*, he told himself. He buried his head beneath his arms. *It's just a dream, a bad dream.*

He wished to God he could wake up.

* _ * _ * _ * _ *

Chicago, May 1893

Reese Sullivan stood on the concrete sidewalk in front of the main office of the Diamond Detective Agency, his head tilted well back as he stared up at the ten-story, red brick building. A gray Stetson shaded his slate-colored eyes, the hat a strange topper for the store-bought suit that looked too new and too small.

Somewhere in his early forties, Sullivan looked younger. He was more fit, more formidable than the gaggle of white-skinned men who passed him—at some distance—on either side. They would approach him, falter, and then—intimidated as much by his unusual height as some intangible sense of foreboding—sidestep to give him more room. So he stood, like an angry wasp being passed on both side by a wary army of piss ants, wondering why in Hell any man in his right mind would ever consider working in, or even visiting Chicago; let alone spend his life living among all the noise and confusion. *The seemingly endless mass of people.*

Sullivan bunched his shoulders and plowed through the steady stream of pedestrians that blocked the doorway. The ornate portico with its Greco-Roman columns and plastered facade offended him, almost as much as the people who crowded beneath the archway in an attempt to escape the wind. From the small lobby, he watched them for a time, staring after them as they scurried down the street clutching their hats or their skirts, only to duck into a similar alcove for another rest before beginning it all again. And all around them, the swirl of city soot and grime, industrial dust-devils blowing through man-made canyons devoid of a single blade of grass. There was an ugliness Sullivan could not forgive, something man had willingly created, and dared to call art.

"Reese!"

The word echoed down the broad marble stairway, full of good humor and genuine affection. Sullivan turned. It spite of his sour mood, he smiled. The fact that a woman secretary sat at the desk in the small receiving room just to his right did nothing to temper his greeting, and without the expected amenities, he moved past her into the corridor separating the cluster of partitioned cubbyholes that served as offices for the clerks and desk-bound investigators.

"Son-of-a-bitch, Roy," he called. "You're beginning to look like all the rest of them!" The nod in the general direction of every other man in the room was neither subtle nor politely subdued.

Joyfully anticipating a continued sparring, Royal Torrance drew himself up to his full five-foot-ten and remained where he was at the top of the stairs. "And just what the hell is that supposed to mean!?" he demanded. Like Reese, he was playing to the audience of fledgling detectives still foolish enough to believe in legends. He descended a single step: Moses coming down from the mountain.

Reese was already mounting the stairs by two. He reached the place where Torrance was standing, and even one step below was still taller, his chin well above the other's nose. "What it means, Royal," he began, the earnest words of mock reproach just as loud as he intended, "is that you're as lily white as some Kansas City whore. Damned near as prissy, too." Judiciously, he raked Torrance bottom to top with a deliberate eye. He reached out, fingering the man's immaculate starched collar. "I can remember the time when you weren't afraid to get out in the sun," he intoned, "or scared of getting a little dirt under your fingernails."

Torrance snorted. "And *I* can remember when you knew how to read," a handful of papers appeared from inside Torrance's vest pocket, the tell-tale, yellow stock used by Western Union, "and maybe even how to tell time." Dropping the papers over the side of the staircase like so much confetti, he thrust out his right hand. "You're late, Reese," he groused. "By about five years."

Sullivan accepted Torrance's hand. "It could have been six," he countered. Shoulder to shoulder, the two men climbed the stairs.

Torrance's office suite was on the third floor. He was breathing hard when they reached the landing, but trying vainly not to show it. His first words came in a series of short puffs. "I—don't—know—why you're so damned hard-headed about a once a year trip back to the home office," he panted. He stood aside as Reese entered the room, and then followed him inside. The quiet nagging continued. "Once a year," he repeated. It really had been five.

If Sullivan was paying any attention, or if he felt any remorse, it didn't show. A subtle change had occurred in him, as if he realized he was no longer on stage and the brash bravado of a *dime novel* detective no longer necessary. Already, he had helped himself to a cigar from the silver humidor on Torrance's neat desk, and was earnestly seeking a bottle. He paused in his rummaging just long enough to pilfer a match, the air around his head turning blue-gray and thick with the smell of sulfur and rum-soaked tobacco. The smoke followed him as he resumed his search for the brandy.

The decanter was in the bottom drawer of the oak filing cabinet behind Torrance's chair. Sullivan withdrew the jug and a single glass, which he filled to the brim. The drink went down easy in one swallow, and was followed by another. "The bank in El Paso wouldn't honor the last voucher I turned in for wages and expenses, Roy. You care to tell me why?"

Torrance wiped his nose with his fist. "It was the only way I could get you here without sending out the troops," he mumbled. He avoided Sullivan's eyes and nodded toward the portrait on the wall opposite the windows. "Besides, the old man wanted to see you."

Reese Sullivan turned his head. He saluted the grim countenance in the painting, but not with his glass. "Then he should have rolled out that Pullman car he's so damned proud of, and pointed it south." His eyes narrowed as he studied Franklin Edward Diamond's painted likeness, the canvas one of five hung at various points throughout the building. *Three hundred pounds of flab topped by a bullish head with rat-like eyes and a bearded chin.* The man was nothing at all like his father, who founded the agency, as stark in contrast to his sire as he was to the portrait of Lincoln hanging beside him in a twin, gilt-edged frame. Turning his back on his employer's scowling icon, Sullivan continued. "Pinkerton does it. Pinkerton even manages to maintain a string of offices west of the Mississippi.

"And he pays his men their due." He put his glass back on the desk, upside down. "On time."

Torrance felt a sudden need for a drink. "Christ, Reese," he breathed, taken aback. Sullivan was the only one of Diamond's agents who had never signed a long term employment contract. In that, he was the one exception to the rule; an exception Diamond only grudgingly allowed. It was also, Torrance knew, a situation Diamond wanted desperately to rectify. "You haven't had an offer? I mean..." He paused just long enough to pick up Sullivan's glass, refill it, and drain it in a single swallow. He regretted it was only brandy, and not something more potent. "I'll top anything Pinkerton has offered," he said finally, well aware that in this, Diamond would support him. "Anything."

Reese Sullivan was at the window. As big as Royal Torrance's office was, it was still too small and too confining. He stared out across the city to the haze above Lake Michigan, concentrating on the sky instead of the rooftops. "I had to take a note at the bank to cover this year's planting of the hay and grain crops, Roy. And then I had to hire extra help to play midwife to mares *I* planned to watch foal. That wouldn't have happened if the money Diamond owes me had been paid when it was due, Roy."

Visibly relieved that it was only the money on Sullivan's mind, Torrance found a glass of his own and poured two more drinks. "We'll clear up the note, Reese, and make good any interest. But you've got to give a little, too. The agency pays you a good salary and I don't think even Pinkerton could top your bonuses. All we ask is that you sign a contract like the rest of the men, and once a year, like everyone else—"

Sullivan cut him off. "Does *everyone else* get the same kind of assignments, Roy?" His voice took on a quiet, close-lipped monotone. "Have you got one other man who plays it so close to the edge? Without the fancy suits, the two dollar steak dinners, and a backup man waiting in the alley?"

The reminder that Diamond Detective Agency wasn't always so selective about its clientele or the methods used to serve their needs was the last thing Royal Torrance wanted to hear, or to acknowledge. "Your choice, Reese," he said defensively. He gestured at the plush surroundings, the oak paneling, carefully grouped chairs, and matching settee. "This could have been your office. Your job. Diamond offered it all to you after his father died, long before he ever considered me. You know it, and—more importantly—*I* know it," he fumed. His voice softened, but the anger was still there. "Just like I know you could still have it, if you just said the words."

"I didn't want it then," Sullivan retorted, the words coming through clenched teeth as he realized they had this same quarrel before—fifteen years before— "and, if I remember right," a scathing sarcasm added bite to his words, "neither did you! I sure in hell don't want it now!"

"Then what the hell do you want?" Torrance shot back. It was funny, how a man's pride could still smart after so long a time.

"To do the job the way I see fit," Sullivan answered. "Without all the interference, or the demand for a yearly pilgrimage to pay homage to a man who won't even talk to me face-to-face, but expects me to come more than a thousand miles to kiss his ass!" It was good to finally say the words. *To have the opportunity to say them.* "Pinkerton has made an offer, Royal. And you can tell Diamond I'm damned well going to consider it!"

Torrance knew instinctively that the man was not lying or playing games. Eager to end a conversation that was close to becoming a real argument, he skillfully maneuvered around the subject they had been discussing and marched headlong into a new plain. His tone conciliatory, "Will Cody is in town, Reese. Has a whole arena to himself, just off the Midway at the Fair. *Buffalo Bill's World Congress of Rough Riders.* Whatever the hell that is." This time when he poured the brandy, his hand was steady. "Might be worth the price of a drink to look the old reprobate up, talk over what used to be." Memories of another time and another place evoked a broad smile, and Torrance chuckled. "Hell, Reese! Maybe he'll offer both of us another job!!"

There was the sound of soft laughter as Sullivan shared Torrance's unspoken memories. Once, to snare a Chicago physician with a Bluebeard's penchant for wealthy widows, they had joined Cody's show, following the murderer East and then on to Europe. Reese surreptitiously arranged for the man and his new wife to have box seats at a show in Germany, and then—as part of the act—roped the unsuspecting killer, and made his arrest. The stunt provided Cody with extensive front page publicity on both sides of the Atlantic. Intent on making the capture a part of his act, the old rake offered both Reese and Royal Torrance a job right on the spot, with glorious promises of a future in show business that would rival even Annie Oakley's.

Reese, who had been deathly ill during the entire voyage to England—and even sicker when they crossed the channel to the Continent—was less than gracious in his refusal of Cody's offer of instant fame. Still, he had enjoyed the time he spent with the man, genuinely respecting his ability to work a crowd. Prince or pauper, Bill Cody knew how to entertain them all. Sullivan had no doubt that, drunk or sober, the old rascal was still the best show in town. "If we're going to buy that old faker a drink, it had best be a whole bottle," he observed dryly. "Which he'll finish all by himself."

Torrance stifled a hearty laugh. "I don't think so," he grinned. "Last I heard, the little lady had hung him out to dry." Considering Mrs. Cody's size and reputation, the euphemism was redundant. Even now, well into middle age, she had a notorious streak of jealousy and a temper to match. More than one wag had suggested she could outshoot, out swear, and outfight the legendary frontiersman. With one hand tied behind her back. "They've been here since before the Fair opened, and Cody hasn't stepped out of line. Not once."

Sullivan was trimming the end off another cigar. "Have you been there?" His glass was on the desk again, upside down.

"To the Fair?" Torrance joined his friend at the window. "Opening day," he answered. "We're handling some of the security for the foreign exhibitors. It's really something, Reese. Civilization from the beginning to the end," he philosophized. "Statues and fountains, buildings right out of some..." He searched his memories for a comparison. "They look like temples, Reese. Stereopticon pictures of the ruins in Italy and Greece come to life.

"And that's just the beginning. The rest..." Torrance's round face became almost boyish. "Electric lights—the President turned them on—and a mechanical, moving sidewalk."

Hearing Sullivan's loud guffaw, he continued. "Swear to God, Reese! You get on the damned thing, stand stock-still, and it moves you right along." A smooth, sweeping motion with his hand marked the path. "And the Ferris wheel! Sixty people to a car the size of a Pullman sleeper," this time his fingers traced a generous arc, sweeping downward to close a large, upright circle. "You can see the whole shindig from the top of that thing, you have the guts to do it, and for only fifty cents!"

The man was beginning to sound like a carnival barker, a puckish grin creasing the skin behind his ears as he continued. His voice lowered to a hoarse stage whisper, like that of a genuine bally-hooer trying hard to sucker the last dollar out of some barefoot, country boy too shy to sample his wares. "They've got a dancer there, Reese. A woman they call Little Egypt. Wears nothing but veils and does some dance they call the *hootchi-cootchi*." He traced the outline of a woman's torso with both hands, lovingly, as if she were beneath his fingers, his palms cupping imaginary breasts the size of large melons. "They say she dances naked at private parties the bigwigs throw over at the First Ward." His voice dropped. "And anywhere else, if you've got the scratch."

Reese was trying hard not to laugh. "What I've got, Roy, is an itch." He scratched the back of his neck with a crooked finger. "The same one I get every time a man gets behind me. Or tries." The smile that had been pulling at the corner of his mouth disappeared just as quickly as the jovial fire that had momentarily warmed his eyes. "What do you want, Roy?" he breathed. "Just what the hell does Diamond want?"

There was a noise as Torrance exhaled, and another as he took a deep breath. Carefully, he averted his eyes and moved away from the window. "I already told you, Reese," he answered. "He wants to see you and to talk to you about..." The words stopped. Torrance shook his head, inwardly relieved that he didn't have to lie. He really didn't know what Diamond had in mind; at least nothing beyond the man's wish to have Reese firmly under contract. He found his voice the same instant he was able to meet Sullivan's gaze head on. "Diamond will be here in the morning, Reese. You can talk to him then." He grinned and nodded at the clock. It was precisely twenty-eight minutes before noon. "I meant it about Bill Cody, and the bottle. We time this right, we can all drink our lunch. With a little luck, maybe even our supper!"

The feeling that he was going to be ambushed still gnawed at Sullivan's belly. It was clear Torrance had nothing more to say. At least, not now. Sullivan stared at Torrance for a time, and then decided it didn't matter. "Who's buying?" he asked.

For the first time since they entered his office, Torrance's smile was real. A bit of the old defiance burned far back in his brown eyes. It had been a long time since he and Reese had been on a tear. *Too long.* "The old man," he answered slyly, jerking a thumb at the picture on the wall. "For the drinks, and any other damned thing we might choose to go after."

The thought that Diamond would be footing the bill filled Reese with a degree of satisfaction. Chicago boasted some of the finest restaurants in the world, and an even greater number of first class bordellos. And, of course, Bill Cody. Eager for the sights and sounds of horses and the men who rode them, Sullivan opened the door and ushered Torrance into the hallway. "You're going to pay top dollar for the pleasure of my company, Roy, and for that bottle you're going to buy for Cody. I just want you to know that, before we start."

Torrance patted his pocket to make sure he had his wallet and checkbook. "I've got an expense account, Reese," he laughed. "I don't intend to buy even one drink. But Diamond sure in hell is going to know that you're in town!"

Chapter Two

They visited Cody's show outside the Exposition Grounds twice. Once in time to buy the man lunch, and again several hours later when a spring squall blew in off Lake Michigan and flooded out the evening's performance. They were just in time to drag the man away from the clutches of an enthralled young advocate of Free Love who had been passing out tracts at his front gate. She proved to be a persistent little thing. Undaunted by the weather, she unsuccessfully tried to follow them through the mud to Torrance's private carriage. Not all that unattractive, in spite of the starched bloomers and bobbed hair wilting beneath the onslaught of an almost torrential rain.

Reese couldn't help but think of the young woman now. He was seated at a felt covered poker table in the back room of one of the more expensive sections of *Hinky-Dink,* McKenna's First Ward Bagnio, watching as Royal Torrance and Bill Cody bid for the favors of a questionably attractive whore long past her prime. It didn't make sense, paying for something they could have had for free only two hours before, and he shook his head. He dismissed the men and concentrated on his cards.

He had just filled out a king-high, heart flush when Torrance collapsed into the empty chair at his right.

"Cody beat me out," he moaned. "The old bastard gave her a look at that California nugget he wears on that gold chain around his neck, and she damn near carried *him* up the stairs." Ignoring the disgruntled glares of the other card players, he sighed, still talking to Reese as if they were they only ones there. "That's twice he's snookered me, Reese." He held up two fingers, using his other hand to bend one down when he saw four, and continued. "That little Chinese girl down on State Street, and now this one." The second sigh was even more audible than the first. "Pats that one on the fanny, gives her a little bow like she's some damned imperial princess, kisses her hand, and then..." He belched, the air around him ripe with the stink of Kentucky bourbon, and rattled on. "I swear to Christ, Reese. If God ever gave the old son-of-a-bitch half a chance he could bed the Virgin Mary herself, and all the nuns in Chicago. Twice!"

Reese Sullivan inhaled sharply and closed his eyes. He folded his cards and laid his forehead against his clenched fists. It seemed an appropriate time to pray, but he couldn't recall any incantations that fit the situation. There they were, in a bordello owned by a Catholic Irishman—a true son of the old sod—with half the Irish-Catholic population of Chicago in attendance and intent on doing a full Saturday night's worth of sinning, and Torrance...

Sullivan's melancholy musing was cut short by the wicked, distinctive snap of a switchblade. It sounded above a silence that descended over the entire room with Torrance's last utterance. More ominous because the knife was heard but not seen. Reese laid down his cards, and put his palms flat on the table. "He's drunk," he said to no one in particular, yet speaking to every man in the room. As if drunkenness were an excuse for the man's stupidity.

The dealer sitting to the left of Reese smiled. The glint of gold showed as his lips pulled back in a grimace which resembled a pit bull's snarl. "My big sis is a nun," he said nonchalantly. "And little Mary, the baby? She's goin' to be takin' the veil herself, come fall." The smile grew.

Suddenly, the gambler leaned forward in his chair. He extended a long fingered hand and fondled the braided leather headband on Sullivan's flat-crowned Stetson, the hat laying between them on the table; a grey wall that was about to be breached. When he spoke again, the words came softly, and they were harsh. "I don't like your hat, mister," he whispered, flicking the Stetson's brim with his forefinger. The brogue was so thick now it made the words almost indistinguishable. "It's an ugly thing, not fit for a real man. I did not like it when you came in, and I really don't like it now.

"As for your friend with the foul mouth and dair-ty mind..."

Torrance sat stock-still in his chair and considerably more sober than he'd been only moments before. "Reese," he breathed. His eyes darted around the room, touching each face, marking each pocketed hand.

Suddenly, a voice boomed out of the near darkness in the far corner. It carried throughout the room, grandly articulate and full-throated. "I believe, sir, you have made a disparaging remark about Mr. Sullivan's hat." Bill Cody, still dressed in the white buckskins he had worn during the afternoon matinee stepped into the circle of light that radiated from the high ceiling. The soft glow of the single electric bulb hanging above the felt-covered table bathed his face and smoothed the wrinkles, making him look young again. He swept his own Stetson from his head, the shoulder length silver hair beneath it as iridescent as a halo, and held it up for all to see. "If you find fault with Sullivan's hat, then, by God, sir, you find fault with mine!"

All hell broke loose as Reese Sullivan used Cody's interruption to his advantage. With both hands, he pulled the card table hard to the left, unseating the man with the gold teeth and knocking him from his chair. He followed the table across the floor, aiming the toe of his boot at the man's mouth. It was a vicious blow, calculated to strike the gambler directly below his nose, and his aim was true. There was a shower of blood and spit, followed by the sound of the man's gagging as he choked on his own teeth.

A raucous shout sounded, and a dozen more thugs entered the melee, the burly crew McKenna employed to keep order in their own peculiar fashion. Dust flew as brass knuckles glinted beneath the artificial light from the incandescent bulbs, the thick metal laced intricately across fists the size of small hams. They struck out with regimental efficiency. Reese ducked, and knew a certain degree of sweet satisfaction as the blow that was aimed at his right ear glanced off the end of Torrance's already bleeding nose. He turned his head to hide the smile, but it was too late.

"And just what the hell is so damned funny?" Torrance roared. He danced away from another punch and whirled to meet his adversary, his anger at Reese fueling the fist he brought up from his knees. The blow landed solidly, and he stepped back to take aim with another. The second punch was just as good as the first.

Reese had his own problems. Stunned, he watched as the giant of a man who faced him picked up an unconscious comrade from the sawdust littered floor. The big Irishman tucked his friend under his right arm, no compassion in him as he aimed the man's bald pate at Sullivan's belly. He charged, moving across the floor with a grace and speed belying his size, the human torpedo he held cradled in his arms as rigid as a piece of steel.

It appeared for a long moment that Sullivan was rooted to the spot where he stood, and seemingly ignorant of Torrance's shouted warnings to look out. Counting, he inched imperceptibly to the left.

There was a pillar at Sullivan's back, a twelve-by-twelve shaft of solid oak. The shadow of the foot-wide beam loomed at an angle across the floor just to his right. He kept to the left outside edge of it for a time, and then—suddenly—stepped into its dark path. Gracefully, he spun sideways.

The lumbering giant, his hands still full, was unable to stop. Miscalculating, he bolted past what he thought to be an easy target, so close he could feel Sullivan's breath on his cheek, and slammed into the rigid beam. He hit head on, stopped dead in his tracks, his still unconscious burden shooting from beneath his crooked arms to sail with deadly precision into the cluster of now silent goons who had been cheering him on. They went down like ten pins, a tangle of feet and arms, the air filled with the sound of their cursing.

Sullivan wasted no time. He grabbed Torrance's sleeve and pulled him toward the nearest door. "Bill!"

Cody was holding court from atop a billiards table, his stance that of a fencer. He waved to Reese with a pool cue, leapt from the table, and then used the stick to clear his own path to the doorway. He paused just long enough to swing the cue at the one overhead light still burning. The tinkle of glass sounded, and the light died as the room dissolved in darkness.

The old man was laughing when he joined Reese and Torrance in the alleyway. "I forgot how much fun you were to have around, Reese!" he panted.

Sullivan was leaning against the damp brick wall, welcoming the wet cold against his back. There was, he mused, something seriously wrong with a man who chanced having his brains beat out without the benefit of being paid for the risk, especially when that man was fool enough to consider it amusing. He took it as a sure sign of Cody's approaching senility. "Fun," he snorted. Tasting blood, he instinctively licked the small cut at the corner of his mouth. "I'm getting too old for this kind of *fun*."

Torrance's chest rose and fell in tempo with his friends. He spoke, the words coming in short puffs as he gradually regained his breath. "The whore, Bill," he said finally. "How was she?"

"Not as old as she looked," the other answered. Even in the darkness, it was obvious he was smiling.

"Jackasses," Sullivan groused. He led the way out of the alley. "Between the two of you, you don't have the good sense to pour piss out of a boot!"

Torrance ignored his friend's show of bad temper. Sullivan had been winning at the poker tables, and the majority of those winnings were behind them on McKenna's floor. "You know, Reese? It's just like it used to be. You getting into trouble, me getting you out!" He laughed and poked Sullivan in the ribs. It felt good to pretend they were young again.

Sullivan's retort was lost in a chorus of angry shouts. The noise of a dozen pair of feet echoed in the alley behind them, the sound coming closer.

Together, the three men sprinted toward the buggy that waited just beyond the entrance to the dark passageway. Spurred on by their pursuers, they cleared the litter at the end of the alleyway and bolted for the open door of the curtained brougham.

Except for Torrance. The liquor he had consumed was working again. He let out the blood-curdling cry of a young Comanche buck that had just taken his first coup, and gamely attempted a running mount on a horse placidly standing still.

Sullivan and Cody stopped dead in their tracks, too winded to laugh, yet unable to stop the laughter from coming. Together, they watched in awe as Torrance sailed up and over the back of the bay gelding on the leeward side of the two-horse hitch, and beyond. He landed in the street, belly flopping against the pavement like a squashed toad.

Cody reached him first. One eye on the alley, he helped the man up, grateful when Sullivan arrived to bear the bulk of Torrance's considerable weight. "If he was sober, Reese, he'd be dead!"

"If he was sober," Reese countered, still laughing, "he might have had the good sense not to try!" Together, they lifted Torrance into the buggy, and ordered the driver into a full run.

* - * - * - * - *

The sound of distant thunder roared through Reese Sullivan's head, the noise of the rain against the window pane as intrusive as the stop-and-go *whir* of a large fly he could hear but not see. Even something simple such as turning his head to look at the clock pained him. He cursed himself for drinking more than he had intended. At an age when he should have known better, he abused a forty-two year old stomach with the drunken gusto of a twenty-year old brain. And now he was paying for his folly.

Gingerly, he turned his head a second time. Royal Torrance was in the chair at his right, looking every bit as sick as Reese felt. It took two tries before Reese could get the words out, and even then they sounded as if they were wrapped in cotton. "Did we ever eat? Or did we do all of this on an empty stomach?"

The mere mention of food, eaten or uneaten, turned Torrance a sickly blue-grey. He rubbed his tender belly, puzzled that there was as much pain without as within. "The last thing I remember," he began, "was you and Bill Cody challenging that jackass with the gold teeth to a duel over your damned hats." Head cocked, he hesitated. "At least, I think that's what I remember." His brow furrowed as he tried to recall what really transpired, and more pain followed the lines across his forehead.

"It wasn't any duel," Sullivan whispered. "And damned sure nothing that Cody and I started." The memory of Torrance's attempt at a running mount brought a smile. "The big trouble came around midnight, when we finally poured Cody out on the floor of his wagon back at the fairgrounds. That's when the old Sioux decided he wanted to go play, too, and you promised we'd take him."

Torrance had trouble remembering, and then it came back to him. They had escorted the old chief through some of the most infamous bordellos in the city before settling in for the night at the fashionable house run by the Kentucky-bred Everleigh sisters. Too sick himself to do anything but hope, he watched as the old buck sated a sexual appetite that had been dormant for twenty years.

It was a humbling experience, watching a seventy year old man with no teeth gum his way through a half-dozen of the most elegant and experienced whores in the city. The ancient renegade seemed to grow stronger and more virile with each tumble, and at three in the morning was still going strong. In the end, Torrance had to pay the bartender fifty dollars to slip the chief a drink laced with *chloral hydrate*, and it still took the combined efforts of Reese and two others to get him into the carriage.

Torrance cast a jaundiced eye in Reese's general direction. "You know what that old horse thief told me when I asked him why—after all the places he's been with Cody—he waited twenty years to have a woman?" He didn't wait for Sullivan's reply. "That he didn't know you could buy one just for the night, and he wasn't about to risk getting stuck with a passel of white wives." He slowly shook his head, as if afraid his brain would collide with the sides of his skull. "And me thinking the old fool had made some holy vow to the great Manitou; a promise that he'd abstain." He sounded disappointed that he hadn't really been responsible for the man's fall from grace.

Sullivan laughed. Between the Irish Catholic rowdies at McKenna's and the Sioux spirit man from Cody's show, Torrance had succeeded in offending most of the known gods, and all of the existing saints. "I take it back, Royal. You haven't gotten soft, you've just gone crazy."

Torrance waved the remark aside. "And you, Reese?" The man's mood had changed, and the playfulness was gone. For all the frolicking the night before, Reese Sullivan had yet to succumb to the wiles of even one soiled dove, and Torrance wondered why. "You gone crazy, or just too old to give a damn?" He smiled, but there was a certain edge to the words, as if he had felt—and resented—Reese's moral scrutiny.

"I make it a rule never to pay for what I can get for free, old son." Sullivan's tone matched the other's. "Not trouble, not advice, and sure in hell not women."

Wisely, Torrance let it go. Reese Sullivan had known the torment of a bad marriage, something Royal Torrance had momentarily forgotten. He made an attempt at idle conversation: "Diamond's late," and cast a baleful look at the grandfather clock in the corner. Everything from the slow drag of the brass pendulum to the audible jump of the minute hand seemed magnified by the oppressive silence.

Sullivan stared at the door. He hadn't expected Diamond to arrive on time. The man's lateness was all part of the ceremony, the long wait he always imposed on any of his men who had fallen into disfavor. His tardiness was in direct proportion to his disdain for those he felt had wronged him. So far, Sullivan's transgressions of the past five years amounted to exactly two hours and forty-five minute of enforced penance, and he had no doubt it would round out to an even three.

He stood up, working the kinks out of his long legs. It was a short walk to the place where Torrance kept his supply of brandy, and he poured himself a generous drink. "Roy?" He held up the bottle.

"How do you do it, Reese?" the other marveled. He shook his head, at the man and the offer of the drink.

Sullivan turned and busied himself with the glasses. In spite of a sore gut telling him otherwise, he knew he hadn't drunk nearly as much the night before as Torrance thought. "You get used to it after a while," he lied. "Half the men I hunt end up trying to hide themselves in the bottom of a bottle of rotgut." That much was true. And while those men got drunk, and careless, Reese Sullivan stayed sober.

Just as he had when he and Torrance had gone on their first tear. And for the same reason. To find out what the man knew, and what it was he was so obviously trying to avoid. Only this time it hadn't quite worked. He decided to try once more. "I asked you yesterday, Roy. Twice. What does Diamond want from me?"

Torrance continued to stare at the clock, his eyes moving back and forth with the swinging pendulum. "He just wants to see you." The words, mentally rehearsed many times in the past week, came automatically and without much thought. It was so easy to give voice to a lie when the words contained even a germ of truth.

"And that's all?" Reese held his glass of brandy between his palms, working it back and forth, his gaze concentrated on the amber liquid as it whirl-pooled away from the center of the snifter and climbed up the sides to be dammed by the beveled rim. He kept playing with the glass, defying gravity and making a game of keeping the liquor contained.

Torrance had given up watching the clock. His eyes closed and he rubbed his forehead at the bridge of his nose with his clenched fist. When that didn't help, he began massaging his temples with the fingertips of both hands. "Look, Reese," he began weakly. It was obvious he was struggling with the words in his mind before he said them, his shoulders drooping as he weighed each one and put them in the proper order. There was a lot to consider. His friendship with Reese, and the long years they had been together as partners in the beginning.

His future with Diamond. Finally, after a long silence, he cleared his throat, still trying to fight the conflicting feelings that had tormented him the night before. "I'm getting married," he began. Standing up, he faced Sullivan, his gaze fastened on a spot on the wall behind the man's head, desperately wanting Reese to believe he was looking at him. The ruse didn't work, and he averted his eyes. "It's Clarise Diamond, Reese."

Sullivan's right eyebrow rose slightly. Franklin Diamond had never married. He had chosen a martyr's role instead, raising his younger brother's children and lavishly supporting his dead brother's wife. The relationship had been a source of more than one off-colored joke: most of them told by Royal Torrance. "The old man's niece," Reese breathed. He waited for Torrance to say more, and when the man didn't, he prompted him. "And...?"

"Diamond offered me a partnership."

Sullivan inhaled, and there was a subtle change in his posture. "For a man who said he didn't want any of this," he encompassed the entire office with an ambiguous wave, "you're doing a damned good job of making sure you aren't going to lose it." His eyes narrowed as he stared across at the man he considered his best friend. "How much of this hinges on me signing a contract?" he asked quietly.

Torrance was unable to hide his relief. There was a visible change in him, an easing of the lines of his face. "I'm going to marry Clarise, regardless, and still get the partnership. But your signing will go a long way towards showing Diamond I've got some real influence with you—something he's never had—and it'll make a hell of a difference with the other men. In all these years, Reese, I've never asked you for a favor. I'm asking you for one now."

Sullivan was quiet for a long time. "The woman," he began. "Do you love her?"

The question—the fact that it was Sullivan asking—caught Torrance completely off guard. Still he didn't hesitate in his answer. "Enough to want her to know I'm marrying her for herself, and not because her uncle dangled a carrot in front of my nose. That's why I need your signature on a contract. To give me some leverage with Diamond, and to show Clarise there are things I can accomplish that..."

"...Diamond can't." Sullivan finished. "You're talking about seven years of my life, Royal." That was the standard term of a Diamond agency contract.

Torrance was at his desk. He opened the top drawer and took out a sheaf of papers. "It's a good contract, Reese. An immediate and substantial raise, all the work the Agency can throw at you and none of it east of the Mississippi, unless you want it." He grinned, remembering their trip to Europe with Cody. "And nothing across the big water."

Sullivan was turning the pages. He hated the complex *party of the first part* jargon lawyers always used so capriciously. "And the trips East?"

Torrance thumbed through his own copy, and displayed the appropriate clause. "Every other year, with the meetings in the off years to be held at a place you choose. You get to negotiate salary the same way, and the Agency has no claim on any..." for want of a better word, the man used the one he personally felt conveyed the proper meaning, "...*indulgences* you might lay claim to along the way." Torrance was obviously pleased with himself and the way he had anticipated the points Sullivan would choose to dispute.

"And Diamond is willing to go along with this?" Sullivan was finding it hard to believe that Diamond could have seen the document, let alone approve it.

"He doesn't want to lose you, Reese," Torrance declared truthfully. "In spite of all the hell he raises."

Sullivan was still hesitating. All things considered, it wasn't a bad contract, and a hell of a lot better than the one Pinkerton offered him. And Allen Pinkerton made it more than plain he didn't want his men involved in any incidental bounty hunting. But there was still a feeling deep in the pit of his belly. He shrugged the discomfort away as something left from the night before. "I'll sign, Roy," he said finally, taking the pen from Torrance's desk. It was more a gesture of friendship and trust than a complex business decision.

There was an awkward silence as both men struggled with their mutual inability to put their feelings into words. Sullivan was the first to speak. "You can consider it as my gift to the lucky bride," he grinned. "A small token of esteem for her new husband, and none at all for her bastard of an uncle."

Jubilant, Torrance put his signature on the line below Sullivan's. "I could have shit gold bricks and it wouldn't have impressed the old man as much as this!" he declared. He offered Sullivan his hand.

Reese's fingers closed around Torrance's in a firm handshake more binding than any written contract. "At least it's improved your mood," he observed wryly. The expression on Torrance's face was one of puzzlement as much as query. "Ever since I got here, you've been acting like you had a bug up your posterior," Reese continued. "Or something stuck in your craw that needed to be spit out."

Torrance nodded a single time, a gesture of acknowledgment he knew would suffice as an apology. "I needed a favor, Reese. I didn't know how to ask."

The mechanism in the tall clock began its slow grind, and the chimes sounded. It wasn't until the clock struck just one time that both men realized they had been in the office for five hours. The appointment with Diamond had been for eight a.m. Precisely. Intent on leaving, Reese Sullivan picked up his hat. Royal Torrance did the same.

The door to the outer office opened. Franklin Diamond stood at the threshold, his massive bulk dwarfing the two agents at his back. He dismissed them both with a perfunctory wave of his hand, never looking at them, and waited to speak until he sensed they were gone. "It's been a long time, Reese," he greeted affably. He still had not moved.

Reese put on the Stetson. "Five years," he answered. *One year for each hour Diamond had kept him waiting.*

His point made and understood, Diamond nodded. He moved across the room, shouldering his way between the two men as he made his way to the chair behind the desk. He sat down and settled in, the sound of metal against metal as the springs in the chair compressed, the annoying squeak continuing as he rocked back and forth. "Well?"

Reese's eyes narrowed as he suppressed a sardonic grin. In the twenty-five years he'd known Diamond, the man had never changed. The arrogance was as profound as it had ever been.

Torrance was the next one to speak. He was gloating, and it showed. "Reese signed the contract, Frank. As a personal favor to me." He laid the papers on the desk.

Diamond's jaws tensed at Torrance's use of his first name. He made a long ceremony of reading and re-reading the document, and then, as if conceding, initialed each page. And then he smiled. "I'm pleased, Royal, to know I'm as keen a judge of a man's abilities as I've always been." The smile grew. "I had every confidence you could persuade him to sign." Somehow, the words did not sound complimentary.

The rumbling in the depths of Reese Sullivan's stomach began again, more earnestly than before. He exchanged a harsh look with Royal Torrance, and then swung his gaze back to the man in the chair. "Meaning?"

Diamond had taken out an ivory nail pick. He leaned forward, his elbows on the desk; his gaze fastened on the tips of his fingers. "Why, nothing, Reese. It's a give and take world. We've both made some compromises, some mutual concessions." He dug a bit of oily grime from beneath his thumb nail, and wiped it on the blotter on Royal Torrance's desk. "You do understand the terms of the paper you just signed?"

Reese nodded. "No work east of the Mississippi, no assignments on the continent—or anywhere else overseas—no yearly meeting here in Chicago." He watched the man's face. "No interference in my outside work, salary negotiable every other year. Same time *I* pick the place for our meeting." Silently, he vowed to make it someplace as close to Hell as he could get.

Diamond nodded. "For the next seven years." He smiled briefly at Torrance, whose mood had darkened considerably, and then swung his gaze back to Reese. "Realizing, of course, that when I give you an assignment falling within the provisions you just outlined, you cannot refuse it."

Sullivan inhaled. A passage in small print that he glossed over when reading the contract came back to haunt him. It hadn't seemed like so much at the time. After all, what the hell was there he could face that he hadn't confronted a dozen times before? "Have I ever refused you, Frank?" Outside of Torrance's *faux pas* of moments before, Reese Sullivan was the only man in Diamond's employ who had ever dared to address him in the familiar. *Your father was Mr. Diamond, Frank, and he's dead.*

"No, Reese." Diamond's smile was devoid of any real humor, but filled with pompous contempt he could not conceal. "I just want it understood that you won't refuse me in the future. I want your word on that." He extended a beefy paw.

Sullivan declined the gesture, refusing the man's hand. "You just got my word, Frank," he breathed. "When you answered my question."

Diamond's eyes burned bright for a moment as he withdrew his spurned fingers. "And you are, of course—as my father was fond of pointing out—an honorable man." His gaze shifted from Sullivan's face to the clock, and then to the watch he had just withdrawn from his vest pocket. He snapped the time piece shut. "There's someone waiting in my office, Royal. A client."

He smiled benignly. "Or rather, a *family* who wishes to become a client. *Reese's* client. I want you to ask them to come in."

Torrance hesitated. He looked at Diamond, and then at Reese Sullivan, as if waiting for Reese to give him some sign. When none was forthcoming, he crossed the room to the twin sliding doors that separated his office from Diamond's private suite. He disappeared briefly into the muted light beyond the threshold, and then—retracing his own steps—awkwardly backed out. Pulling the doors closed, he stared at his employer, his face ashen. "You bastard," he whispered. Half-turning, he faced Sullivan. "Reese, I didn't know..." His voice was full of apology and apprehension.

Diamond was out of his chair. He strode across the room, roughly pushing Torrance aside as he flung open both doors. "Mrs. Underwood!" he called. "If you and your son would please join us..."

Reese Sullivan's face clouded, the blue eyes somehow appearing to change color until they were the same dark grey as a piece of flint. A spark of raw fire burned far back beneath the hooded lids. He drew himself erect, his back stiffening as the woman stepped through the door and into the room.

She was dressed in black, swathed head to foot in the muted rich silk and lace netting of a woman in deep mourning, and followed closely by her son. He stayed beside her until they were inside the room, and then moved to her side to take her arm; a protective shadow for a woman who needed no protection. *Who, in spite of her frail demeanor and dark widow's weeds, had never needed any protection.*

"Your next assignment, Sullivan," Diamond announced. "Find the men who murdered Mrs. Underwood's husband," he paused, enjoying the next, "—this poor lad's father—and return the things that were stolen from him."

Reese stared directly into the woman's eyes. The dark veil did nothing to hide or diminish the cornflower blue orbs which dominated her face, and served only to heighten the pink sheen of her full, moist lips. As much as it pained him to admit it, she was as beautiful as she had ever been, still possessed of the flawless white skin and soft blond hair that had, for a long time, driven him crazy with a need no other woman could satisfy. His greeting was polite, purposely restrained, and he was grateful his voice did not betray him. "Vanessa."

The woman was equally skilled in hiding her feelings. "Reese."

Sullivan forced himself to look away, the turmoil he felt deep inside his chest increasing as he glanced at the well-built but foppishly pale young man who stood at Vanessa's side. Not one detail of the youth's demeanor escaped his quick head-to-toe scrutiny; from the healing scar on his pale cheek, to the immaculately manicured nails, polished brown shoes, and hand-tailored, starched shirt.

There was an arrogance in the youth. Sullivan could see it in the way he carried himself, and in the imperial stiffness of his back; so like his mother. As if, by some divine decree, they inherited the right to issue orders, instead of earning it.

A flicker of contempt registered briefly on Sullivan's face as his eyes swept the youth a final time, his gaze settling squarely on the other's face. Their eyes locked—collided—and Reese found himself staring into pools of blue ice that mirrored and magnified the rage burning within his own. *No*, he thought, reconsidering. *Not rage. Hatred.* Coldly, he dismissed the younger man, looking through him as if he were no longer there, and then swung his gaze back to the woman.

Sullivan stared into Vanessa Underwood's veiled eyes for a long time without speaking, until a passion he thought long dead ignited an old fire and flamed deep in the pit of his belly. "No," he said softly. He turned to face Diamond, and repeated the word. "*Hell, no.*"

Diamond stood rocking back and forth on the balls of his feet. "You have a contract," he crowed. "And I have your word as a gentleman." His lips parted in a smile that mocked Sullivan to the very core of his being.

"I lied," Reese answered. He turned and started toward the door.

It was a move Diamond had not anticipated. "You have a contract!" he roared, repeating himself. He followed Reese through the door and into the hallway. "Do you hear me? *You have a contract*!!" And then, unable to catch up, he shouted at Torrance. "Stop him!" he ordered.

Instinctively, Torrance reached out. He had followed the man's orders too long not to obey. "Reese," he pleaded.

Sullivan turned. Just long enough to land a haymaker on the button of Royal Torrance's chin. A second blow caught him right in the mouth. The man went down; hard. He caught himself on the railing. "Reese!"

The word echoed against the marble walls, sounding again and again. An echo of Royal Torrance's strong tenor at first, and then, as Diamond joined in, the high pitched wail of a wounded ram. "You come back here, Reese," Diamond shouted. "Damn you! You come back!"

The chase continued down the stairs to the second floor landing. Torrance was on his feet, using the back of his hand to stem the flow of blood from his torn lip, his shame at inadvertently betraying a friend giving him the stamina to keep pace. It was more difficult for the obese man who followed him. Diamond collapsed in a heap midway down the broad staircase leading to the first floor. The woman simply watched from the third floor balcony.

But not her son. Trey Underwood followed in Torrance's wake, their leather heeled shoes beating a quick staccato against the pink Wisconsin marble. And still they could not catch up.

Sullivan was already at the bottom of the stairs. He turned, daring them to follow him; a cold smile coming as he saw Torrance and the younger man come to a dead stop, neither one of them able to meet his gaze. Franklin Diamond was behind them, leaning heavily against the railing at the first floor landing. The man was waving a copy of the contract in his clenched fist, his chest heaving as he attempted to vent his anger. Finally, his voice returned. "Sullivan!"

Reese answered the man, his words coming with a deadly quiet that carried just as far as Diamond's almost feminine screech. "You know what you can do with that contract, Frank."

Diamond went wild. "You're finished, Sullivan. Do you hear me? *Finished.* There isn't an agency in the country that will touch you. I'll keep you in the courts until you beg me to let you come back! Do you hear? *Until you beg me..."*

Sullivan turned his back on the man. Unimpeded, he strode down the wide corridor leading to the front door, pausing at the entrance to the lobby as a covey of eager trainees moved in to block his way. They formed a loose half-circle around him, nervously standing their ground as they debated what to do.

The man on Sullivan's right dropped his hand, his fingers disappearing inside his coat to grope at the tell-tale lump just above his belt on the left side. "Mr. Diamond wants you to stay put, Sullivan," he gloated, certain he had stopped the man.

Reese smiled across at the man. As if caught, he started to raise his hands, lifting them slowly until they were even with his waist. He bunched his left shoulder, releasing the mechanism that propelled the sleeve gun down the underside of his forearm and into his palm. "Don't be a fool," he breathed. The man backed up a full pace, and threw his hands high above his head.

Instantly, Sullivan swung around. In a move as effortless and as natural as pointing his finger, he took direct aim at Franklin Diamond's forehead.

A chorus of stunned gasps sounded as everyone in the room inhaled, the ensuing quiet worse than the noise of their breathing. Forty pairs of eyes shut tight against the certain reality of what was to come. Sullivan used their panic and the blind silence. Unseen, he raised the gun slightly, thumbed back the hammer, and fired.

Overcome, the agent to Reese's right fainted, a dark stain appearing at his crotch as he hit the floor; the acrid scent of urine permeating the still air. The remaining five scattered, seeking refuge behind the marble columns at either side of the wide staircase.

Above Diamond's head, in the framed, life-sized portrait hung in the alcove at the landing between the first and second floor, a scorched hole appeared. *Directly between Franklin Diamond's painted brown eyes.*

Before the wisp of blue-grey smoke cleared, Reese Sullivan was out the door. Like a wraith, he disappeared into the dense crowd and was gone.

Chapter Three

The large, three story brownstone stood on a wide, well-manicured lot in an old neighborhood once home to the same millionaires who now lived in the *splendid little castles* on Lake Shore Drive. A restored survivor of the Great Fire of '71, it still bore signs of the intense flames that nearly destroyed the city. One section of the wrought iron fence that surrounded the two acre plot had been left in place as a stark reminder of nature's (perhaps God's) fury. The warped, rusted uprights bent inward on the concrete footings, as if the metal had sought to escape the fire, the intricately worked sprigs of iron ivy bearing leaves that had once lain flat within the framed grillwork, leaves now curled tight like a closed fist.

Inside the house, in the large study on the first floor, Trey Underwood watched as the physician finished knotting the final suture that closed the ragged tear on Royal Torrance's swollen upper lip. The man had refused the opiate the doctor prescribed, stoically accepting the pain as if he deserved it.

"You're probably going to lose that molar, Royal, and—in all likelihood—the tooth beside it." The physician shook a finger at the man. "You would think, at your age, a man would have sense enough to refrain from this kind of foolishness, or at least be intelligent enough to duck."

Torrance pushed the man's probing fingers away. "You can't duck what you don't see coming," he observed. The stitches made it difficult to talk. He kept his words to a minimum. "You can bill Diamond," he announced, getting up out of the chair.

The doctor started to protest then thought better of it. "Diamond," he repeated. He shrugged and began putting away his instruments. He snapped the bag closed then left the room without bothering to say his farewells.

Torrance went into the small bathroom built into a space that once, long ago, had served as a closet for the adjoining bedroom. He stared into the mirror above the porcelain sink, gingerly fingering the still raw cut that ran at a sharp angle from the corner of his mouth to a point even with his right nostril. He turned his eyes from his own image to the somber reflection that stared at him from over his right shoulder. "He always did pack a hell of a wallop." There was no rancor in his voice, or his words.

Trey Underwood's jaws tightened then relaxed. "I wouldn't remember," he said uncharitably, the bitterness adding an edge to the words. "Where do you think he is now?"

Something in the younger man's face set Torrance's teeth on edge. "Why?" he asked.

Trey smiled, the warmth failing to reach his eyes. A truly wise man always answered an unwelcome question with a question of his own. He decided to play the game. "Why not?"

Torrance bent over the sink and splashed cold water onto his face. When he finished, he took his time with the towel. His mouth was beginning to hurt again, worse than before. "Look," he began. "I'm not going to play games with you. I don't have the time, or the inclination. I don't know where Reese is right now, and if I did, I wouldn't tell you." He shouldered his way past Trey and went into the bedroom.

The next few minutes were spent opening and closing drawers as he looked for a clean shirt to replace the one that was stiff and brown with his own blood. When he was done changing, he nodded toward the door. Without speaking, he led the way down the hallway to the parlor and to the front entrance. He pulled the door open; as subtle as a bull in the china shop.

Trey stopped the door with a well-placed foot. "I want to talk to him," he declared. It was more a demand than a request.

Torrance was having none of it. "I don't give a tinker's damn about what you want! This is *my* house, and I don't recall having invited you for a visit." He waited for the younger man to move his foot, and when Trey didn't, used his shoulder to swing the door hard against the wall.

Trey stared through the opening out into the street. What Torrance was saying was true. He hadn't been invited. In fact, to locate the place, he had found it necessary to wait for the driver of the hansom cab who took Torrance home after his abrupt departure from Diamond's office. Then he bribed the man to make the drive a second time. Ride included, the extended excursion through a maze of back streets he didn't know cost him twenty dollars, plus a great deal of time he didn't feel he could spare.

The young man could feel the warm flush of his temper crawling up the back of his neck, the heat rising to color his cheeks. The blood fired skin paled by long weeks spent in the military hospital at Fort Yuma, and turned his face a deep crimson. Except for the long scar beneath his left eye where the condor marked him. The ridge of still healing tissue drew a long white line that reached from the corner of his eye to his chin. Absently, he fingered the wound. "Diamond said there was only one man working for the Agency that could do the job, and that Reese Sullivan was that man." The words came in a soft whisper. "If that's the truth, then I want to talk to him."

Disgusted by the young man's tenacity, but certain he wouldn't leave without being answered, Torrance slammed the door shut. "Oh, it's the truth," he declared. "Only problem, *boy*, is that Reese isn't working for Diamond anymore. But, then, you were there. As smart-assed as you appear to be, I'd think you'd be able to figure that out." He didn't know what riled him more. The youth's way of making him feel suddenly old, (*How the hell could so much time have passed so quickly?*) or the fact that Trey somehow managed to follow him home and intrude into a world few others even knew existed.

"And you?" Trey asked suddenly. "Would Sullivan work for you?"

Torrance laughed. There was genuine humor in the sound; dark humor. "For me? Probably." He changed his mind, rephrasing his answer. "Reese would work *with* me. If I wasn't still working for Diamond," he finished.

Trey was unable to hide his surprise. "I heard Diamond tell you—"

"That I was fired," Torrance interrupted. "That was today. Tomorrow, when he's had some time to think about it, he'll change his mind." The man's smug grin matched his words. "Right now, I'm the only thing standing between Franklin Diamond and..." *to hell with it*, he thought. He had pussyfooted around the kid long enough, "...the only thing between Franklin Diamond and your father!"

Trey Underwood's head snapped up, his blue eyes suddenly bright with the same fire Royal Torrance had seen earlier in Reese Sullivan's orbs. So intense was the anger, the young man's face visibly changed, a hardness in his features making him look much older. "My *father*," he repeated. Coming from his mouth, the word sounded dirty. "Reese Sullivan may have planted the seed," he breathed, "but he sure in hell didn't stay around to tend the crop!"

Torrance ignored the outburst. "Whose idea was it?" he asked finally. It was a question that had bothered him from the first moment he saw Vanessa Underwood sitting in Diamond's waiting room. "Who the hell put it in your head that Reese would be the one to go after Underwood's killers?"

Trey's hand closed around the glass doorknob, as if he were afraid Torrance would force him out. "Diamond told us we needed a man who knew the desert. A man who could get into Mexico, get the job done, and get out. The fact that Reese Sullivan was the man he picked didn't matter to either of us. Not Vanessa, and not to me.

"I want the men who murdered my father, Torrance." Trey's voice shook with emotion. "And if Reese Sullivan is the only man who can find them, then..." He paused, an old wound festering deep in his soul—a wound he thought healed—began to hurt again. Steeling himself, he willed the pain away. "I'd hire the devil himself if that's what it took. At any price he named. You tell Sullivan that, and you tell him I want to see him!"

Roughly, Torrance shoved the younger man aside. He pulled the door open a second time and nodded toward the dark street beyond. "I'm not telling Reese anything, boy. And if you've got half a brain in your head, you won't try to tell him anything either." Torrance was tired, and the fatigue showed in his voice. "Go home, Trey," he breathed. "Go back to where ever it is you and your mother have been living, and pick up the pieces. But stay away from Reese." The next words came after a long pause. "He deserves better," he said cryptically. Before the younger man could respond, he shoved him across the threshold and out onto the broad front stoop.

Trey found himself outside facing a door that had not only been shut, but locked. He swore, softly, and then, even more determined than before, began walking down the street. At the corner, he hailed a liveried coachman. *There were just so many hotels in Chicago*, he reasoned. *Sullivan had to be at one of them*. It was only a matter of time until he found him.

* _ * _ * _ * _ *

The Palmer House had been built anew after the Chicago Fire, and reflected the wealth and prestige of its builder, Potter Palmer. Now, twenty-two years later, it hosted an elite clientele of Fair goers from all over the world. *Fit for Prince or President* its lavish brochures proclaimed, a picture of Palmer and a relaxed Ulysses S. Grant testifying to its truthfulness. The building was also fireproof.

Vanessa Underwood, still clad in the black widows weeds she had worn in Diamond's office, stood at the entrance to the hotel's dining room. She surveyed the interior with an approving eye, relishing the gleam of sculpted metal and onyx that dominated the room. It was, she knew, an exact and fastidious replica of the grand salon in the palace of the Crown Prince at Potsdam. The gold fixtures and ornaments glowed warmly against black and white marble floors as highly polished as the mirrors that lined the walls. There was nothing obscene in this kind of wealth, she mused—unless it was that it belonged to someone else.

"Mrs. Underwood?" A hand tugged lightly at the woman's elbow.

Startled, she turned, her cheeks pink with the flush of embarrassment at being caught off guard. And then, amused at what she saw in his face, she smiled at the bellboy, a provocative tilt to her head. "Yes?"

The youth's blush rivaled the woman's, and then surpassed it. For some foolish reason he could not remember, he had assumed her to be much older, and certainly not so attractive. "The gentleman you inquired about. Mr. Palmer said to tell you that he is staying here, but that he doesn't seem to be in his room." The boy paused, sorry he didn't have more to say; at least, nothing more he'd been instructed to say. "Ma'am," he began again, reluctant to leave her. "If there is anything else I can do..."

Vanessa smiled. She knew better than to laugh at a man, even one as young as this. "You may show me to his room," she whispered, taking the boy's arm and patting his sleeve. "And you can let me in." She led the way to the elevator.

Without any thought as to the right or the wrong of it, the young man did as he was asked. But there was a certain amount of agony in him as he ushered her down the long hallway to the corner wing of the top floor, and a great flood of envy. "Mr. Sullivan's a lucky man," he thought aloud, wanting the woman to hear his words. He bowed and stepped away from the unlocked door, careful to remove the pass key.

Vanessa Underwood stepped across the threshold. "Once," she said, more to herself than to the youth at her back, "he was a *very* lucky man." She shut the door and leaned against it, listening to the slow drag of footsteps as the boy went away.

"In your opinion, Vanessa." The voice whispered to her from the dark corner, as harsh as the sound of the Texas winds that had bred it. There was a soft *click* as the man uncocked the pistol he had been holding, and then another noise as he slid it into an unseen holster.

Reese Sullivan stepped out of the blackness beside the tall dresser that stood against the wall. He was only partially dressed, his massive chest and strong arms brown and bare in the dim twilight that streamed through the half-drawn draperies. He was carrying the sheathed Colt, the full cartridge belt draped over his shoulder as if he were expecting trouble. "Diamond." Without saying anything else, he eased down onto the bed, stretched out, and began rolling a cigarette.

The woman nodded. She had been aware of the tenuous affiliation between Reese and Franklin Diamond for more years than she cared to remember. It rivaled their own passionate love/hate relationship and had somehow prevailed. "You could invite me to sit down, Reese."

"I didn't know you intended on being here that long," he countered. He scratched his thumbnail across the top of a match, the flame bathing his face briefly before he inhaled, then flickering out. Somehow, the fact that she had chosen to come did not surprise him.

The woman's lips compressed in a tight, dry line before smoothing into an enigmatic half-smile made even more attractive by the muted light from the low burning gas light beside the door. "I want to talk, Reese." She made a place for herself at the foot of the bed, her back straight, and her feet solidly on the floor.

Sullivan studied her profile for a long time, trying to read the face behind the veil. The lace netting on her small hat had been carefully arranged in a series of soft folds that veiled her eyes, but not her mouth, or the attractive curve of her small chin. A study in shades of shimmering black silk and alabaster skin, she was like a delicate figurine that had been created out of an especially fine clay, and then fired and painted by a master's hand. Even after the long day, not one hair was out of place, nor was there one flaw in her decoration. It would have been easy to hate her for her perfection, if once, long ago, he had not loved her. "What do you want, Vanessa?"

There was the soft rustle of silk as the woman shifted slightly. "Just what Franklin Diamond told you I wanted. To find the men who conspired to kill my husband, and steal his belongings." Her face showed the proper amount of sadness, but she said the melancholy words dispassionately and very unlike a woman seeking revenge.

Sullivan immediately recognized her indifference. "Why?" He took a long drag on his cigarette, and waited for her answer.

"They took something from him," she replied. In this place, with this man, there was no need for pretense. Her husband was dead, and there was no point in reflecting on what was, or could have been. "Something I want back."

"And?" Another single word query, and another long pull on the smoke.

"And I want you to do it without involving my son." For the first time, she turned and faced him.

There was no humor in Sullivan's short burst of quiet laughter. "*Your* son?!" The cigarette lost its flavor and he pinched it out between his thumb and forefinger. The brief spate of pain added an edge to his words. "I saw the register at the Drake, Vanessa." He wrote in the air with an extended forefinger. "*'Trey Underwood'*", he mocked, " ... not *Danforth*," (her maiden name),"...not even..."

"Sullivan?" she finished for him. She made no effort to hide her resentment. It had been a bitter divorce, several years in the making, made worse by Sullivan's rage and his foul accusation regarding Trey's true parentage. She had never forgiven him for accusing her, any more than she had forgiven him for cataloging her indiscretions. She had been unfaithful, but not until after Trey was born. *Not until she had taken him away from the ranch; far away from the suffocating loneliness she had endured for five long years*. The fact that she had chosen to leave Reese without telling him, or that she left with another man ...

Reese had intended to say *Trey Danforth Underwood*, the name the young man had used upon entering Harvard. *Not that Vanessa would have ever thought he had known*. Beyond the money he sent for the young man's care and support—even that had been handled through the bank and his attorney—he had never once written her, or inquired about the boy's well being.

Sullivan rose up from the bed, drawing his legs up and pivoting to the right in a conscious effort not to touch her as he stood up. He kept his back to her. "I want you to give me a reason, Vanessa," he held up a tanned finger, "just *one* single reason why I should do what you want."

She rose up from the bed. "I can give you ten," she answered quickly. "Ten *thousand* reasons." She was beside him now, uncomfortably close to his right shoulder.

Without turning his head, Sullivan cast an eye at her. She was holding a bank draft in her hand, the stiff paper neatly folded in half, long ways, so that only his name, not the amount, was visible. "Five thousand dollars now," she intoned, using her thumb nail to unfold the document so that he could see what was written, "the balance when you bring me what I want." Hesitating, she waited for him to respond and when he did not, continued. "You'd take the job for half this, Reese," she breathed, tracing the five thousand with her finger, "if it was someone other than me. Surely, for four times the amount..."

He reached out and took the draft in his hand. It was a considerable sum of money, regardless of its source. Money he needed. And still, he hesitated. *A bird in the hand*, he thought ruefully. This bird would go a long way towards paying off his debts in El Paso, with a few eggs to spare. *If only it wasn't Vanessa's.*

"Reese?"

The woman's voice roused him from his dark musing. Toying with the check, he faced her, as if he were still trying to make up his mind. And then, prompted by a feeling he didn't really understand, he took the woman in his arms, and kissed her.

It was a long kiss, the probing kiss of a lover—*two lovers*—and, after the initial shock at his boldness, she did not resist. She felt herself drawn to his naked chest, the heat of his flesh warm against her covered breasts and beneath her gloved fingers. Deep within the woman, an old hunger flamed to life, and she returned the kiss, yielding to his touch, and wanting more.

Then, suddenly, he drew away. "I want you to understand, Vanessa," he whispered hoarsely. "It's for the money. Nothing more than the money."

She felt his hands slip from her shoulders and waist, and raised her eyes to see something in his face she had never seen before. A sense of relief spread over his countenance, easing the harsh lines at the corners of his mouth and his eyes. *It was*, she realized, *as if he had just recovered from a long illness, and was finally well.*

A smile touched her mouth, but there was only sadness in her eyes. She had taken it for granted he would always love her, the way he had in the beginning, and for all those years after she left him. It was a sureness in that love which had given her the sense of power she felt in Diamond's office, and here, when she first came to this room. But now...

"For the money," she echoed dully. *How well she understood the hunger that could drive even the very strong to do something they didn't care to do, just for the money.*

Sullivan was back on the bed. "I want this cashed before I leave," he announced. He tapped the check with his finger. "And I want a paper saying that you'll pay the balance when the job's done."

Absently, the woman nodded her head. "And Trey?"

The question caught Sullivan off guard. He quickly recovered. "I didn't see his name on the draft, Vanessa. Which means, as far as I'm concerned, this isn't any of his business."

Business. She thought how appropriate the word sounded. "He intended, if you took the job, on going with you," she sighed. When she faced Sullivan, there was a genuine concern marring her features, a tightness around her mouth that made her face seem drawn. "He blames himself for what happened to his fa..." too late she stopped herself then hurried on, "for what happened to Wes It's become an obsession with him—this need to find the men responsible.

"I don't want him to go, Reese. I don't want him to find..."

Assuming there was more to be said, Sullivan waited for her to continue. She did not, and the things that were unspoken remained unspoken. Sullivan noted the silence, and filed it away in his mind. "Potter Palmer will cash the draft, Vanessa." He reached for the shirt hanging on the bedpost and slipped it on. "I can leave here tonight. As for Trey..." After all these years, it seemed strange, saying the young man's name. "You can tell him any damned thing you please," he finished.

She caught his arm before he opened the door, a firmness in her touch that matched the determination in her words. "I'm going to tell him you said *no.*"

Sullivan made no attempt to hide the wry smile. He reached out to her, almost as if he were going to caress her cheek. Instead, his hand moved to lift the dark veil away from her right ear. Before the woman could pull away, he took hold of the black earring she wore, and worked the pearl-sized pendant between his thumb and one finger. Using his thumbnail, he scratched the dull gem, his smile growing. The unmistakable gleam of a diamond shone through the paint, the stone the size of a large pea. "Did you ever really love Wes, Vanessa?" *Or me, or the boy?*

As if she could read his thoughts, the woman struck out. The slap exploded against Sullivan's cheek, the sound amplified by the emptiness of the dimly lit hallway. "Yes, I loved him! Just as he loved me," she rasped. "And, more importantly, just as he loved Trey!" She left him then, shaking loose from his grasp and almost running down the passageway in her determination to escape him.

Sullivan stared after her. He touched the place where she had struck him, his knuckles moving back and forth across the still warm ridges beneath his left eye. *It was,* he mused bitterly, *as it had always been between them; the harsh words, the pain.* And, in the end, one of them running away.

* - * - * - * - *

There was something feral and sinister about the city in the long, dark hours between midnight and dawn. As if once the sun's warmth had dissipated and the rats came up out of the sewers in search of food, the cold fog from the lake and the river drove the people out of the streets and into the shadowy world behind their bolted doors and barred windows. It was the only time Sullivan felt an affinity for the place, or for its unseen people.

He was being followed. He sensed, rather than saw, the two men who began trailing him when he exited the Palmer House. There was no doubt in his mind as to who sent them, or what they were instructed to do. So he made a game of it, taking them on a long chase through a part of the city he knew only from the exacting maps Potter Palmer had given him. Relentlessly, he led them down the silent brick canyons to a place he'd known intimately as a boy of fourteen.

Sullivan felt a chill as he passed through the massive gates marking the entrance to the Union Stockyards. The fact that he was expected and greeted by the guard on duty aided him in carrying out his little charade for the two shadows still following him, but it did nothing to erase the swell of memories that assaulted his mind. The gate slammed shut behind him, the clang of steel jarring his spine and making him jump. He reached for his tobacco. His hand was shaking when he rolled the cigarette, and he had to fight to control it.

"Headin' home, Reese?" the man in the gatehouse asked amicably. His voice carried on the cool night air and echoed against the darkness. He opened the door and stepped down from the small office, and offered his pipe for a light.

Head bent, Sullivan dipped the butt into the pipe's bowl, drawing hard on the cigarette to get it started. Between puffs and rising embers of spent tobacco, he said, "In the morning, Jasper." He patted the bedroll he had slung from his shoulder. "Right now, I just want to find a place for this, and have a talk with the crew boss who brought those longhorns up from Texas for Bill Cody."

Jasper Bent laughed. "Old Tank Hubbard," he said. Conscious of the noise and the way his words carried, he lowered his voice to a near whisper. "He *drove* them, Reese! From Fort Worth, up the old Shawnee Trail to Kansas City!! Damnedest thing I ever heard. The old bastard must be nigh on to seventy-five years old, and he made the whole ride!" Bent shook his head. "Old outlaw like that..." Suddenly, the man's voice rose. "Dammit, Reese! You arrested him once!"

The darkness hid Sullivan's grin. "Yeah," he replied. "Once." On two other occasions he had let the old man go. He left Bent standing open-mouthed on his office stoop, and disappeared into the moon-lit yards.

* - * - * - * - *

Twin ribbons of steel marked the path to the place where the stock cars were lined up on a siding in long rows pointing west. Steam rose up from the manure littered floors, escaping into the night between the painted slats and carrying a curiously sweet scent of dried chips and fermenting hay. Sullivan followed the smell, trailing a gloved hand along the sides of the cars as he passed; longing for the feel of an animal beneath his fingers. *God, how he wanted to go home.*

The soft yellow glow of a single kerosene lantern appeared ahead of him, the light spreading in a tall rectangle beside the tracks, and Sullivan's pace quickened. The beam came from a small window in the last coach, an old boxcar converted into living quarters for the gandy-dancers who had lived aboard the trains when the railroads were still pushing west. Now it served as a temporary bunkhouse for the stockmen who rode with their beef to the eastern markets; and in this instance, as a makeshift home for the rugged old man who chose to shun the teeming city streets and the crowded hotels.

Sullivan hoisted himself up onto the platform at the rear of the car. He knocked twice on the door and waited, and then knocked again. The light went out. When the door opened, he found himself staring into the business end of an old Navy Colt, the barrel only inches from his nose. With one finger, he pushed it aside. "Hell of a welcome for an old friend, Tank," he observed. The gun disappeared.

The interior of the car grew light again, and Sullivan stepped inside. He could smell chicory brewing on the wood cook stove in the corner, the riper smell of a honey-pot assaulting his senses and making him conscious of his old aversion for small spaces. He left the door slightly ajar.

"Well, boy," the voice boomed. "You goin' to stand there all night?"

Tank Hubbard's greeting was primed by copious amounts of a home-brewed whiskey he referred to as varnish. He kept quart jars of the potent liquid in his cavy sack, using the brew for everything from a cure for ringworm to canker sores.

And to toast special occasions. This was one of them. He looped an arm around Sullivan's shoulder, and guided him to the table. "Hear tell you and Diamond parted company." Two tin cups sat at its center, and he used a teaspoon of the homemade mash to wash them out.

"Didn't know you could read chimney smoke, Tank." Reese was quick to cover his mug with his hand. He preferred, under these circumstances, to pour his own.

"Cody sent a man here looking for you. Figured you might jump at the chance for honest work." It was Hubbard's turn to laugh. "I'd have given my teeth to see it, Reese."

Sullivan toed out a chair and turned it around. His back to the wall, he sat. "It isn't over, Tank."

Hubbard wiped his lips with the back of his hand. He poured himself a second drink, filling the cup to the brim. "Diamond's looking to take his pound of flesh?"

Reese nodded. "I'm being tailed." He took his first drink and felt his eyes water.

The old man's eyes narrowed. "How many you think there are?"

"Two," Reese answered. "Maybe more."

"Hell, boy," Hubbard complained. "You won't even need any help." The disappointment was real, and he eased it with another long drink that emptied his cup.

"Not in taking them," Reese breathed. He started to take another drink and changed his mind. Already, his lips felt raw, and he wet them with his tongue. The air inside the boxcar seemed increasingly hot. "But in keeping them...?" He grinned across at his companion, the smile growing as he saw the older man's watery eyes come alive.

Hubbard stroked his beard. He was a big man, raw-boned and red from long hours in the sun. Sixty years of hard work had left their mark on him, but the eyes were as young and as bright as a boy's. "What've you got in mind, Reese?"

"I need a rope," the other answered. "And then I'm going to need an empty corner in one of your stock cars."

Hubbard's laughter boomed into the silence. "Damn, Reese! You going to let me take them home? For pets?"

Reese shook his head. His mood became more serious, and he reached out to touch Hubbard's arm. "I don't even want them to see you, Tank." His hand closed around the man's arm. "If Diamond thinks you're involved, he'll come after you. He could arrange to have you put away, old man. For a long time."

The old timer shook his head. "He'd have to find me first, Reese. And you don't work for him anymore."

Sullivan was flattered by the compliment, but adamant in his determination that the old man not take any risks. "Just tell me which car, Tank. And then keep away from it until we're west of the Mississippi."

Hubbard gave a reluctant nod. "You could just kill them, Reese," he murmured.

Sullivan stood up. He shook his head. "Diamond would just send more. I want them alive, Tank, and able to talk. Ten words from a man who's had the fear of God shoved down his throat is worth a hell of a lot more than a dead detective Diamond can turn into a martyr."

Hubbard capped the liquor jar he had just emptied, and tossed it on his bunk. "I got a good *reata*, Reese. A thirty footer that old Mex braided for me when I was in Huntsville." He got up and began rummaging in the trunk at the foot of his bed.

Reese joined the man in his hunt. The old drover's entire life seemed to be jammed into the chest. He picked up a framed picture and stared at it, aware that Hubbard was watching. "Sarah?" he asked. The girl in the faded tintype was young, and fresh, and very pretty.

"The summer I met her," Hubbard whispered. There was something reverent in his voice and his touch when he caressed the print. "She's gone now, Reese," he said finally, burying the picture beneath a stack of shirts. "One winter too many in the Texas hills.

"She's gone, and I wish to God I was with her."

There was nothing Sullivan could say. He took the braided rope that Hubbard was holding, and cleared his throat. "I'm going to be leaving this," he said softly, shrugging his shoulder to unload the bedroll he had been carrying.

"We're leaving early, Reese," Hubbard reminded him. "Rolling out at first light."

Sullivan nodded. "I'll be here," he promised.

Chapter Four

Reese Sullivan had made a mistake. He knew it when he saw four silhouettes where there should have been two.

The men stood at the end of a long passageway between two of the larger stock pens, framed by the muted lights from the rows of shanties in Packingtown. They were talking, small puffs of white vapor ballooning above their Derby-covered heads as if they were characters in one of John McCutcheon's cartoons in the *Daily News*. Sullivan strained to hear them, swearing to himself when the words remained nothing more than a rush of jumbled whispers.

He hunkered down and peered around the corner post, watching as the quartet separated and went off in pairs; two east, two west. Tracking them by ear, he listened attentively as the cattle in the two corrals began to bawl. The animals began to mill, turning to move in a ragged line, twenty abreast as they instinctively bunched to be driven by the men outside the pen.

For a time, the beeves in both pens moved away from Sullivan. And then, as the four detectives completed the back half of their circuits, the animals came about. Reese watched them, and when the lead steer in the corral to his right nosed its way past him, he moved.

The moon had disappeared behind an island of gray clouds, the noise inside the pen covering the scrape of Sullivan's boots as he climbed up the eight-foot high fence and scrambled onto the board walkway. Bent low on one knee, he tested the causeway, feeling the give of the two, inch-thick, foot-wide planks beneath his feet. From the small amount of slack, he reckoned the braces to be at two foot intervals along the unbroken fence, mentally allowing for larger gaps where the narrow walkway would pass over the four-foot wide entrances to the chutes. Satisfied, he dropped down onto his belly to wait.

Beneath him, the cattle continued their endless round. Dumbly, they began piling up against the fence, the cows in the rear mounting the cows in front, one animal climbing up on another as Diamond's men rounded the last corner to meet and head back to their starting place.

The racket from the pens increased. Two separate bunches of spooked bovines faced each other across the six foot passageway that separated the enclosures, their panic intensified by the darkness and their inability to see. The potent musk of the aroused animals filled the air as the brindle mossback in Sullivan's pen snorted a challenge to a younger, more vocal maverick across the way. Tail high in the air, the young bull began butting the fence, both animals bellowing back and forth as they began their strut.

The four men in the passageway stopped as Jess Cochran reached out to pull at his partner's sleeve. "Jesus, Logan, they aren't going to bust out, are they?'

The older man laughed. "Didn't you ever hear of a *stam-pede*," he joshed, the words coming precisely and with a trace of a Boston accent. "If you talk long enough, and loud enough," he paused, ominously watching as the other bit the end off a cigar, "or strike a match..."

Cochran almost choked on his cigar. He started to throw it away, and then changed his mind, as if afraid to let it hit the ground. "What the hell is so important about Sullivan, anyway?" he grumbled.

There was more laughter as Logan Masters considered his answer. Of the four, he was the only one who knew Diamond's real motive for going after Sullivan, and just how things would go once the man was caught. It was information he chose not to share. "He scared the juice out of Diamond," he said finally, juice sounding so much more refined than piss. "And Mr. Diamond doesn't like being scared."

Cochran was still feeling peevish. "So?" A small man in his late twenties and given to pacing, he felt hemmed in by the high fences, the constant movement of the beeves making him even more disagreeable than usual.

"So we're going to find him," Masters answered patiently. "And teach him some proper manners." Something in the man's voice told Cochran that he would be wise to shut up.

From his perch, Sullivan watched as Masters began issuing orders in a hushed voice that demanded attention. "We're going to split up again," the man announced. "Only this time, we're going to take it one pen at a time.

"We'll start here," he continued. He resumed walking, heading for the place where they first started. The other three men fell in behind him.

On the walkway above, Reese snaked after them. Masters was still talking. "Jeffries, you stay here," he instructed when they reached the first corner. He led the other two men around the post and headed for the next. When they reached it, he dropped off the second man, Vern Webster.

They made the turn, heading for the third corner of the corral. It was getting darker, and they were moving away from the sparse lights that burned in the shanties in Packingtown. Cochran could feel the hot breath of the few steers that had, for some reason he didn't comprehend, followed after them.

"I don't like this," he complained. And then, "Oh, shit!" as a spooked cow backed up to the fence and let fly. "Work my butt off five years to get out of that damned office, and for what!? To scrape cow shit off my pants in the middle of the night..."

Masters had heard enough. "Quiet!" he ordered. He jabbed a finger in the direction of the next corner post. "You'll stay here. I'll go on ahead, and then when I give the word, we'll make the circle."

Cochran swore under his breath, but did as he was told. He leaned up against the fence, and watched Masters' back as the other man made his slow walk to the end of the corral.

Sullivan was directly above Cochran. Head raised, he lay rock still, biding his time and watching as the man in charge used his hand to signal his terse commands. Two jabs in the direction they would go, and then a single wave to Cochran when they were to advance.

Cochran began his slow march, unaware that above his head, Sullivan moved with him. Masters had already disappeared around the corner ahead of him, and aware of his sudden aloneness, Cochran began to mutter. "All this bullshit just because the old man's nose is out of joint," he grumbled. "I get my hands on Sullivan..."

The man never had a chance to finish. He heard a faint, unfamiliar rustle above him and looked up. The last thing he saw was the toe of a high-heeled boot; and the last thing he heard, the distinctive hiss of Sullivan's borrowed rope.

* - * - * - * - *

"Cochran!" The hoarse whisper sounded for the third time as Masters and the others cautiously rounded the corner. "*Cochran!!*"

One of the three lit a match. "Where the hell is he?" Jeffries demanded. His voice rose in an urgent whisper, an insolent edge to the words that had not been there before. "Dammit to Hell, Logan. He just didn't take wing and fly!"

Masters was on one knee on the ground. The first match had gone out, so he struck another. Straightening the crease in his pants, he stood up. The light spread. Cochran's footprints followed along beside the fence line to a point almost directly in the middle, and then stopped; as if he had been snatched from the face of the earth. The detective moved forward for a closer look, going down on his knees again as he probed the ground.

"He was above us, the whole time," he breathed, talking more to himself than the others. He stood up. Together, all three men backed away from the fence and into the shadows. They took shelter in a three-sided shed.

"Sullivan!" Masters called the name aloud. Nothing. He tried again. "Sullivan!" His eyes swept the top of the fence. He reached inside his jacket with his right hand, and drew his pistol; a small, short-barreled Remington .38. "We know you've got Cochran, Reese! And *you* know we're going to get him back." He paused. "Reese!" There was still no answer, just a solid *thunk* as a frightened steer charged the fence. The animal's long horn snagged between the bottom two planks, splintering the wood, the hook gleaming yellow-white, like bone in the muted moonlight. A white-ringed eye stared into the darkness.

Masters wiped cold sweat from his upper lip with the back of his hand. Something that seemed so simple at the onset was becoming increasingly difficult. They had been so careful, so discreet in the way they had watched Sullivan; had followed him. *Right to the place he led them.*

The realization of what happened made Masters smile, his mouth parting in a wry grin. Sullivan had chosen his position well. The moon was behind him, and it had begun to wane, thin shafts of light filtering between the rows of tall buildings at the man's back. Pale streams of moonlight poured into the pens below the catwalk, washing across the backs of the milling beeves before it spilled through the slatted fencing to illuminate the broad alleyways and the packed floors of the open sheds.

Conscious of the light, Masters backed up. He pulled Jeffries and Webster with him. "We've got to get him off that walkway," he whispered.

"And just how do you plan on doing that, chief?" Jeffries asked the question, the words filled with a thinly veiled sarcasm. A twenty year veteran with the agency, he was Masters' subordinate, and resentful of the younger man's undeserved authority. *Another of Franklin Diamond's snot-nosed college graduates.*

Masters' jaws clenched. A shared animosity was all he had in common with Jeffries, a man he considered too entrenched in the past to be of any real use in a world of photographs, fingerprints, and forensic laboratories. "You've got a big mouth, Kyle," he said softly.

Jeffries snorted. "Not as big as yours," he countered. "*I* wasn't the one who told Diamond how easy it would be to take Sullivan here in the city. *Out of his element, so to speak, sir,*" he mocked. "Not me.

"Fact is, sonny," he continued, pausing just long enough to spit a stream of tobacco juice between the younger man's feet, "I'm the one that told you..."

The jibe hit its intended mark. Masters' jaws began to work, and he stopped Jeffries rantings with a single wave of his rigid right hand. He'd had his fill of Reese Sullivan stories, and of Jeffries' smug reminders of the man's reputation for a short temper and a long memory.

As for Sullivan's fame among his peers as a man hunter extraordinaire... He was sick of hearing about that, too. It was the precise reason he promised Diamond something more than his desired pound of flesh. He had pledged to beat Sullivan at his own game; to beat the man and kill the legend. *It was a promise he intended to keep.*

Masters resumed speaking. "We're going out the window," he announced. "Webster and I." He began rummaging at the back of the shed, knocking on the barrels stacked against the wall. "And you, Jeffries. You're staying here." One by one, he began rolling kegs toward the front of the shed. Silently, Webster followed suit. They kept it up, moving the barrels and stacking them two high.

"Now what?" Jeffries whispered. The caustic edge was gone from his voice, replaced by a genuine concern. He didn't like the idea of being alone, and it showed.

Masters handed the man his Remington and the two fully loaded cylinders he always carried in his pockets. "You're going to keep Sullivan busy." When Jeffries started to protest, he ignored him and continued. "I want him to think that we're all in here," he explained, his tone that of a man speaking to a half-wit child. His fingers dug into the man's shoulders. "Take your time. Spread out your shots, and aim high." When he was certain Jeffries understood, he let go. He turned to the other man waiting in the shadows.

Webster nodded a silent *all clear* and jerked his head toward the open window at the rear of the shed. Almost as an afterthought, he raised his right hand waist high. He was holding the bail of a large, capped can between his bent fingers, and a layer of torn burlap sacking hung from his shoulder. The cloth was heavy, damp; the wetness emanating the pungent odor of kerosene.

Masters grinned. He turned away from Webster, and stood for a time at Jeffries' side, his eyes probing the darkness beyond the line of barrels. Sullivan was nowhere to be seen. The detective cleared his throat. "Reese!" He called the name knowing there would be no answer, but still he had to try. "You're only delaying the inevitable, Reese. You know it, and I know it!" A steer snorted. Another answered with a muted bellow. But there was no sound from Sullivan. Masters waited. Inside his head, a clock ticked away the long minutes, until the inner alarm went off and set fire to his rumbling belly. "Then I guess we do it the hard way!" he shouted.

Backing away from he barrels, Masters flashed five fingers at Jeffries, closed his fist, and flashed five more. *Ten minutes*, he mouthed, touching his nose with one finger. *Exactly ten minutes*.

Webster went out the window first. He waited for his comrade. Then, single file, they made their run.

Hidden by the darkness, Tank Hubbard watched as Masters and Webster exited the window and began skirting the line of sheds that marked the entrance to the yards. There was, he knew, still one man inside. "You should've known Diamond would have the cards stacked in his favor, Reese," he scolded, as if Sullivan were there and could hear him. "But it's goin' to be all right, boy. Me and old Henry here are goin' to watch your back." The old man stroked the rifle's brass breech. Then, his feet whisper quiet atop the packed manure that littered the earth all around the stockyards, he headed for the shack Masters and Webster had just left.

* - * - * - * - *

Reese Sullivan was inside one of the corrals. Gingerly, he moved among the restless beeves, his gloved fingers skimming gently over sweat-streaked hides as he crooned his soft greetings. "Whoa, boss," he whispered, passing alongside a belled cow. He kept his hand on her neck, guiding her through the other animals as he headed for the opposite side of the pen. Unconcerned, the corralled beasts let the old cow pass, paying the man no heed. Sullivan turned her loose when he reached the far corner.

Cochran was there. Trussed and tied like a calf about to be deballed, he hung suspended from the corner joist that supported the narrow walkway. He looked the fool, his arms tightly bound to his sides, his legs secured at both the ankles and his knees.

Sullivan toed his way up the fence until he was even with Cochran's shoulders, and checked the man's gag. "Your friends plan on taking you back," he breathed in the man's ear, and a glimmer of hope radiated from Cochran's eyes. "The hard way," Sullivan finished.

Cochran's pale orbs closed in despair. He felt, rather than saw, Sullivan depart, bits of wood and flakes of dust filtering down from the walkway above his head. *Damn you!* he cursed silently. He struggled vainly against the rope that bound him, and swore again. *Damn you to Hell!*

But it was not Reese Sullivan that he cursed. Not this time. It was Logan Masters and his damn plan to take the man who had humiliated Franklin Diamond. *No matter what the cost.*

* - * - * - * - *

Tank Hubbard's mother was Cherokee. He inherited none of her physical features, but all of her stealth. It was said by those who knew him, or of him, he could cross a floor littered with broken glass and eggshells, and no one would hear him pass. Now, of an age when other men grew feeble, or were unsure, he was quieter still. He moved like death.

He was through the window and inside the shed before he spoke. "I'd wait a bit, if I was you," he announced.

Jeffries sucked in a big lungful of cold air and felt the hair on the back of his neck rise, and then wilt. He dropped his pistol. The urgent need to relieve himself worsened as he felt the cold barrel of Hubbard's rifle skim the hollow beneath his ear. "Christ," he blurted.

There was the sound of soft, ancient laughter. "Not even close, sonny!" Hubbard poked the man's neck with his rifle. "But I might arrange a meeting," he offered, "you don't do as you're told."

Jeffries eyes flicked sideways. His head never moved. The man holding the rifle remained a dim presence just beyond his line of sight. "In my pocket," he said, assuming Hubbard to be one of the stockyard's company guards. They carried rifles, just like George Pullman's private army over in Pullman City; and they were just as cocky when an outsider trespassed beyond their iron gates. "My papers, and a letter from my boss to your..."

"Boss?" Hubbard laughed again. The laughter stopped as suddenly as it had begun. "Sullivan," he breathed. "You and those other yahoos. You came here after Reese Sullivan."

Surprised, the detective's head swung sideways, and then back. Eyes front, he spoke again. "You're mixing into something you got no business sticking your nose into, old man," he warned. "This is between..."

"Reese and Frank Diamond," Hubbard finished curtly. He sighed. "Only problem is, you're here and Diamond ain't." Coldly, he lifted the rifle's barrel, and then brought it down. Jeffries fell into the dirt at his feet.

Hubbard stepped over the man's body. "Left you behind to play army," he observed. He bent down and picked up the Remington. The two extra cylinders were in easy reach on top of a small keg abutting a line of larger barrels. "Well," he reasoned, "no sense disappointin' your friends."

Using the pistol, the old man began firing. Low, into the dirt and filth mounded beneath the bottom rail at the corner of the fence.

Logan Masters swore; profusely. "Son-of-a-bitch!" Jeffries had started too soon, and he was firing too low. "This way!" he ordered, grabbing Webster's arm. Together, the two men sprinted into the darkness and ran towards the pens.

* - * - * - * - *

The shots came as a surprise. Instinctively, Sullivan flattened against the planking beneath his belly and scanned the sheds for the source of the fire. One man, he reckoned, using a single pistol and moving right to left and then back again as he peppered shots in a one, two, three cadence. The knowledge brought a wicked smile. If there was only one man in the shed, then there were two who were out looking. Sullivan liked the odds. It sure beat the hell out of four to one.

Only one thing puzzled him. The shooter's foolhardy aim. It was clear from their earlier behavior that they had figured out where he was -- that he was above the pens—and still the man kept firing low.

Suddenly, there was a dull *o ooof,* and then the pained bleating of a wounded steer. Reese could hear the animal as it fell, the soft *whoosh* as it folded up and collapsed onto the ground. There was a long, tense silence—even the shooting stopped—and then a new sound lifted from inside the barricaded shed.

The clear, eerie cry of an old Johnny Reb pierced the unnatural quiet, echoing above the cold mist again and again until the dark yards became for a moment another place and another time. And then the firing resumed. This time, it was the distinctive roar and flash of a .44 caliber Henry. Tank Hubbard called out to Sullivan. "They're in the alleyway, Reese! Give 'em hell!!!"

One by one, the wounded cows inside the enclosure began to bleat and stumble. The smell of blood reached out to Sullivan, filling him with savage memories that refused to be stilled. Pistol drawn, he stood up and ran along the causeway, firing into the cattle below his feet as he pounded toward the wide gate at the far corner of the pen.

Logan Masters and Webster were trapped. They stood back-to-back in the passage, debating which way to run. Hubbard was no longer shooting into the pens. Ten shots of the sixteen rounds in his rifle's breech had wounded as many steers, and he concentrated now on the entrance to the alleyway. *And Sullivan...*

Sullivan was behind and above them. He appeared briefly at the top of the fence, a dark shadow against a darker sky, and then disappeared.

"Jesus!" Webster whispered the word, and in a momentary return to his childhood, crossed himself. He felt Masters at his back, and turned to face him.

The sweet, salty smell of blood swept both men, the sensation made worse by the sudden swell of panic within the pens. The cattle strained against the dry timbers in a futile effort to escape the scents and sounds of death, and the wood began to give. Sullivan helped them along. Dropping down from the walkway, he swung open the gates.

Logan Masters saw the cattle hang for a long moment in the wide breech that opened in the high fence. Packed tight, the animals could not move. Then—like ants crawling one over the other—they began pouring through the gate.

"The kerosene!" Masters reached out to his companion. Dumbly, the man refused to surrender the tin. Masters pried his fingers loose. "We can turn them!"

Webster's momentary terror faded. He let go of the can. Deftly, he pulled the burlap sacking from where it had been slung over his shoulder and spun it into thick, over-sized wicks.

Masters touched a match to the damp fabric; his face bathed in the sudden orange glow as the coarse fibers ignited. "Throw it!" he shouted. Obediently, Webster made the toss. Just as quickly, Masters lit the second tube of sacking, and then the third. And then he tossed the can. It arched high into the air, spewing kerosene.

A trail of blue-white flame erupted in the can's wake. Snaking across the straw-littered earth, the line of fire raced to meet its source. The pail landed squarely in the path of the wide-eyed beeves.

The stream of fire on the ground diminished, and then flared brighter. Orange-tinged flames fed on the flood of fuel that poured from the can's open spout, sputtered, and turned a pale blue. There was a brilliant flash of white as the sides of the can contracted, and then suddenly expanded.

The explosion ripped into the ominous quiet, a huge fireball erupting three feet above the ground as the rusted can disintegrated. Bits and pieces of searing hot metal rained from the sky, the sharp firebrands becoming lethal bits of shrapnel that tore through the beeves thick hides to bore into flesh and bone. The cows bolted and stampeded into the yards, their herd instinct diminished by the deeper need to escape the fire.

Webster screamed as a piece of hot metal pierced his right thigh. He went down, and was momentarily pinned against the bottom rail of the fence by a panicked steer. The animal never stopped. It simply changed course mid-air and ran on. Webster struggled to stand up, only to face a new terror. A finger of blue tinged flame raced across the packed earth and up the leg of his trousers, fed by the kerosene he had spilled, and he frantically beat it out. "Logan! Help me!!"

Master's stared at his partner, and then at the disappearing herd of crazed steers and beyond. *Where the hell was Sullivan?* And then he turned to face the sheds. Almost reluctantly, he offered Webster his hand.

* _ * _ * _ * _ *

Tank Hubbard cursed. From his place behind the barrels, he could see the commotion in the yards. Tall shadows cast by the flames danced against the face of the board fences, the distinct figures of the two men trapped in the alleyway, and then the black jumble of the horns and hooves of the rearing cows. The explosion came then, and with it a shower of hot sparks that pinged against the corrugated tin roof of the shed. Instinctively, Hubbard ducked his head and shielded his eyes, then peered out again into the renewed darkness.

The noise of the explosion had roused Jeffries. He rose up briefly on all fours, and then lay back down, a wave of nausea sweeping him as the smell of scorched hair assaulted his senses. Slowly, it came back to him; where he was, what had happened. *The reason for the throbbing pain at the base of his skull.*

The detective turned his head, his eyes slowly adjusting to the dimly lit interior of the shed. He could see Hubbard and the quick up and down pumping of the man's right hand as he levered another shell into the Henry's chamber.

Hubbard's gaze was fastened on the two shadows still trapped in the causeway. He swung his rifle to his shoulder, both men centered in the *v* sight as he chose his target and took aim. The big man first, he reasoned, the one called Masters, and then the little banty rooster who followed so closely in his wake.

Grinning, the old man squeezed the trigger. The hammer fell on an empty chamber. Hubbard quickly worked the lever. Once. Twice.

The Henry had jammed. The long tube below the barrel was hot, the mechanism that fed the cartridges into the breech refusing to work. *Hell of a note*, he mused. He swore again. At the rifle, and at the long dead Yankee he had taken it from at Manassas. "Work, you son-of-a-blue-bellied-bastard!"

Jeffries moved. Rising up, he charged Hubbard's back. The force of his attack shoved the old man forward, into the barrels. Hubbard's cursing was more profuse now, the surprise giving way to anger. He lifted his arm up and back, his elbow connecting with the side of Jeffries' head.

Hubbard felt Jeffries' fingers close around his left wrist. He turned slightly, twisting until the detective's soft belly was exposed, rising up on his knees as he regained his balance. He dropped the rifle, freeing his right hand, and reached for the knife.

The knife's haft protruded from the top of Hubbard's high boots, the rawhide bound grip molded to fit his long fingers. He pulled the blade free and up in one swift, effortless sweep and drove it home.

Jeffries felt nothing more than the sensation of being punched in the stomach. And then he sensed the warmth. It crawled across his skin, growing cold as a different kind of fire began to burn inside his gut. His fingers growing numb, he touched the place where the heat seemed most intense, and knew that he was a dead man. "For a damned shanty Irishman," he murmured, a bemused look of surprise coming when he no longer felt the pain. He fell, face forward into the dirt.

Without warning, the two wooden barrels directly in front of Hubbard crashed inward. Startled, as much by the noise as the new attack, the old drover scooted backwards and stood up, half expecting to see a crazed maverick poking its head through the opening. Groping for the rifle, he gripped it like a club, and poised for the swing.

Logan Masters dove through the gap, his shoulder crashing into Tank Hubbard's chest. The unexpected force of the blow lifted the older man off his feet, and he tumbled backwards. Masters straddled him, blind rage guiding his fingers to the man's throat. His thumbs pressed hard against Hubbard's windpipe as he lifted the old man's head up and then smashed it back down against the hard plank flooring.

"Logan!" Webster clawed at Masters' shoulders. "*Logan!*" There was no response, only the dull thud as Masters slammed Hubbard's head against the floor yet again.

Finally, Masters let go. Breathing hard, he eased back onto his heels. He was still on top of Hubbard, and made no move to stand up. His eyes flicked across Hubbard's pale face, and then to the crumpled figure sprawled beside them on the ground. Only then did he realize that the man between his legs was not Jeffries. Slowly, he stood up. "Get him on his feet," he ordered.

Webster started to argue, and then changed his mind. The pain in his own leg forgotten, he bent down to examine Hubbard. Bright purple lines above the man's collar traced the image of Master's long fingers, the blood pooling beneath the flesh where his thumbs had dug into the hollow of Hubbard's throat. "Old man," Webster breathed. He touched Hubbard's shoulder, and then shook him. "Old man?"

Hubbard's great body convulsed, his chest heaving as he began to cough. Bright red blood colored the spittle that foamed at the corner of his mouth, and he reached up to touch his throat. The cough worsened.

Logan stared down at Hubbard's still form, no compassion in him as he realized what the man had done, and for whom. He pushed Webster away, and once again straddled the old drover's body. With the toe of his shoe, he lifted Hubbard's right leg and moved it aside, exposing the man's vulnerable crotch. "I want Sullivan," he whispered. He saw Hubbard's eyelids flutter. "You're going to help me get him."

The kick was quick, vicious, and cruelly calculated to inflict a maximum degree of pain.

Unable to stop himself, Hubbard screamed.

Chapter Five

Sullivan was hurt. He leaned heavily against the fence and touched his left side just above his belt, grimacing as his fingers came away bloody. Still, he considered himself lucky. The steer had hooked him on the run, turning him completely around without knocking him down. There hadn't even been any pain, just the feeling that the wind had been knocked out of him, and that, suddenly, he needed to rest. He closed his eyes, and for the third time in as many days, wished himself home in Texas.

Hubbard's tortured scream roused Sullivan from his brief moment of indulgent self-pity. The fatigue that had consumed him when the wound in his side throbbed against his fingers was swept away by a surge of renewed purpose. He opened his eyes to a heaven bright with the cold light of more stars than mortal man could count, the air around him seeming alive with their brilliance. His other senses responded, the aroma and sounds of the smoldering bits of burlap sacking that littered the passageway reaching out to him, and he began to move.

Tank Hubbard screamed again.

There was a terrifying agony in the old man's cries, as if they were being wrenched from his very soul. Sullivan's jaws tightened, and his pace quickened to a steady, ground-eating lope.

He knew the Yards well. He had been there, from the fall of 1863 until Christmas Day in 1865, when the big gates finally opened for the first time. He had come in chains, a young, teenaged prisoner of war, the Confederacy's gift to the enterprising Yankees who bought cheap labor from the corrupt guards at Camp Douglas. For two years—six months beyond the end of the War—he wallowed in the muck and the mortar, building walls, laying the rails for the spur tracks that led to the world beyond. *While he watched his two older brothers die.*

Old memories burned deep in the man as he made his way around the pens to the rear of the row of sheds just beside the tracks. The rage came back, the same anger that kept him alive when he was a boy, and he used it.

He heard Hubbard cry out again, the shriek ending almost as soon as it began. A new sound came, from the same source but somehow seeming far in the distance, the strangled coughing of a beaten man who was fighting for air.

Sullivan flattened himself against the back wall of the shed. Gun drawn, he inched his way to the window and peered inside. A single kerosene lantern illuminated the small circle where Logan Masters and Vern Webster stood, the soles of Kyle Jeffries shoes also visible in the small circle of light.

Hubbard was lying on the floor between Masters and Vern Webster, the bulk of his weight resting on his elbows as he struggled to rise. His face was gray and contorted, the pain deep in his groin etching deep blue lines around his nose and beneath his eyes. Fresh blood trickled from the corner of his bruised mouth, and he lifted a trembling hand to wipe it away.

The soft, dispassionate drone of Logan Masters voice carried into the darkness beyond the window. "You're making it hard on yourself, old man," he cajoled; as if he really gave a damn for the man who lay at his feet. "And for what?" He laughed. "A *fellow Texan?*" There was no attempt to hide the ridicule. It was as if Masters thought that true loyalty was something only a Harvard man—perhaps, even someone from Princeton—was worthy of, or could understand. He hunkered down beside Hubbard, resting on his heels as he continued to torment the man with his words. His fingers toyed with Hubbard's red neckerchief. "Sullivan doesn't give a damn about you. The only thing he's interested in now is saving his own..."

Contemptuously, Hubbard spat. Still capable of drowning a piss ant with a stream of tobacco juice, his aim was true. The nicotine-laced spittle found its mark, landing dead center in Masters' open left eye.

Humiliated at something he considered the ultimate insult, Masters face went chalk white. For a long moment, in spite of the pain, he was still. Then, the color flooding his cheeks, he went mad. "You bastard!" he roared. He fell forward on his knees, his shoulders bunching as he grabbed at Hubbard's throat. "You ignorant, ill-bred bastard!!"

Hubbard felt Masters fingers close tightly around the red scarf, and then a terrible wrenching at the base of his skull as the stout fabric was twisted into a finger-thick cord that cut off his wind. Feebly, he tore at the man's fingers, unable to cry out as the neckerchief was drawn tighter. The bright red cloth disappeared beneath the graying folds of slack flesh above Hubbard's collar.

Vince Webster clawed impotently at Masters' shoulders. The viciousness of his companion's attack on the old man sickened him. "Logan!" He shouted the man's name a second time. "He's no good to us dead, Logan!"

As if a switch had been turned, Logan Masters regained control. He relaxed his grip just long enough to raise his right fist and bring it down hard against Tank Hubbard's lax belly only inches below the old drover's belt. The pain pushed another loud cry from behind the man's clenched teeth.

Unheard, Sullivan slipped through the open window at the back of the shed. There was little sound now; only the intense breathing of the two detectives, and the labored gasps of the strangling Tank Hubbard. Sullivan thumbed back the hammer on his revolver. The noise of steel working against steel filled the small shack. "Let him go, Masters," he breathed. "Now."

Masters back stiffened, and for a moment he froze. A smile flickered briefly across his lips as he realized his good fortune. His instincts had been right. Hubbard was Sullivan's Achilles heel. Without turning away from the old man, he spoke. "I'll kill him, Sullivan," he breathed. A single quick flip of his wrist changed the position of the cloth rope around Hubbard's neck, the knot strategically positioned across the old man's wind pipe. "If you don't drop the gun *now*, I'll kill him."

Sullivan's voice matched the other's. "Then he'll be in Hell to open the gates for you, *chacal*."

Logan Masters head snapped to the left. The last thing he saw was Reese Sullivan's smile.

Sullivan fired. Point-blank, the slug tore into Masters face directly between his eyes, the impact lifting the man up and away from Tank Hubbard's chest. His dead fingers slipped away from the bright red cloth that encircled the old drover's neck and he collapsed onto the floor.

An unnatural quiet filled the shed. White vapor rose up from Masters' still form, the shimmering mist drawing the blue-tinged smoke from the barrel of Sullivan's revolver and hovering above the man's body in a strange, macabre halo that mirrored his image.

Ghost-like, the steam dissipated, carrying the dead man's soul into the blackness beyond.

Stunned, Vince Webster backed up a full pace, his hands shooting into the air as he collided with the side wall of the shed. He had just witnessed an execution. Sullivan had the advantage from the moment he stepped through the window, and yet he had killed Masters. *With no more remorse than if he had swatted a fly.* A sharp crack sounded as Webster's head hit a two-by-four stud, and he dropped a hand to rub at the pain. Instinctively, Sullivan followed the sound. Crouching, he swung to his right, his pistol cocked and waist level.

Webster's heels smacked against the wall as he pressed even closer to the rough planking at his back. He raised his arms even higher. "Jesus, Sullivan," he croaked. His eyes flicked to the cold body beside Jess Hubbard and then back to Reese Sullivan's face.

Straightening, Sullivan uncocked his pistol. His stance was still the same, a cat-like awareness that made him seem more animal than man. One eye on Webster, he knelt down beside Tank Hubbard. He felt for a pulse, his fingers gentle as he probed the flesh at the old man's neck. A sporadic flutter whispered beneath his fingertips, the same erratic pattern that marked Hubbard's labored breathing.

"Tank?" Sullivan bent forward. The pale light from the lantern heightened the gray cast to the older man's skin, dark bruises appearing at his throat and on his right cheek.

Hubbard coughed, his shoulders shaking as the air rattled in his lungs. His lips parted, moving noiselessly as he struggled to find the words. Another great cough came, shaking loose the blood and phlegm, a new trickle of red coming as he gestured for Reese to raise him up. Unmindful of the taste in his mouth, he lifted a weak hand to wipe his chin. "Took your own damned sweet time, boy," he rasped. He forced a grin, his eyes focusing and coming to rest on Masters' still form. He kicked out at the body, a grim satisfaction in him as he heard the dull thud of leather against dead flesh.

"I've got to get you out of here, Tank." Sullivan had been busy, his hands moving swiftly over the old cowboy's lean frame. The damage he could feel—the broken ribs—concerned him less than the wet rattle that emanated from deep inside the man's chest.

"You still got business to take care of, Reese." Hubbard nodded at the place where Webster stood hugging the wall. "This yahoo, and the stray that's still out there..." His eyes narrowed as he stared out into the yards. An eerie orange glow was growing beyond the barrels, and he could hear the faint crackle of smoldering straw. "Reese."

Sullivan sensed the controlled panic in the old man's voice. He chose to ignore it. "I've got that maverick tied up in the pens, Tank." He handed the man his revolver. "It's going to take me about five minutes to get him tamed and bring him home..." Worry for the old man made the humor brittle.

Hubbard grimaced and rose up on one elbow. The pistol felt unusually heavy against his palm. "You're gone more than the five, Reese, I'm going to have to kill him." He nodded toward Webster.

Sullivan sprinted into the darkness. He returned with Jess Cochran in tow and a full minute to spare.

* _ * _ * _ * _ *

The first rays of a rising sun painted the eastern horizon a pale pink, the color muted by the black soot belching forth from a hundred chimneys as the city came alive. Coal stoked the flames in the factories north and east of the Chicago River, the same coal that fed the fires in the great locomotive that steamed out of the rail yards and onto the main line heading west.

Trey Underwood stared out at the skyline, watching as window after window in the tenement across the street began to wink in varying shades of yellow. He could see movement behind the curtains and the shades, his gaze lingering on the lace-veiled window directly across from his own. A young woman—he presumed her to be young—bent forward at the waist to brush a full head of long hair, her unfettered breasts rising and falling with each sweep of her arm.

"It's quite disconcerting, Trey; for a mother to wake up and find her son indulging in an old man's sport." Vanessa Underwood's voice cut into her son's brief reverie. She stood at the threshold of the doorway that separated their rooms, her long, ash-blond hair loose around her face and shoulders. "I raised you to be something more than a *voyeur*, Trey. And your father..."

The young man turned away from the window. "My *father* checked out of the Palmer House last night, with five thousand dollars of our money." He was immediately sorry for the words and the tone of voice he used when he said them, but too angry not to go on. "Why, Mother?"

Stunned to learn that he knew, Vanessa Underwood withdrew into the fragile facade she created long ago to engender compassion from men who threatened her sense of control. The fingers of her right hand toyed with the long curl at her shoulder as she chose her next words. It was a unique experience, finding it necessary to play the same game with her son she had played so often with so many others. In the past, she had always been able to control him with a look or a subtle raising of her eyebrow, but now...

Her recovery was quick, and she pulled herself erect. "We're going home, Trey. I would suggest that you get your clothing packed, and make whatever calls you feel are necessary to say a proper goodbye to your friends from school. As to anything else..." She faced her son. "I have no intention of discussing Reese Sullivan with you. Not today. Not ever." As far as she was concerned, the matter was ended.

Trey said nothing. It had been thirty-six hours since he last slept, and he felt as if every single hour had been ten. "I don't want to quarrel with you, Mother. I'm too damned tired, and too..." Something in the woman's face made him stop. He knew she wasn't listening to him.

It was, he knew, pointless to go on. She had made up her mind, and nothing short of an act of God would change it. He shrugged his shoulders. "I'll say my good-byes, Vanessa."

There was a moment of awkward hesitation as the woman realized he addressed her by her given name. An eeriness in the fact that his tone—the inflection in his voice as he said the words—sounded almost identical to Reese as he had spoken to her the night before. She immediately dismissed the thought, attributing it to her own fatigue. Then, content that she would ultimately have her way, she withdrew.

Trey watched as his mother left the room, knowing from the way she carried herself that she considered herself the victor. For as long as he could remember, she had been this way; this delicate looking creature who ruled with an iron will. Her own father, when he was still living, and later, Wes Underwood.

The young man realized he had been no different from the others. He had spent his life silently agreeing to her demands, following the lead of his elders and avoiding the rages and the tears. The thought sickened him. He was only three years shy of twenty-one, damn near a man full grown, and still afraid of his mother's tantrums.

Unconsciously, he rubbed at the long scar on his right cheek, tracing the place where the condor had marked him. The memories of that day in the desert north of Yuma came flooding back, and with them a very different kind of fear. It was the same gut-tearing panic that haunted him in his early morning dreams, the insidious terror which chewed at him from within. That he was not man enough to find the men who murdered his stepfather; the same men who had beaten him and left him in the desert to die.

Trey's hand shook as he wiped the sweat from his forehead. Somehow Vanessa and her rages didn't seem so formidable now. He laughed—a bitter irony in the sound. *God pity the poor fool who had the misfortune to be the one who would tell her he was gone.*

* _ * _ * _ * _ *

The locomotive crawled out of the siding, waved on by a solitary switchman. He tripped the lever, watching as the strips of steel slipped smoothly into place, the noisy *clack-clack* sounding as the engine picked up speed and pointed its nose west. There was nothing out of the ordinary as far as the trainman was concerned, just one more cattle train making the turnaround trip to Kansas City and beyond. It was only a matter of time before the slatted cars returned to the stockyards, filled with the western beeves Armour and Swift turned into steaks and chops.

For want of anything better to do, the reformed gandy-dancer counted the cars as they rolled past. Fifteen empty stock cars, a Santa Fe reefer, and two crew cars. *Two?* The man scratched his head. Wasn't any of his damned business. He waved at the departing train, dismissing it, and trudged back to his shack.

And then he saw the smoke. The train forgotten, he sprinted towards the yards and sounded the alarm.

* _ * _ * _ * _ *

Tank Hubbard's hands were cold when Reese Sullivan reached out to adjust the man's blanket, the flesh beneath his fingernails the color of blue clay. He was dying, by inches, the punishment he had taken inside the shed at the Stockyards drawing harsh lines around his mouth and eyes.

Sullivan sat on the edge of the man's bunk. There had never been a question of calling a doctor, or getting Tank to a hospital. The old man would have none of it. *Just take me home, boy. Home.*

"Sullivan?" Vince Webster intruded on Sullivan's thoughts, a hesitancy in the man's voice clearly bespoke his apprehension.

Reese stood up, spreading his legs as he adapted to the back and forth sway of the crew car. "You have a problem with the accommodations, Webster?" Feeling a need to keep his hands busy, he began rolling a cigarette.

"You can't keep us trussed up like this!" There was a sudden flurry of activity as the man struggled against the ropes that bound he and Cochran back-to-back. "Dammit! You got no right!"

Sullivan took a long draw on the freshly built smoke. "How many more?" he said finally, the words coming on a thin stream of blue smoke.

Webster stopped struggling against the ropes. Stubbornly, he stared straight ahead, focusing on a gap between two planks in the side of the car. It was as if he'd been struck deaf and dumb.

Jess Cochran had been similarly afflicted before, but not now. The youngest of the four detectives who had pursued Sullivan, he was also the most affected by what happened. That, and all the stories he had heard from Webster and the others about Sullivan's methods of dealing with men he considered his enemies.

"There aren't anymore," he breathed. He felt Webster tense, the ropes that bound their arms suddenly cutting into the flesh above his elbows as the other man jerked violently to the left. Shutting his eyes against the pain, he continued. "Logan Masters," he murmured. "He told Diamond that you were only one man, an *old* man, and he didn't need an army to take you down." The laughter came then, a sardonic laughter that sounded harsh and accusatory. "The sorry son-of-a-bitch," he swore. He shook his head, his tone changing to match the expression deep in his dark yes. "We're dead men, too, aren't we, Sullivan?" he asked.

Sullivan said nothing. He pinched out the butt of his dying smoke, and went back to resume his vigil beside Tank Hubbard's bed. The old man's breathing was more labored now, the wet rattle deep in his chest louder than before.

Hubbard's eyes were staring into the distance, as if he could see far beyond the confines of the converted boxcar. He was talking, his mouth moving rapidly as the words poured forth from a mind that had regressed to another time. He called out, summoning people Sullivan did not know, naming towns that had been born, and boomed, and had died. And then, finally, softly, "Sarah?"

Reese Sullivan cursed. His hand was on the old man's shoulder, and he slipped it beneath his head. He could feel Hubbard dying beneath his fingers, the substance that was the man draining away to leave behind nothing but the broken shell of something very fragile and very old.

There was a sharp *phfff* as Hubbard suddenly inhaled. He held the single breath a long time, stubbornly clinging to life as his chest expanded and his back arched. He tried to rise up from the cot. Then, the air leaving him, he simply slipped away. It was, Sullivan thought bitterly, a hell of a way for a man to die.

For a long time, Sullivan sat holding Hubbard's head cradled in his arm. The old man had been many things in the seventy-odd years he had lived. Trailblazer, pioneer. Lawman. Outlaw. But above all, he had been a *man*; a decent man and a good friend. And, Sullivan realized—facing for the first time his own mortality—one of the few men left old enough to call him *son*.

Gently, Sullivan let go of the old man and stood up. The silence in the boxcar was broken by the sound of weathered canvas as he picked up Tank Hubbard's sun-bleached slicker and shook it out. He worked slowly, drawing the stiff cloth around the old outlaw's shoulders, his hands steady as he knotted the rawhide *reata* that bound the shroud in place. He could feel Cochran and Webster watching him, and purposely prolonged the grim chore. Time, so often his enemy, had become his ally.

Sullivan knew from the rhythmic *clickity-clack*—from the amount of time it took for the front and rear wheels to pass over the gaps where the twenty-four foot spans of steel were joined— the train was slowing down. The decrease in speed was barely perceivable at first, becoming more obvious as the train snaked to the right. They were approaching a siding, with no customary signal from the engineer. Sullivan knew the reason. Webster and Cochran did not.

Neither man said anything when Sullivan approached. He bent down, Tank Hubbard's big "*Texas toothpick*" seeming to grow from his fingers. "We're going to take a walk, Webster," he announced. "Just you, me, and the old man." A single flick of his wrist sliced the cord binding Webster's feet.

A loud banging on the back door of the car filled Webster with a brief spate of hope and he scrambled to his feet. Unsteady, his legs cramped from the long hours he had been tied, he lurched forward.

Red-faced, with a wild mane of red hair that matched his cheeks, Benjamin O'Toole stuck his head in the door. He held a bucket in his hand, and he waved it back and forth like a signalman's lantern. He looked right through Webster as if the man were not there. "Brought fresh water, Reese, for the old man..." The words faded as he spied the tarp-encased body on the narrow bed. "Jesus," he breathed, crossing himself.

"I'm going to need some time, Ben."

O'Toole nodded. "You take all the time you need, Reese." Shaking his head, he withdrew.

Webster's hoped for salvation followed the engineer out the door. He faced Sullivan. "You own the train, Sullivan," he raged, "or just the man that stole it?"

Sullivan said nothing. He nodded toward Tank Hubbard's body. "Pick him up," he ordered

Webster hesitated. His choices, he knew, were extremely limited. *To die here and now, or...* As long as he was alive, he reasoned, there was always the chance he could get away. Resolutely, he went to the bunk, and hoisted Tank Hubbard's remains on his shoulder.

The train had begun to move when Sullivan returned to the crew car alone. He said nothing to Cochran, choosing instead to let the man's fears create the demons that would haunt him and eventually rob him of his manhood.

* - * - * - * - *

Sullivan's mood was black. An unscheduled layover in Kansas City had set him on edge, his concern turning to cold anger aimed more at himself then anyone else when he found out the delay had been caused by a wait for a private car on loan to a friend of George Pullman's son. There had been a tedious ceremony when the palace car joined the train, the engine, tender and one other car uncoupled to allow the Pullman a place at the front end. A second delay came when Reese's car was also unhitched and relegated to a place at the rear.

O'Toole had brought him the word: "Word is it's just a pair of smart-ass college boys, Reese, headin' west to play cowboy for the summer!" He ended his brief commentary with a limp-wristed wave, sashaying away like an over-aged dancehall queen.

Reese didn't give a damn about the two faggots. The four hour wait in a full prairie sun was excruciatingly long, and he paced the distance between his car and the dripping reefer more than a dozen times. Tank Hubbard's body was inside the boxcar, resting atop a chunk of last winter's Lake Michigan ice and a layer of clean straw. He intended to take the old man home, just as he had promised, and not as some stinking, bloated mass of rotting flesh robbed of its final dignity.

At last, the train began to move. Sullivan swung aboard the crew car, his elbow crooked around the side railing as he stood on the end platform and leaned out to watch the steam engine. Puffs of white steam erupted like twin geysers, the great wheels disappearing behind the vapor as they spun and sparked against the rails. Then came the familiar *ka-punk, ka-punk* as the engine chugged forward and each car lurched against the couplings. The train curved southward, gradually picking up speed as the engine neared its top speed of fifty miles an hour. Sullivan remained on the platform until the wind and soot drove him inside.

Jess Cochran waited. He sat propped against the side of the car, the fear that had gnawed at his belly subsiding and becoming something new. There was a coldness in him now, a stoic acceptance of what was to come. He was a dead man—as dead as Masters, Jeffries, and Webster. It was only a matter of time.

Reese lit yet another cigarette. He struck the match against his thumb nail, and then changed his mind. He pinched out the flame and broke the stick in two. He addressed the younger man without looking at him. "You know, don't you, that the old man was worth more than all four of you put together?"

Cochran laughed. "Do you really think I give a damn?"

Sullivan's eyes narrowed. "You will," he promised.

* - * - * - * - *

Three hundred miles out of Dodge City, Kansas, somewhere between Trinidad, Colorado and Hell, the train stopped to take on water and wood. They were in the high desert mountains, inside New Mexico Territory, in a land where the temperature would vary as much as seventy degrees between night and high noon.

A loud grating sound tore into the natural quiet of the place as Reese Sullivan reached up and opened the sliding door on the refrigerated car. The cold air rolled out to greet him, the damp white vapor feeling good against his skin as he hoisted himself up into the dark interior.

Vince Webster lay in a far corner, inside a dark hole between two great blocks of ice, as still as the shroud-covered corpse that had been his only companion since Kansas City. Wrist and ankles red and raw from the stiff remnants of baling twine Sullivan used to bind him, he was pale, his lips the same color of blue as the deep furrows on either side of his nose. His jaws locked as he tried to choke back a great sob, and then, unable to help himself, he began to weep. There had been rats in the car, scurrying about and over him in the darkness, their incessant chirping evoking terrifying memories of a ghetto childhood in New York's Hell's Kitchen. "For God's sake, Sullivan..."

Reese pulled the man upright. There was no gentleness in him as he ushered the man toward the open doorway. Involuntarily, Webster recoiled, the bright rays of a setting sun scalding his eyes. Bodily, Sullivan lowered the man to the ground, the muscles in his neck and back straining the soft chambray work shirt and pulling the seams at his underarms until the threads seemed about to burst. His burden increased as Webster lost his balance and fell forward onto his knees.

Sullivan jumped onto the ground. Roughly, he jerked the man to his feet. Using a well-placed knee as a prod, he forced Webster away from the car and into a clump of thick chaparral.

Webster stared out across the desert plateau. As far as he could see, there was nothing, not one sign of human habitation. The sheer desolation of the place—the barren brown rock and sand—tore at him. It was, he felt, as if he and Sullivan were the last men on earth. He was going to die here, and no one would ever know.

There was a dull thunk at Webster's back and a strange tingling in his hands and fingers as the cords that bound his wrists fell away. Gingerly, he wiggled his fingers, reluctant to make any sudden move. Then, feeling Sullivan's hand on his shoulder, he froze.

Reese turned the other man away from the sun. "East", he said, pointing the way.

Webster's eyes widened in sheer terror as he realized Sullivan's intentions. "No..." he whispered. The dry, brown emptiness spread out before him, broken only by the shimmer of thin fingers of steel that disappeared into the horizon in two directions. He would have preferred a gun to this. Visions of a lingering death tore at him. He had already been a full day without water or food, and ahead of him..."No..." he begged.

The train had begun to move again. Sullivan felt the earth beneath his feet rumble as, one by one, the cars passed him. He swung aboard as the crew car came abreast.

Webster dog-trotted beside the car, trying desperately to catch hold. Twice he stumbled, recovering his footing and running even harder than before. "Sullivan!" he screamed. Gasping for air, he sprinted beside the boxcar. He reached out.

Sullivan swung out from the side of the car. Carefully gauging the distance, he kicked out at Webster's head. He caught the man just above the left ear and sent him sprawling into the dirt and gravel beside the tracks.

Weeping, Webster rose up on his knees. The desert seemed to increase in size as the train grew smaller. "Sullivan-n-n-n!!"

Following the sound, a dazed Jess Cochran trudged up the embankment, each step jarring his aching head. Five feet away from the other, he stopped. He stared hard at his partner, noting each sob that racked the man's body, each change that occurred in the man's posture. "Vince," he called softly.

Webster was still on his knees. Without rising, he turned toward Cochran, his hand trembling as he reached out. Relief flooded his countenance, but the hysteria had not eased, and he was still crying. "He's left us to die. Damn him..." There was no fire in the words, only despair. "What the hell are we going to do?" Webster asked the question as if Cochran were the only man who could answer it.

Cochran helped the man up, grimacing as Webster leaned heavily against his shoulder. The fight was gone out of the man; all the bravado and big talk Cochran had heard mile after mile when they were bound together with Sullivan's rope. "Hell, Vince," he mocked, "we're going to get even, just like you said." The sarcasm added an edge to the man's words. "Get loose, find Sullivan, and kick his ass." He laughed. The sound stopped as soon as it came. There was a fleeting, sobering memory of a madman he had once escorted back to a state run asylum northwest of Chicago. His laughter had sounded the same.

Stubbornly, Cochran forced himself erect. He was still alive. And, he decided, he wasn't about to die. Not in the middle of some damned desert; and sure in hell not for an asshole like Frank Diamond. "We're going to walk," he said resolutely, pointing towards the eastern horizon. "And when we get to the first town, we're going to wire Diamond for our wages.

"And then, Vince, we're going to tell him to shove this job up his ass."

* _ * _ * _ * _ *

Just across the line into Texas, the train made its final unscheduled stop. Unable to wait any longer, Sullivan and Ben O'Toole laid Tank Hubbard to rest three feet beneath the rocky soil. It took them another hour to build the cairn. And then they got back on the train, and Reese Sullivan got drunk.

Chapter Six

The woman stood apart from the others who waited on the station platform. Something more than distance separated her from the clusters of impatient shop keepers and ranchers and their wives. An occasional glance in her direction brought a knowing smirk from the men or a contemptuous frown from one of the women.

Eva Delgado accepted the judgmental scrutiny with a wry smile. In appearance, she looked no different than the half dozen or so Anglo women; at least, in her mode of dress. The difference came in her bearing and the subtle coloring of her skin and hair. *And her eyes.*

The orbs were neither blue nor brown. Green, flecked with sparks of amber and topaz, their color was enhanced by the long, black hair that tumbled over her shoulders and down her back. Like strands of fine silk thread, it drew the sun, glistening blue-black against her smooth cheeks. Half white, one-fourth Mexican and one-fourth Comanche, she was beautiful, a sensual and exotic blending of three races; and reviled for that beauty.

She didn't care. With a directness she knew would be interpreted as brash impudence, she returned the sharp appraisal of each man and woman, and one by one, they averted their eyes.

The long wail of the steam engine reached out to the crowd waiting on the platform and there was a steady shuffle of feet as everyone moved out of the shade in anticipation of the train's arrival. Eva joined the others, moving through them toward the very end of the platform.

Cavy sack slung over his shoulder, Reese Sullivan swung down from the rear steps of the last car before it rolled to a complete stop, the momentum of the train carrying him forward at a brisk trot. And then he saw the woman.

She ran toward him, lifting her skirts to expose trim ankles and mocassined feet, her long hair lifting away from her face like a black banner. Sullivan caught her, sweeping her into his arms, the sweetness of her freshly washed hair filling him with a sense of home. The kiss was long, hungry; neither one giving a damn who saw, or what they might think.

They parted, but still held hands. "Two," the woman said, answering the question before he asked it. She laid her head against Sullivan's shoulder. "A filly, and a little stud colt out of the red mare from Bannerman's." She tried hard to hide the smile.

Sullivan drew her close and kissed her again. "Don't be so smug," he scolded. "You had a fifty-fifty chance on that one."

"You still owe me five dollars," she countered. They had made a bet on the Bannerman mare and the foal she would throw. The woman held out her hand and wiggled her fingers.

"Later," Sullivan teased. "After I take a look and make sure." Then, unable to keep his hands off the woman, he pulled her close and kissed her again.

"You would think, old man, that I'd at least rate an introduction."

Sullivan froze. The voice came at him from his left and to the rear. Soft, arrogant and irritatingly familiar. One hand on each of her shoulders, he gently pushed Eva away, searching her eyes and seeing a look that was something more than surprise, but not the alarm that would have spurred him to a different reaction. Still, he kept her at his back as he turned around.

Trey Underwood stood a scant foot away from Sullivan. Neatly dressed, freshly washed, he looked as if he had just stepped off the pages of Harpers Magazine. The smile was just as real, and just as empty. "I don't believe I've had the pleasure..." the pause was intentional, and he made the word sound obscene, "...Madam."

Eva Delgado moved from behind Sullivan's back and stood at his side. "Reese?"

Sullivan's jaws were working. He should have checked the Pullman himself. His face mottled, and then turned white, the anger growing as he became painfully aware of his disheveled appearance and the three days of dirt. *The gray in his beard.* "This," he began, staring hard at the younger man, "is Eva." The sudden flicker of amusement in Trey's eyes, the snide grin that tugged briefly at the corners of his mouth, did not escape the man's notice. His voice whisper soft, he continued. "And this, Eva, is—"

Eva Delgado stared directly into Trey's blue eyes, one eyebrow arching as her gaze shifted briefly to Reese's grim countenance. The resemblance was unsettling, and undeniable. "Is Trey," she declared. She extended her hand.

The gesture was unexpected. Trey hesitated, surprised that she knew his name, and then took the woman's hand. "Trey Underwood," he finished, purposely stressing the last. He took pleasure in her touch, and held her hand longer than the social amenities required; then, inspired by what he was seeing in his father's face, he lifted it to his lips, and kissed her fingertips. "My pleasure, Mrs.—"

She cut him off. The electricity between father and son was as intense as lightning during a summer storm. "It's Delgado," she announced. If the young man intended to play games at Reese's expense, or hers, he was sadly mistaken. "Eva Delgado." There was a moment's hesitation, and she continued. "I am your father's whore." She was smiling when she said the words, a different kind of humor far back in her eyes when she saw Trey's cheeks flush. Satisfied, she turned from him and took Reese's arm. "Let's go home, Reese," she murmured. She was still smiling when she turned back to the younger man. "Trey." It was, he realized, an invitation to join them.

Sullivan stared at the woman's profile for a time. He swung his gaze to his son then pointedly, in spite of what Eva intended, to the Pullman. Not one spoken word passed between them, but the meaning was clear. *Get out.* He turned, and led the woman away.

Trey watched as Sullivan and the woman climbed into the buggy. He was still watching as they drove off. "Not this time," he breathed. Catching the arm of the man unloading his bags from the Pullman, he announced, "I'm going to need a hack."

The man's brow knotted. "You mean a buggy? Livery stable. Across from the hotel." He held up the two valises. "Hey, boy? What about these?"

Trey tossed the man a silver dollar. "Later," he called.

* - * - * - * - *

Sullivan watched as the woman rose up from the bed. It never failed to amaze him, the grace she displayed when doing ordinary things. Walking. Doing the dishes. Scrubbing his back. Climbing in and out of their bed. "Eva." He crooked a finger at her and tried to coax her back.

She was already putting on her blouse. "He'll be coming, Reese," she said gently. The next word, "*soon*," was muted by the soft fabric of the skirt that she slipped over her head.

"Like hell," he declared. He sat up, drawing the sheets around his knees as he watched the woman finish dressing. "If he's got any sense at all, he got back on that train and is already heading home to his mother."

Eva was shaking her head, remembering the look on Trey's face; the Sullivan stubbornness she saw in his eyes. "He's your son, Reese." She sat down on the foot of the bed, her hand warm against his leg as she stroked his right ankle. "It's not in him to come this far and then simply turn around and run away just because you told him to go home."

Sullivan reached out to the table beside the bed. He made a fruitless search for tobacco, and then swung his legs over the edge of the bed. "I don't want him here, Eva."

The woman laughed, a gentleness in the sound. And love. A great deal of love. "You've always wanted him here, Reese." She chose her next words carefully. "You were just afraid he would never want to come."

There were times when Sullivan wished the woman didn't know him so well. This was one of them. "It's wrong, Eva." He was unable to hide the remorse. "The reason for his being here, it's all wrong..." He shook his head.

"The reason doesn't matter, Reese. What matters is that he is here." She was at the window. "Now." With her right hand, she opened the curtains, and then lifted the sash. Sullivan could hear the muted jingle of harness riggings and traces.

The woman was out the door before Sullivan could call her back. Swearing, he pulled on his pants, and followed after her.

Trey was still in the buggy when Reese joined the woman in the front yard. Once more, they sized each other up, their expressions the same.

Sullivan was the first to speak, and then only one word. "Well?"

The younger man stepped out of the buggy. He didn't waste any words. "You left Chicago with five thousand dollars of Vanessa's money," he began. The words came softly, laced with a bitterness that had been nurtured for a long time. "Since I can assume it wasn't a loan, or anything she might have owed you, I want to know just what you intend to do to earn it."

Reese smiled, but there was no warmth in his face or his eyes when he answered the youth's question. "The same thing I intend to do to earn the other five," he answered.

Trey's jaws tensed, then relaxed. He hadn't known about the other money, and it showed. "Ten," he breathed. He recovered, but the belligerence was still there. "So?" he demanded.

Sullivan's cold smile grew. "So, she hired me to find the men who killed Wes," he declared. "And to bring back whatever it was she thinks they stole."

There was another long silence as Trey digested the words. "You're going into Mexico," he said finally. Diamond's fee for the same job had been a flat two thousand and expenses.

Reese felt Eva tense beneath his arm, and he pulled her close in a quick, reassuring hug. "I'm going into Mexico," he echoed.

Trey turned back to the buggy. He began unloading his bags. Sullivan strode across the yard and grabbed the younger man's arm. "And just what do you think you're doing?"

Trey pulled away. "Right now, unloading the rig." He stared up at his father. "I figure ten thousand entitles me to a room," he said evenly. "At least until we leave."

Eva Delgado stepped between them. "Of course you'll stay, Trey," she announced. Ignoring the fury deep in Sullivan's eyes, she took the young man's arm and ushered him up the stairs and into the house.

* - * - * - * - *

Trey had risen early. In the cool morning air, he explored the cluster of buildings that surrounded the house, taking in the measure of what his father had built. Then, ending his search in the big stock barn, he climbed the ladder to the second floor.

From the loft, he could see everything. The corrals, the manmade ponds in the fields beyond the fences. A bunk house, a second, smaller barn, and an assortment of sheds and pens. And, of course, the main house.

The red brick structure had surprised him. He had lived in the house until he was five, and yet he had no real memory of the place. In the back of his mind, he had always thought of the ranch as being the way Vanessa had described it; a place that reeked of cattle and old leather and sod floors. Instead, he had found nine rooms, the ones he had seen furnished in a simple good taste that gave a new meaning to the word elegant. There were none of the heavy Victorian trappings or draperies that filled the homes in Boston, and no over-blown ornamentation. Simple, clean lines, and furniture that was comfortable to sit in. And no wasted space. *A place for everything, and everything in it's place*, he thought.

A soft rustling, the subtle noise of shod feet slipping across straw, roused Trey from his daydreams. He cocked an ear toward the sound, following it and moving silently across the stacked bales of hay as he headed back toward the ladder.

Saying nothing, he peered over the edge of the two-foot square opening, and watched from above as Eva collected eggs. She moved among the hens, searching out their nests and calling them by name as they flocked around her feet. They scolded her as she stole their eggs, flapping their wings and clucking loudly as she moved from nest to nest.

Trey followed the woman with his eyes. She bent down, her soft laughter rising above the noisy clucking of the hens as she scratched the fat belly of the shaggy-eared puppy that had followed her into the barn. His hind leg strummed the air in rapid tempo to her scratching, his round bottom burrowing deeply into the thick straw as he squirmed happily beneath her fingers.

Immediately overhead, Trey saw the woman bend forward to give the pup a final pat, the cotton blouse she wore drooping at the throat to expose the dark hollow between her breasts. She was wearing only a sheer camisole beneath the buff-colored shirt, a bit of pink ribbon showing against her skin. It made a pleasing picture for the young man; the contrast in color between her flesh and the clothing she wore. There was an early morning freshness to her, the exotic sheen of her skin and hair intensified by the single shaft of sunlight that poured through the eastern window to bathe her in an almost ethereal glow.

Trey watched her rise. He waited until she passed beneath the opening to the loft, and then dropped to the floor behind her.

Startled, Eva spun around. The eggs were cradled in her skirt, and she instinctively dropped a hand to secure them. Dust and feathers flew up from the floor to dance around her face, and she brushed them away. "That was almost the end of your breakfast!"

Trey's fingers plucked a single feather from the woman's hair, just above her right ear. The hand lingered there, and then caressed her cheek. She was, he realized, much younger than he first supposed.

Eva stared up into Trey's face. His palm was warm against her skin, the flesh cooling as one finger traced a line down to her lips. Suddenly, without warning, he drew her close and kissed her. It was not the kiss of an infatuated boy attempting to steal a moments pleasure. The kiss was harsh, demanding; filled with a man's need.

She did not fight him. Nor did she respond. And when he finally let go, she still held a dozen unbroken eggs in her skirt. She backed away from him. "We'll need some cream from the well house. You'll find a small copper tin at the shallow end of the tank."

Angry -- his pride smarting -- Trey grabbed her arm. "And that's it?" he demanded. He didn't know what he expected, but it wasn't this.

She faced him, her green eyes luminous and burning with a quiet rage more unnerving than any tantrum. "You'll want to know it all.

"I'm twelve years older than you, Trey. Thirty to your eighteen; thirty to Reese's forty-two. I have known your father since I was sixteen. And before that..." She smiled, but the anger did not fade. " ... what happened before that is none of your business.

"I love your father. Enough that I have no intention of ever hurting him." She peeled his fingers away from her sleeve, her voice becoming soft, filled with steel. "Nor will I allow you to hurt him."

He searched her face, the words registering and finally sinking in. *Since she was sixteen.* He did some quick ciphering. If she was telling the truth—and he had no reason to doubt her—she had, he assumed, been with Reese for fourteen years. Trey's lips compressed in a tight line.

It had been ten years since Vanessa and Reese Sullivan's divorce was finalized; *ten years since he had last seen his father.* "You bitch," he seethed. The anger he had felt—the feeling of utter abandonment—when he watched Reese ride off that final time, filled him again.

Sensing the younger man's thought, Eva drew back her hand. She meant to slap him, her fingers curling into a tight fist as she stopped herself. Fighting the rage, she concentrated on the pain as she drove her fingernails deeper into the tender palm of her right hand. Anger filled her voice when she was finally able to speak. "Vanessa took you away from here when you were five. She waited until your father was gone, packed you up, and left here with a man Reese considered his friend." She hesitated, hating herself for the bitterness she felt against a woman she had never met.

"I didn't steal your father away from you, Trey, or from your mother. I simply took what she had thrown away shortly after you were born." Her eyes narrowed, cat-like, and she backed away.

He watched as she left the barn, selfishly choosing not to believe her. She was a whore. The when or why didn't make any difference. She had come to the place when Reese and his mother were still married, and had taken Vanessa's rightful place. *His place.*

* - * - * - * - *

They ate breakfast in silence, Sullivan's belly growling as he drank a third cup of coffee. Eva was unusually quiet, and Trey...

His stomach rebelled again. Even the extra cream in his coffee hadn't helped. He gave up and put the cup down. There was an awkward silence as he debated his next words. How the hell did he go about something as simple as addressing the kid? *Son. Boy.* Even using his first name seemed out of the question. "Your clothes," he said finally.

Trey was finishing the last of his bacon. There was a wary antagonism in him when he responded. "What I've got on," he said, smoothing the seams on his linen trousers, "and three other suits in my bags."

Sullivan scratched his nose. He cast a quick glance at Eva, watching her face as he spoke the words. They had argued until long after midnight, until she convinced him of the rightness of the thing. Time alone with his son, no matter what the circumstances. "We're going into Mexico, not to some social function at the Ritz."

The woman smiled.

Reese stood up, going behind Trey's chair and then continuing. "You'll need boots. A slicker." There was a sound as Trey pushed back his chair and stood up. Reese's scrutiny continued, his eyes narrowing as he unconsciously compared his own height to his son's. He still had a good four inches on the boy, as well as twenty pounds. He continued. "A couple pairs of denim pants, twice that many shirts." The list was growing. "Long johns. A poncho. A decent hat." He gave up, shaking his head. "Eva," he finished.

She was clearing the table. "I'll pick up what he needs at the mercantile." She paused in her chore just long enough to measure Trey's frame with her eyes. "From the skin out," she announced.

Trey found the woman's gaze disconcerting. "And now?"

Sullivan was already heading out the door. "We find out if you can ride," he answered.

Trey's hands locked around the back of the chair, his knuckles turning white as he shoved it back into place beneath the table. In the space of a scant two hours, the man and the woman had reduced him to the status of a weanling child. "I can ride," he muttered. "You can bet your damned ass I can ride."

* - * - * - * - *

The longest week of Trey's life followed. There had been no let up, not from the first day, and not now. They did the same thing, again and again—the piddling ranch chores before breakfast, the meal, and then back in the pens.

The chambray shirt Trey wore soaked through at the armpits and across his back. He struggled with the rope, his fingers blistered and aching with the effort of a dozen tries. And all the time, Reese was on his back.

Sullivan's rope sang, whistling through the air to settle neatly over the head of a bay gelding. Rope-broke, the horse came to an immediate stop. "You can be the best rider ever to sit a horse, but it doesn't mean a damn thing if you can't catch one when it's running loose," he observed. He led the bay though the gate and began saddling him.

Once more, Trey's rope dropped impotently across a horse's fat rump. He swore, and reeled in, and knew the frustration of seeing Reese already mounted. Sullivan shook his head, and kicked his horse into a trot. Vindictively, he circled the pen, knowing the horses inside would follow. They bunched and then broke into a run.

Eva watched from the front porch, a weariness in her as she saw the battle of wills. Reese and Trey. Trey and the livestock. It had been a long week.

Unable to stand it any longer, she stepped down off the porch. She caught up with Reese and walked beside the horse. "Why, Reese?"

He didn't answer her question. Reaching down, he scooped her up from the ground. The kiss was the one he intended to give her when they first woke up. It didn't work this time, either. "Because," he began, "maybe if I keep it up, he'll give in and go back where he belongs."

Eva twisted free. "He belongs here," she mumbled, as stubborn in her own way as the man was in his. She dropped to the ground, but did not let go of the saddle. "I'm sick of it, Reese. The constant sniping. Trey walking around with his fists clenched. You turning your back on him and walking away, as if daring him to take a swing at you." There were times when she wished it would happen. Still angry, she grabbed suddenly at the tender flesh beneath the gelding's underbelly, giving it a quick twist as she stepped away.

Sullivan felt the big gelding bunch. Startled, the bay kicked out with its rear legs, its head going between its front legs. Ass-end over elbows, Reese tumbled out of the saddle and hit the ground. Hard.

"Dammit, Eva!" he roared.

She laughed then sprinted toward the house with Sullivan in hot pursuit.

* _ * _ * _ * _ *

There was a smug vindictiveness in Trey as he kicked open the front door. He stomped across the room, heading directly for the front bedroom. And then he pounded on the door.

Sullivan felt himself wilt. Beneath him, Eva stifled a giggle. "I'm going to kill him," Reese hissed. "But first I'm going to cut off his..." The last was stopped by the sudden rattling of the door.

Reese was out of bed and into his pants like a surprised lover caught in another man's bedroom. Bootless, he padded across the floor. He opened the door and found himself face to face with his sweat-drenched son.

"Every one of them, old man," Trey bragged. He grabbed Reese's arm and pulled him to the open front door.

Sullivan stepped out onto the porch. Fifteen horses stood haltered and tethered to the hitching post. Reese raised an eyebrow. "So you can rope," he said. "Put them up. Tomorrow, we'll find out if you can shoot." He turned around and went back into the house. The sound of the younger man's cursing filled him with immense satisfaction.

* _ * _ * _ * _ *

Trey held the packet in his hands. He turned it over, fingering the twine that bound the stack of letters and debated going through it. He hesitated at first, and then worked the individual envelopes free, careful to leave the cord's knot intact. The varied return addresses surprised him, the top two the most intriguing. The first was an official looking document bearing an additional wax seal and a bold signature in the upper left hand corner: *Cade Devereau, US Marshal.*

The second letter—to his surprise—bore the tell-tale logo of Diamond Detective Agency. This missive was not as bulky as the other, but its weight was still impressive. He fingered the logo, his gaze lifting to the kitchen doorway, and then the hallway to his left. This letter interested him the most. *If his old man had been sacked from the agency, then why the hell the apparent collection of documents?* He regretted now that Eva had been with him when the clerk at the Wells Fargo office in town had given him the mail. She was undoubtedly aware of what the package contained, and would be able to tell Reese what had arrived.

He slipped the twine back around the stack of envelopes, sorry he didn't have the time alone to work his usual magic. The past year at school had left him an expert at diverting or censoring the mail his parents were intended to receive, and he had no doubt that he could have opened and resealed each and every letter in the packet without discovery. He balanced the thick bundle against his palm, and swore. *To hell with it.* Turning to his left, he carried it down the hallway, pausing at the door to the one room in the house where he had not yet trespassed. More out of habit than courtesy, he knocked.

Reese Sullivan's deep baritone rumbled from within. "Come."

Trey opened the door and stepped inside. The room came as a surprise; completely different from the spartan domain the young man expected, yet somehow familiar. Floor to ceiling bookcases filled the walls, the shelves lined with leather bound volumes that were as well used as they were well cared for, a semblance of order to the titles and the authors. "Jesus Christ," he breathed.

Sullivan looked up from the stack of papers on his desk. "And Socrates," he announced, "and Homer." He pointed to the shelf at Trey's right.

The humor missed its mark. Trey was too absorbed in the titles. Reverently—books became his one great passion from the very first time he had seen the printed word—he slipped a slim volume from its place on the shelf and opened the cover. It was a collection of the poems of John Donne. A name was written on the flyleaf, the delicate script of an almost feminine hand faded to an illegible reddish-brown.

Sullivan rose from his chair and joined his son. He tapped the faded signature. "James Augustus Sullivan," he said. "An Irish Protestant, doctor, and scholar." The smile bore a generous measure of irony. "And a pacifist." When he saw that nothing was registering, he continued. "Your grandfather."

Trey put the book back on the shelf. The forgotten mail packet still tucked in his belt. He pulled it free and handed it to his father. "A pacifist," he echoed.

Sullivan took the package back to his desk and sat down. "He left Ireland to escape the war between the Protestants and the Catholics. The brother against brother.

"He left Virginia for the same reason, only it was too late." He left the rest unsaid, engrossed in the contents of the thickest envelope.

"Why 'too late'?" Trey asked.

It was as if Sullivan had not heard the question. "Tell Eva I won't be wanting lunch; just an early supper," he ordered.

If Trey learned nothing else in the last two weeks, he had learned that when Sullivan was finished talking, the conversation was ended. He shrugged. *It didn't make a damn anyway*, he reasoned. He'd only had one grandfather when he was growing up, and that had been his mother's father; Senator Emmett Tremayne Danforth.

He shut the door and carried Sullivan's message to the woman.

* _ * _ * _ * _ *

The woman outdid herself. Trey was amazed at the variety of foods she prepared, the meal going well beyond the usual meat and potato fare that Sullivan seemed to prefer. There was a linen cloth on the long table and napkins, as well as an impressive array of silver, china, and crystal. Even candles. And she wore an elegant, emerald green gown.

It matched her eyes.

Sullivan had dressed for dinner, too. Another departure was the wine. He brought a bottle to the table and kept their glasses filled.

Trey watched as Eva trimmed a cigar. She handed it to Reese, their hands entwining as she held the lit match. It was, he realized, as if they were observing some secret ceremony, and he was the uninvited intruder. He helped himself to another glass of wine, and downed it in a single swallow.

Reese's goblet was empty, and he placed it upside down beside his plate. "The men in Arizona," he said finally, the first words he had spoken directly to Trey since the meal started. "What were they after?"

Startled, Trey considered the question; and then his answer. He stared into his empty glass, wishing it was full; seeing instead his own distorted reflection in the goblet's stem. "I don't know," he answered finally.

Sullivan exhaled. He had hoped for more from the younger man, and wondered now if he was lying. "The packet that came today," he began, "the papers from Diamond. Your mother's letters to the agency about what Wes was doing in Arizona, and what was missing when..." *they found what was left of his body*, he finished silently. Aloud, he said, "...they brought Wes back to Yuma.

"There was a notebook," he continued. Something in Trey's face, a subtle flicker in the younger man's eyes made him pause. When nothing was forthcoming from the other, he continued. "A collection of documents that Wes was supposed to have purchased for a client in San Francisco. He made the buy with twenty-five thousand dollars of his client's money, but he never delivered those papers. He—you and he—made the trip to San Francisco, but he never made the delivery. I need to know why."

It took a little time before Trey realized what Sullivan was suggesting. *That Wes Underwood was a thief.*

The fingers of Sullivan's right hand drummed, one-two-three-four, against the table, softly, the linen cloth muting the noise until it sounded like a muffled drum. The sound tore at Trey, unleashing memories of the desert and the bird. The vulture had made a similar sound when it was feeding, a sound that had never completely gone away.

"I'm leaving here in the morning," Sullivan announced, angry at the younger man's stubborn silence. The forefinger of his right hand traced the delicate circle on the bottom of his upturned glass.

Trey had been leaning back in his chair. He came forward, reaching out to help himself—for the third time—to the dark hued wine. "And..?"

Reese studied the young man, willing him to meet his gaze. Their eyes locked, and he continued. "I'm leaving here alone."

The long muscles in Trey's right arm tensed, his temper flaring. Instinctively, he made a fist, the goblet he was holding in his hand shattering; the sharp sting of the glass intensified by the alcohol content of the wine. "Like hell," he rasped. Eva reached out to him, a napkin poised to bind his hand, and he jerked away. "I did it all," he argued. "The roping. The damned nigger chores you meant to wear me down!" He flexed his arm. He had never been soft, and the labors of the last two weeks had simply honed a different set of muscles. His right hand disappeared beneath the table. "Even this!" he hissed. In spite of his bleeding fingers, the Remington appeared with an admirable degree of speed. It was aimed dead center at Reese Sullivan's broad chest.

There was a noise, a sudden explosion that roared from the end of the table. The napkin covering Reese Sullivan's left hand lifted slightly, a cloud of blue-gray smoke coming one with the smell of scorched cloth as the corner of the napkin turned black and momentarily caught fire. Eva Delgado screamed. Trey Sullivan rose up out of his chair, the pistol tumbling from his numb fingers, the dull pain in his right shoulder coursing down his arm to assault the sensitive nerves at his elbow. Instinctively, he probed at the wound with his left hand, his fingers exploring the shirt for the expected wetness. There was no blood.

With his right hand, Sullivan wadded up the napkin. He lifted it away from the concealed pistol. "Double barreled," he intoned. "Made to order by Elliott Firearms." His voice carried the bored weariness of an overworked teacher once again explaining the lessons to a recalcitrant student. "Two fifty caliber hand loaded cartridges." He smiled. "Allows a man to be inventive."

Eva whacked Sullivan's back. "Damn you, Reese!" She rarely swore, and when she did, it sounded all the more harsh. The fact that the slug he had fired was a dummy load—a solid, hard wood pellet meant to stun without maiming—did not lessen her anger.

Trey's shoulder still throbbed. He massaged the soreness, his fingers kneading the flesh and feeling the welt begin to rise. Livid, he stared down at his sire. "You're not leaving me behind!"

Sullivan snorted. "You're not ready." He made no effort to hide the contempt. He was watching the younger man, gauging Trey's moves as he edged back towards his chair. *The pistol.* He waited until Trey was a finger tip away from the weapon and then cocked the Elliott. "Choose the spot, boy."

Trey considered the words, and then backed away. Keeping both hands above the table, he backed into his chair and sat down.

Sullivan nodded his head. "Finally. After two weeks. A single show of self-control and common sense." He stood up. "We're leaving at four." His voice lowered and he jabbed a finger in his son's face. "The next time you pull a gun, you'd damned well better be ready to use it." Without another word, he left the room and went outside.

Trey's entire body trembled. The shaking was so great that the dishes on the table rattled. "It was a test," he seethed. "Just another one of his damned tests!"

Eva Delgado watched as the young man picked up his pistol and left the table. He came back just long enough to get the bottle of wine. She braced herself for what she knew was coming. The back door slammed shut, and then the screen door to the back porch. Twice.

Chapter Seven

Sullivan finished his last cup of coffee while it was still dark. He was dressed for the trail, in soft denims and chambray, his close-fitting leather chaps molded to his lean thighs and hips. Eva helped him slip the heavy wool serape over his head. He preferred the hand-loomed blanket to the traditional rancher's denim jacket, and with good reason. The wool would protect him from the early morning cold, and be useful again later to conceal the two *bandoliers* he would wear when they were well south of the big river.

"Where is he?" It was still difficult for him to use his son's name.

Eva nodded toward the door. "Trey's been ready for hours, Reese. I don't think he ever slept." She hesitated before she said the next, a troubled frown pulling at the corners of her mouth. "He's been drinking. He finished the wine we had at supper, and I heard him looking for another bottle when he finally came in."

Reese cupped the woman's chin in his hand and stroked her bottom lip with his thumb. If he was concerned about his son, it didn't show. "You didn't sleep either," he admonished. He had wakened once, in the middle of the night, and found her sitting up in bed just staring at him.

"I'll make up for it tonight," she promised. It was a lie, but she told it well. She inhaled, the sound unnaturally loud in the early morning quiet. Even the birds were still asleep. "Well, Mr. Sullivan." For his sake, the smile was real.

Arm in arm, they walked through the door. There was time for one kiss, and then he was gone.

* - * - * - * - *

Trey's gut was on fire. He stood just outside the barn door, his jacket open to the morning chill, taking deep breaths as he attempted to put out the flame. Nothing helped, and he was sorry now he had tried to drink himself to sleep. This time—the last several times, he realized bitterly—the liquor hadn't helped.

A horse whickered inside the barn, a second animal snorting in answer. Trey could hear Sullivan talking to the animals, a seldom heard gentleness in the man's voice as he paused at the stall where the three-week old stud colt born in his absence was suckling its mother. "Grow strong, little man." There was a soft *whack* as he patted the colt's rump. "You're going to help me build a whole new blood line."

Hearing the noise and jingle of curb chains, Trey stepped away from the open barn door.

Reese loomed out of the darkness, his breath white against the black morning air. Both saddle horses were behind him, the pack horse trailing at the rear.

Immediately, Trey was aware of another presence. He sensed, and then saw, a blur of blackness at Reese's side, the animal suddenly standing dead still. Ears pricked, the big dog stood with its right front paw upraised, as if it had been frozen in its tracks, the tempo of its panting increasing as the animal picked up a new scent. Only the ears moved, going flat against the dog's head. Without thinking, Trey reached out.

Too late, Sullivan saw the move and called out. "Don't!" The big dog lunged forward, his mouth closing around Trey's inner arm, just above his elbow. The weight of the animal, the incredible power in his broad chest and the sudden fury of his attack, knocked the young man back against the side of the barn. He was held there, pinned against the rough planking by paws the size of a child's open hand, unable to move.

Sullivan snapped his fingers. Just once. The big dog dropped to the ground and obediently came to heel.

"Jesus," Trey breathed. His eyes still on the dog, he held out his arm.

Sullivan examined the torn sleeve. The denim jacket and the shirt beneath were both punctured and wet with the dog's saliva. He took off his glove and felt for blood. Satisfied there was no real injury, he let go. "*As de palas,*" he said, nodding at the dog, the Spanish running together to sound like a single word, somehow lyrical in its pronunciation. Difficult to translate literally and still convey the original meaning, but—Mexican or Anglo—the superstition was the same: *tarjeta de muerte*, the death card. "Ace of spades; the harbinger of death." He mounted his horse, waiting for Trey to do the same. "He answers to *Palas*."

The brief explanation did little to still the questions racing through Trey's mind. He climbed aboard his horse, a profuse amount of relief flooding him when he settled into the saddle. From his place astride the gelding, the dog didn't seem so large. "Where'd he come from?"

Sullivan considered the question, his eyes resting on the wolf-like beast. The dog settled back on its haunches, sitting still, yet conveying the restless energy and eagerness of a moving thing. "I don't know," he said finally. "One day, he was just here." The part of him that was old country Irish accepted the dog's arrival as an omen, a perversion of the ancient belief that a black cat coming unannounced to the door was a sign of good luck. Then, anticipating the question Trey was about to ask, he said, "I keep him penned and away from the house. Until I need him."

They moved out, Trey aware of the way the big dog fell into place beside Reese's horse at a single unspoken command. The pecking order had been clearly established. Sullivan came first, and after him, the dog and the pack horse. And, behind that, Trey.

The young man grinned. He had been a fool to think it would be otherwise.

* _ * _ * _ * _ *

They traveled west, away from El Paso, crossing the *Rio Bravo* and bypassing Juarez as they rode south into the harsh Mexican desert. It was, for Trey, a grim trip back into his recent past. As the sun rose, the sameness of the terrain began to haunt him, the cacti and wind blown rock stark reminders of the sand flats north of Yuma. Each passing mile brought the memory closer, the insidious panic setting him increasingly on edge.

The fear reached its zenith when they passed through a dry wash and came on the remains of a downed burro. There were no flies, no small winged predators. *Just the birds.*

The vultures were feeding. Three hens and a younger male. The staccato *thunk-thunk* of their sharp beaks against the bloated flesh echoed across the small arroyo, their onyx bright eyes sinister and soulless as they fearlessly sated an ancient hunger without regard to the intrusion. Single file, Sullivan and the dog passed them with unseeing eyes, unaffected by the carnage.

But not Trey. He fell back, a macabre fascination in what he was seeing and hearing, his chest filling with the painful sting of bile-raising revulsion. The feeling grew, until—in the heat of the moment—it surpassed the fear. He reined the horse to a halt and coldly pulled his Henry from its boot. There was a moment's hesitation, his lips compressing in a tight line as he attempted to work the rifle's mechanism without making a sound, and then he took aim. The shot tore into the broad feathered chest of the largest hen, and the feasting stopped. The other birds screeched loudly and momentarily withdrew.

Trey watched as the wounded condor spread its wings, its long neck recoiling as it scented fresh blood. The bird teetered drunkenly on jack-straw legs, and then, insanely, tore at the dark hole where the bullet had penetrated. It seemed impervious to the pain, pecking at its own breast as the feeding frenzy resumed. Cannibalistically, the younger birds turned on the older, the dead burro forgotten.

Trey raised the repeating rifle a second time.

There was a sudden clatter of shod hooves against shale and sandstone as Sullivan bore down on the younger man at a dead run, the packhorse trailing behind him. He swung out with his coiled *reata*, knocking the weapon out of Trey's hands.

"Just what the hell is wrong with you?" he roared. The strain of too many years as the hunter and the hunted drew stark lines on his forehead, the fear that he made a mistake tearing at his belly and flooding him with momentary, but very real, feelings of self-doubt. It was as if he had allowed someone to get behind him and toy with him like a cat with a soon-to-be-dead mouse.

Father and son, they faced each other, both of them breathing hard as they fought their separate, inner turmoil. Sullivan was the first to speak, a growing need within him to tame a rage now directed more at himself than at his son. "Trey..." It was the first time he had addressed the young man by his proper name.

Stubbornly, the younger man remained silent. He dismounted and picked up the rifle, careful to keep his back to the man, afraid Sullivan would see his face. *His eyes.* What was there he could say, and still look like a man? The truth was, he had seen and heard the condors feeding, and it scared the piss out of him. The rifle had been a frightened little boy's handful of rocks, a fruitless attempt at bravado. And now the fear was back. He remounted the horse, stuffing the rifle into the boot, and then moving out.

Sullivan stared at his son's back. He made a mistake, he thought darkly, allowing the youth to come with him. And it was too late now to turn back.

* _ * _ * _ * _ *

They made camp at high noon, a full eight hours after their journey had begun. Trey hobbled the stock while Reese put together the army-issue lean-to that would provide them protection from the sun, and none at all from the relentless heat. In silence, they set up camp and prepared their noon meal.

Sullivan ate slowly, a deliberation in him as he studied his son's profile. Trey's untouched plate lay on the ground at his right foot, the scent of the food drawing the smaller desert scavengers, and the dog.

The black was on his belly, stalking the full tin plate as if it were a living thing. The dog would inch forward across the sand, drop low onto his belly, and then rise up again, intent on the hunt. It was, Sullivan mused, as if the dog were consciously playing a game, the same way a pup would chase its tail or stalk a grasshopper. A subtle shift in Trey's posture—the movement of the young man's foot—would interrupt the game, the dog dropping low again and burrowing into the dirt. He would lay still, watching, and then—at some inner signal, unperceivable to the man—begin crawling forward again.

Out of the corner of his eye, Trey caught the dog's subtle movement. Without turning his head, he watched the animal, the curiosity overcoming the wariness. Suddenly, his arm began to ache, the sweat stinging the red ridges where the dog had grabbed him, the pain a reminder of the animal's disposition.

There was a vindictiveness in the young man as he bent down and picked up his tin plate, and no small amount of joy as he began to tear apart the thick pieces of side meat. The dog watched him, the animal's big head coming up suddenly as the scent from the bowl intensified. The black's ears came forward, its nose twitching as it stretched its neck forward and watched the young man pop a piece of meat into his mouth.

A second chunk of pork dropped into the dirt in front of the mongrel, just beyond the animal's front paws. Without rising, the dog strained forward, coaxing the piece of meat to him with his long tongue. The gravy-laden chunk remained just beyond his reach.

From his perch on a nearby rock, Sullivan watched the contest between his son and the dog. Twice he was tempted to intervene, and both times reconsidered. Two things could happen, he reasoned. The dog would yield to the younger man's will, or he would not. Whichever way it went, it was Trey's party, and not his. And still he watched.

The dog's eyes darted between the piece of meat just beyond its nose, and the young man with the plate. He watched as the man ate another piece of meat, and felt his belly rumble.

Trey bent forward. Another chunk of meat lay in the flat of his hand. He showed it to the dog, and with perfect aim, tossed it into the dirt next to the animal.

The black began to dance in place, its paws kneading the ground beneath its belly. Brown eyes, so black they seemed to disappear into its face, stared out at the bits of bacon, saliva forming on the dog's tongue. Twice, half-heartedly, he barked. First at the meat, and then at the man.

Grinning, Trey dropped down on one knee, unaware as his father came forward in his place on the boulder beyond. The younger man reached out, a fresh piece of meat in the gloved palm of his left hand.

Whining, the big dog glanced at Reese Sullivan. The brown eyes begged more eloquently than the sound that came from deep within the animal's throat. Unseen by his son, Sullivan nodded his head.

The dog's neck stretched forward, its mouth opening. Then, gently, as if plucking a flower, the black took the piece of proffered meat and swallowed. Trey laughed, the sound soft, filled with a sense of victory. He reached out with his left hand, ruffling the fur at the big dog's collar. "Beats the hell out of a bullet between the eyes, doesn't it?" he cajoled. Only then did he release the hold on the Remington.

Sullivan relaxed. His left hand dropped away from his holster, and he hunkered down to sleep. A smile tugged at the corner of his mouth, and he hid it with his Stetson as he covered his face against the sun. *It would have been a hell of a choice*, he mused, *which one to shoot. His son, or his dog.*

* - * - * - * - *

Unassisted, Vanessa Underwood stepped down from the rented surrey, her mouth turning downward in a deep frown as she snapped open her parasol and found only a small amount of reprieve from the sun. The place was as dismal and as backwoods as she remembered. All the bitter memories came flooding back, along with her intense hatred of the ranch, the haughty disdain evident in her face. Then, her expression changing to one of stubborn determination, she inhaled deeply. Her son was here, and she wanted him back, and if that meant dealing with Reese, so be it.

The front door opened, and Eva Delgado stepped out onto her front porch.

The woman beside the buggy could not conceal her surprise. She tried, vainly, angry her face betrayed her, and called out sharply to the old man she hired to drive her from town. "If you don't mind," she said curtly, holding out a gloved hand to point at her valise.

The old man proved surprisingly agile. He scooted across his seat and jumped down, a wry smirk touching his lips as he sensed the woman's unease. He pulled her bag from the boot, nodding in greeting to the woman on the porch. "A visitor, *señora*," he called. With great ceremony, he took Vanessa's arm and led her to the bottom of the stairs. He had recognized her from the beginning, but had not let on, his mind reliving the old scandal as if it were yesterday. His mouth opened wide in a toothless grin. "*Mrs. Sullivan.*"

Eva Delgado dismissed him with a single glance "No, Mr. Jennings," she said softly. "Mrs. Underwood." Smiling, she offered her hand. "Vanessa."

Without thinking, Vanessa Underwood reached out. At the last moment, she changed her mind. "And you are...?"

The smile danced far back in Eva's green eyes. *The woman didn't recognize her; didn't even remember that Eva had been part of the household service staff in the early years after Trey had been born.* "Mistress of this house," she answered. She opened the door and stood back.

Stiff-backed, Vanessa marched across the threshold, the silver tip of the closed parasol thumping against the wood floor. This was the house Reese had brought her to as a bride, and now another woman—*a very young woman*—had taken her place. '*How dare he?*' she fumed silently. Her pale cheeks flushed a deep scarlet and the old jealousies, like the forgotten feelings, were resurrected and began to grow.

* _ * _ * _ * _ *

Sullivan pulled up, the gelding dancing beneath him as the sun-crazed gnats burrowed into the folds at the animal's flanks and between its legs. A second swarm buzzed around the bay's ears, and the horse shook its head.

Trey rode at Sullivan's right, the big dog between them. "How much farther," he rasped. The desert had taken its toll, on his skin and his throat.

Reese lifted his arm, the braided quirt dangling from his wrist as he pointed toward the mountains. They were just north of the *San Miguel*, the desert far behind them. Already, the drab browns had turned into the lush greens of the Chihuahuan grasslands, the budding caltrop bright yellow-orange against a bed of emerald. The grasslands stretched as far as the eye could see along both sides of a finger-thin thread of gray water. "Just beyond the river," he said, "twenty miles into the mountains."

Trey stared out beyond the man's pointing finger. The lower slopes of the *Sierra Madres* mountains loomed before him, breathtakingly rugged, newer than the glacier-worn mountains he had known in the East. There was a primal beauty to the place, a wildness that intrigued more than intimidated. Unlike the desert, it seemed alive. Without thinking, Trey urged his horse forward. It was as if he was being drawn by the mountains.

Sullivan fell in behind his son. In the long week they had been on the trail only a few dozen words had passed between them. The younger man remained locked in a world of his own, beyond Sullivan's understanding.

Not that he hadn't tried. But the barrier was there. *The years*, he thought. *Or something more.* He spurred his horse into a trot and moved up to ride shoulder to shoulder with his son. For a second time, he pointed to the narrow pass leading into the mountains. "They call it *Entrada al Infierno*," he began, the words soft and melodic as they rolled off his tongue. "The gateway to hell," he translated.

"And the town?" Trey asked. Sullivan had drawn him a crude map, their second day out.

"*Ciudad del muerte*," Reese answered. "The city of the dead." He shrugged, his shoulders lifting; seeming even more broad and powerful beneath the *serape*. "Bridger calls it Limbo."

Trey's brow knotted. "Bridger?" The name was familiar, but he couldn't remember why. When he was small, a hundred different names had stuck in his memory. Men his father had worked with, or pursued, or told stories about to entertain him. He decided it didn't matter. "How much longer?"

Unable to help himself, Sullivan laughed. It had been the same when Trey was just a child. *How much farther? How much longer?* Or *I've got to pee.* Still laughing, he kicked his horse into a run.

* _ * _ * _ * _ *

Ansel Bridger lowered the telescope, using his palm to collapse the brass banded tube. He stood for a time, staring out across the grassy basin, the telescope thumping softly against his gloved fingers as he debated a future that just took an unexpected turn. "Sullivan," he whispered, genuinely surprised that his men had not known. He swung the glass to his eye again, this time focusing on the second rider. It took him awhile before he recognized the youth, but the resemblance could not be denied. This time when he collapsed the spyglass, he put it away. Then, amused by the way fate had seen fit to toy with him, he mounted his horse.

The two *comancheros* fell in behind. "And now, *Patrón?*" the bigger one asked.

Bridger kept his horse to a walk until they reached the bottom of the small wash. "I go back to the *pueblo*," he said, "and wait to greet an old friend."

Mendoza's eyes narrowed. "And me?" he asked.

Bridger stared into the horizon. "You will go back to the ranch," he ordered. "Until I send for you." Leaving the two men behind, he kicked the big roan into a run.

* _ * _ * _ * _ *

They entered the town at dusk, aware of the many pairs of eyes that greeted their arrival and followed their tracks. Trey felt the hairs on the back of this neck bristle and rise, his right hand lifting to brush the feeling away. When he could not, he turned to face Sullivan. The question died before he could ask it.

A severe change had occurred in the big man who rode beside him. Even the posture was different, the wary way Reese's left hand disappeared beneath the striped *poncho* added to the ominous set of his shoulders. His skin was dark from the long week in the sun, the deep tan transforming his face to an expressionless mask that seemed wrought from finely chiseled obsidian. Above the dark beard, his eyes looked uncommonly bright, as soulless as a pair of perfectly matched blue marbles, his gaze all encompassing.

It was as if he could see through the adobe walls, or—Trey realized—through a man.

Uncomfortable, Trey turned away, his own eyes busy as he surveyed the drab surroundings. The town was a curious maze of buildings, all of them old, seemingly impervious to decay. Adobe brick, baked and bleached by the sun, from the ramparts of an ancient *presidio*, the outlines still definable in the back walls of the structures that had been built abutting the original fortress. Some of the older buildings, he saw, rested on half-buried foundations, a distinct difference in the ancient rock that fit together without any sign of mortar.

The inhabitants of the small city were also a blending of the old and the new. *Mestizos* prowled the streets, an arrogance in them as they brushed aside the fragile, much smaller dark-skinned *indios*; both of them yielding to the Mexicans.

There were others in the streets, Trey noted. Peering out at them from the gloom between the narrow alleyways and from inside the darkened doorways. Anglos, trying hard not to be seen.

Sullivan placed a hand on Trey's right forearm, and felt him freeze. "There," he said. He indicated the place with a single nod of his head.

Trey's mouth opened in disbelief. A single building loomed before them at the end of the long *paseo*. The mica-flecked white stucco walls shimmered beneath a half-dozen *faroles* hung suspended from a ceiling which created the floor of the second story balcony. Not one mote of soot marred the glass-encased lanterns, the beveled crystal forming prisms where the wrought iron frames joined the glass panels. Color radiated from the spectrums at the base of each lamp, the muted hues washing across the face of the building to create a myriad of tiny rainbows.

Unlike the other buildings within the compound, floor to ceiling windows flanked the wide doorway. And from beyond the front door, Trey heard music. Soft, unexpectedly genteel. A remnant from another time and another place.

"What the hell?" he breathed

Sullivan dismounted. "There are two things I want you to remember." He took his time tying off his mount and the pack horse, speaking softly, as if the walls could hear. "Ansel Bridger is different from any man you've ever met," he spoke with the assumption that Trey had no reason to remember the man, "or ever will meet. Physically," his eyes narrowed as he considered the next, "as well as in the way he thinks. The second thing—" he hesitated again, staring up into his son's face and trying to convey everything with a minimum of words, "—this is his town, and these are his people."

Trey threw his leg over the saddle horn and slid to the ground. "You make him sound like some kind of old world lord." He was shaking his head. "He could have picked a better kingdom," he observed, seeing only the dirt and the poverty.

Sullivan laughed, sardonically. "There isn't much better than when you own it all. And all the people in it." Calling the dog to him, he headed for the open front door.

* _ * _ * _ * _ *

Ansel Bridger stood in the shadows at the back of the long room just beyond the arched doorway leading to his private quarters. Secure in his surroundings, he was unarmed. He lounged against the cool adobe, his brown eyes studiously exploring the faces of his many patrons, not one man escaping his examination. He held them all in contempt, these ill bred *desperadoes* who robbed and plundered north of the border. They would make a raid—a bank, perhaps, or an occasional merchant rumored to have some secret hoard—and then run from the law. To this place, to spend their paltry treasures drinking his watered wine and screwing his jaded whores.

The quadroon laughed, softly. The outlaws had made him a very rich man.

* _ * _ * _ * _ *

Sullivan picked a table in the rear of the room. A drunk was asleep in the chair against the wall; a sunburned youth with a hint of peach-fuzz bleached the color of ripened corn. He sprawled across the table, his arms spread above his head, a lost soul drowning in a sea of cheap whiskey. The boy didn't look to be anymore than fourteen, but already the face bore the tell-tale signs of too much drink and not enough food.

Trey reached out to touch the boy's shoulder, and felt himself rudely shoved aside as Sullivan picked the kid up by the collar and belt and dumped him unceremoniously in the dirt on the floor.

They sat, Reese taking the chair recently occupied by the young drunk; the big dog slipping beneath the table to lie at his feet. And then they waited.

Trey was on his third tumbler of *mescal* when he saw Sullivan's eyes narrow slightly. He felt the dog stir and heard the quick panting, and then sensed the strong presence at his back. Setting his glass down, he half-turned in his chair to stare up into the brown eyes of a face somehow very familiar, and very out of place. His mouth dropped open, but he could not find the appropriate words.

Sullivan reached out to lay a restraining hand on his son's arm. "Ansel," he greeted. The smile seemed to crawl across his face before reaching his eyes. "You'll have to forgive the boy. It's his first time away from the big city." When he felt Trey tense beneath his touch, he increased the pressure on the younger man's wrist. And then he stood up and extended his hand.

Trey rose up out of his chair also. He was surprised to find himself considerably taller than the man who stood only a scant foot away.

Ansel Bridger was short. He stood only a half-inch above five-feet-six, a man of considerable bulk without one ounce of flab anywhere on his compact body. A full beard and a lionesque mane of long, curly black hair framed his dark eyes, the orbs the same color as his mahogany-colored skin.

On anyone else, the man's short legs would have been described as those of a bantam cock, and would have been ridiculed. But not on Bridger. Trey recognized instinctively that no one but a dolt would ever make fun of Ansel Bridger.

"Well," the man breathed. He released Sullivan's hand, and extended his ham-sized fist to the younger man.

"Trey," Sullivan urged softly.

The young man's mouth was suddenly dry, and—for a moment—his voice failed him. He recovered quickly, suddenly bothered by a gut- wrenching feeling of apprehension that tugged at his memory, yet something he did not fully comprehend. "Mr. Bridger." Trey felt the massive fingers close around his hand, and sensed a strength more animal than human.

"It's been a long time, boy."

Trey could not conceal the surprise. "Sir?"

Bridger's lips parted in a gregarious smile. He liked the *sir*, recognizing it for what it was: the inbred good manners exhibited by the grandson of a United States Senator, and the learned respect of a young man for his elders. "You were little more than a toddler the last time I saw you," he said affably. It was a convincing lie, well told. "It was wrong of me to assume you would remember."

He dismissed the young man, turning his attention back to Sullivan. "You'll need a room, Reese. And something more fitting than this..." He picked up the green bottle from the table and held it up to the light.

"What I'd like right now, Ansel, is a bath, a shave, and a hot meal. And later..." He didn't have to finish.

Bridger nodded, the thick curls at his forehead bouncing above his eyes and ears. "We'll have dinner together, Reese." It was not a request. He took a watch from his pocket. "Eight o'clock."

Sullivan nodded his head in acceptance. And then he summoned the dog.

Trey followed the man and the dog across the room. He could feel Bridger's eyes on his back, his shoulders lifting as he tried to shake the sensation that something was chewing at the base of his skull, something which had been there before and had hurt him. His eyes swept the room, searching the faces of the men who turned away from his scrutiny, marking their wariness and the way they watched him after he passed them by. *What the hell is this place?* he pondered. *And who the hell is Bridger?*

Chapter Eight

"You should have told me he was a crossbreed," Trey groused. He pulled off his right boot and grimaced at the rank odor of his sweat-damp socks.

Sullivan sat in the tub, working up a thick lather as he shampooed his hair. He disappeared beneath the water just long enough to rid himself of the suds and then resurfaced again to shake the water away. "And you have a problem with that?" Sullivan had lived too long to be bothered with the bigotry and petty snobbery his ex-wife indulged in during their marriage. It was clear from his tone he was not going to tolerate it in his son. Easing a crick in his neck, he leaned back in the tub and let the steam work, waiting for the young man to respond.

Trey piled the pillows up at the head of the bed and lay down. He was too tired to argue the new theories on the intellectual dominance of the white race that were his mother's most recent religion. "He reminds me of..." His brow knotted as he tried to remember.

"Dumas," Sullivan suggested. It didn't matter which one. Father or son, the two writers had—like Bridger—retained the mark of their Negroid heritage in coloring and features. The water sloshed as he raised his legs and rested his heels on the rim of the tub. "You were studying literature," he continued. "I would have thought you could have managed to acquaint yourself with at least one of the Dumas' before you were kicked out of school."

Trey's head snapped up. He came up off the bed suddenly, his face turning gray as the *mescal* raced from his stomach through his veins and to his head. "I wasn't kicked out," he protested. It was a poor lie.

Sullivan grabbed a towel and stood up. "Like hell you weren't." He stepped out of the tub. The pain in his legs was not as bad as it had been before, but the subsiding aches did not mellow his temper. "You didn't even make it through the first semester without being put on probation." It had been eating at him for some time, Trey's failure to apply himself at Harvard. *Or at anything else, for that matter.* "You weren't at the school a month before they had you up on charges for being drunk during class, and for starting a brawl with one of your instructors. And then there was that 'incident' with the 'lady' you hired to entertain a bunch of your friends in your room."

The younger man went on the defensive. He was also surprised to discover his long absent sire had access to information his mother had been so good at covering up. "I didn't get kicked out!" he repeated. The term the professors had used was 'academic probation', with a strong recommendation he take the remainder of the year off, and try again the next fall.

From the look on Sullivan's face, it was clear he wasn't convinced. Abruptly, he changed the subject. "I want you to make yourself scarce after supper," he declared. When Trey started to object, he held up a hand and silenced him. "I came here to get information that only Bridger can give me. I don't want you around..."

"You've made that clear," Trey muttered. The liquor he consumed earlier was working, teasing, and tormenting an already testy disposition.

Sullivan closed his eyes briefly, silently wishing they had taken two rooms instead of one, instinctively knowing it would have been a big mistake. "Bridger doesn't like an audience. We'll eat, you'll find something to do, and you and I will talk about it later." He began dressing. "I'll send up more hot water," he nodded toward the tub. He took another long look at his son, his eyes narrowing. "And the barber," he finished.

There was a distinct *click* as Trey pulled himself erect and snapped his heels together. He stood at attention and saluted.

Sullivan ignored his son and headed for the doorway. He stepped across the threshold and slammed the door shut.

* _ * _ * _ * _ *

They ate dinner at Bridger's *hacienda* a mile north of the old *presidio*. It was a leisurely meal, with Bridger surprisingly congenial. To Sullivan's amazement—and contrary to Bridger's usual custom of doing business immediately after dispensing with the polite courtesies—the man was extremely solicitous toward Trey. He made a point of drawing the young man into their discussions, playing the role of the benevolent host, and spicing the conversation with anecdotes about the men and women who found their way to his city. Through it all, Sullivan remained aloof, content that there was always tomorrow.

At some prearranged signal, the liveried servants withdrew and Bridger poured the final brandy himself. He leaned across the table, filling Trey's glass for the third time, but neglecting his own. Sullivan placed his hand over his own goblet, declined the offer, and settled on a cigar from the silver tray at Bridger's elbow. "I'm going to take a walk," he announced. He coaxed the dog out from beneath the table and took his leave.

Bridger waited until the man was gone, the *pock-pock* of Sullivan's leather heeled boots against the tiled floor in the outer corridor diminishing and finally fading away. "You were surprised, Trey," he began. "At the food," he gestured expansively with his hand, "and with my humble..." his smile was almost paternal "...*estancia*?"

Trey toasted the man with his half-empty glass. "With everything," he answered honestly. They had toured the house before dinner. A private museum, it was filled with carefully tended treasures and artifacts, and Bridger knew the history of each piece. He had taken a considerable amount of time to explain the antiquities, extolling the craftsmanship of the long-dead ancients, making love to the gold with his hands as he displayed each relic. It had been a mystical journey into Mexico's distant past, a sojourn Trey enjoyed.

"Do you believe in legends, Trey?" Bridger asked suddenly.

The query caught the younger man off guard. He recovered quickly. "You mean like Saint George and the dragon?" he grinned, a boyish innocence in the smile and the answer. "Or the proverbial leprechaun's pot of gold at the end of the rainbow?"

Bridger laughed. The sound rolled from deep within his broad chest. Then his mood changed and he became solemn. "All fables are based somewhat on historical fact, Trey," he observed. "Fairy tales, the Greek myths. Even the nursery rhymes your mother read to you when you were a child." He paused, pouring himself a drink and lifting the bottle in invitation. With Sullivan gone, there was no real need to be discreet. "Your father believed in legends," he said softly.

Trey held out his glass. He was still sober enough to realize the man had spoken in the past tense. "My father?"

Bridger nodded his head. "Wes Underwood." He saw something flicker briefly far back in the younger man's eyes. "I've known Reese for a long time," he began. He was almost whispering now, framing his words in such a way that made the half lie sound like the truth. "Before you were born, and long after he left your mother." He smiled sympathetically. "I knew your stepfather, too."

The last was unexpected, and it showed in Trey's face. "But how...?"

Bridger lounged back in his chair, the fingers of his right hand tracing the intricate carving on the nub of the arm. "We all worked for Diamond, in one capacity or the other," he answered. "Reese, Torrance, and I in the field, and Wes..." He paused, carefully considering how far he should go. *How much the younger man might remember if prodded too far.* "Wes was Mr. Diamond's..." he was speaking now of the old man who founded the agency "...legal advisor." *And chief toady,* he finished silently. Aloud, he said, "He was an important man with the agency, Trey, and—unlike the rest of us—wise enough to know to leave when the old man died. Wise enough to strike out on his own."

It was strange, Trey reflected. How little he actually knew about the adults who had governed his life when he was a child. His memories of Reese were fragmented and bitter, and he had never known Wes Underwood was anything other than junior partner in a law firm with offices in Boston and San Francisco. He helped himself to the decanter of French cognac. "You said my father believed in legends," he uttered. "What legends?"

Bridger sighed, his great chest lifting then falling. "El Dorado," he said finally. He stared out the window into the darkness now, beyond the night. "Montezuma's lost treasure. Hernan Cortez' plundered hoard." The list grew. "*Cibola.*" For a moment, he seemed lost in his reverie, as if he had lived through the centuries, among the people and the places he named. "Maximilian's gold and Mad Carlotta's pilfered riches. It's all the same, you know," he breathed at last.

"And my father?" Trey prodded. Something in Bridger's face—his eyes—set the younger man on edge. For the first time in a long time, he finally had enough to drink.

Bridger's smile returned. "Your father discovered the secret to where it was hidden."

It took a copious amount of time for Trey to digest the older man's words. He shook his head, too taken aback to ask how Bridger could be so sure, or for that matter, how he even knew what Wes Underwood discovered.

Bridger removed the stopper from the decanter, and poured both of them another drink. His mood seemed different now; all business. "You accompanied Wes on his trip west," he began. "You spent two days in San Francisco at the home of a man named Levi Schuster—your father's associate—and a week in a rather seedy part of the city searching for a man claiming to be an illegitimate son of the House of Hapsburg."

He saw Trey's eyes narrow and continued. "You found him," Bridger emptied his glass in a single swallow, "and with twenty-five thousand dollars that belonged to a client of your father's, purchased a certain collection of documents Wes decided to keep for himself."

There it was again, Trey reflected. The mystery client and the twenty-five thousand dollars Sullivan had mentioned the night before they left El Paso. *The money Wes Underwood supposedly embezzled.* "You seem to know a hell of a lot about things that aren't any of your business, Bridger," he observed. "And I don't like you calling my father a thief!" Like the other, he downed his drink in one gulp.

Bridger didn't miss the liquor induced animosity in the younger man's voice. His jaws tightened then eased into the familiar smile as he lifted his empty glass in an equally empty toast to the younger man. "I only know what Reese has told me," he announced. The smile broadened. "He's the detective. The assumption about Wes is his."

Trey's face hardened, his eyes smoldering an ash gray beneath narrowed lids. He'd been a fool not to realize Reese had been in contact with Bridger all along. "I don't give a damn about his assumptions," he whispered. "The only thing I give a damn about is..."

The scrape of a sulphur-tipped wooden match against plaster resounded as Reese Sullivan suddenly appeared in the arched doorway. The stick flamed briefly, illuminating the man's face as the air around his head turned blue with the smoke of a freshly built cigarette. "You about ready to call it a night, boy?" He asked the question, but it was clear from his tone that he expected no answer; just Trey's compliance to his suggestion.

Bridger turned in his chair. It struck him, how Sullivan could leave so noisily, and return with such stealth. "The night is young, Reese!" he cajoled. He tried tempting the man with the bottle.

Sullivan shook his head. "I guess I'm just getting old, Ansel." He nodded at the uncleared table and the remnants of their evening meal. "If I had stayed there much longer, I'd have fallen asleep in my chair!" The smile came easily. "I'm sorry."

Bridger waved the apology aside. "My priest is only thirty, Reese," he grinned affably. "My dinners put him to sleep, too."

Sullivan chuckled. "And your confessions, Ansel. Do they put him to sleep as well?" He winked at the man and laughed again.

Bridger was on his feet now. Waiting until the big dog came to heel at Sullivan's left, he took the man's arm and led him into the hallway. "Why, what would I have to confess, Reese? I am nothing more than a simple innkeeper, providing food and lodging for the weary traveler. Does that make me responsible for their mischief, or accountable for their sins?" Sullivan's sacrilegious retort was lost in another gale of shared laughter.

Angry at being left behind, Trey hurried to catch up, his pace slowing abruptly when he stepped into the darkened hallway to be confronted by the helmeted figure of an ancient *conquistador*. And then he recalled the suit of armor. Cursing himself for not having remembered, he side-stepped the display and headed down the corridor in pursuit of the others.

The two men stood in the center courtyard, their heads together in deep conversation. The conference ended immediately when Trey approached. For some reason he could not fathom, their sudden silence offended him. "I'm going back to the *cantina*," he announced.

Sullivan grabbed his arm before he could pass. "Not tonight," he declared.

"And why the hell not!?" Trey demanded.

"Because I said so," Sullivan answered. He turned back to Bridger. "Tomorrow?"

Bridger dipped his chin. "Tomorrow," he echoed. "You know my terms, Reese."

Sullivan returned the nod. "Just as you know mine," he breathed.

With his son in tow, Sullivan departed.

Bridger watched their retreat and knew from their posture and stride that they were quarreling. *So much at stake*, he mused. So much that could go wrong if he were careless.

The thought brought a smile. He inhaled, deeply, his massive chest filling with the clean night air. Above him, a multitude of stars danced, and he raised his face to receive their cold light. They sparkled like diamonds suspended on wide ribbons of black velvet, and he reached toward them with open hands. Then, laughing, he closed his fingers against his palms and shook his fists in arrogant defiance of a distant God and His withheld treasures.

"No more," Bridger challenged. "You will deny me no more!"

* - * - * - * - *

It had been a long night, and would be an even longer day. Trey had risen well after noon to find Reese's bed made, the only sign that the man had been in the room the open cavy sack and an orderly pile of dirty clothes. That and the note: *Stay put.* Like he was some snot-nosed brat that didn't know how to behave in public. He wadded the note and tossed it onto Sullivan's neat bed. He hadn't listened to the man the night before when he told him not to go back to the saloon, and he sure in hell wasn't going to do his bidding now.

He took his time dressing, his fingers fumbling with buttons that seemed too big for the buttonholes. *One more night*, he philosophized, *one more morning hang-over.* At least the headache had gone away. *Glory be to the gods of the grapes.*

* - * - * - * - *

Sullivan moved about the *pueblo* freely, the wary transients giving him wide berth, visibly concerned with his presence. The dog helped. The animal padded noiselessly at the man's heel, or lay at his feet, something menacing in the way the black sniffed the air as each man passed. As if he were recording the scent and filing it away.

The town was, Reese noted, as it had always been. Even in the bright light of day, there was a sense of night about the place and its people. Everyone lived in the shadows, scurrying from one dark saloon to another, never staying too long in one place.

Sullivan paused to roll a cigarette. He stood with his back against a wall, shielding the match from the morning breeze and watching the rat-like burrowing of a dozen nondescript men. It was easy to spot the newcomers. They traveled in pairs, twin shadows moving as if they were conjoined at the shoulders, carefully sidestepping the solitary men who chose to decline the company of others.

These were the men who had been in Limbo the longest. Sullivan could number the days they had spent in Bridger's purgatory by the degree of gauntness that marked their faces and the way they moved. They went about their meager business like dim ghosts on a haunt, lacking the money or the will to leave. Bridger would be recruiting them soon, Sullivan reckoned. Sending them on forays deep into the interior as hired mercenaries, members of the disposable army Ansel Bridger rented out to whatever political or private entity possessed enough gold to pay the freight. And as such they would die.

Sullivan shook the grim thought away. There wasn't a man in Limbo who wasn't here of his own choosing, he reasoned. They chose to come, and if they were too weak, or too stupid to leave, then so be it.

He ended his long day at Bridger's saloon. It was clear when he walked through the wide front door that he was expected. The table in the back of the room—the same one he and Trey had been seated at the day before—was empty save for a single cut-glass bottle and a tray with three down-turned glasses. Sullivan accepted the silent invitation. He took his seat, and waited.

It didn't take long. Bridger joined him almost immediately. "Only one shadow tonight, Reese?" he smiled, acknowledging the dog with a single nod of his head.

"Until he finds me," Reese replied. Using his foot, he pushed out the chair on his left, watching as Bridger settled in. "Town's pretty quiet, Ansel," he said. His eyes never left the man's face. All day long, it had been gnawing at him. The things—the people—he should have seen, and didn't.

Bridger smiled. He nodded at a well-dressed man at a table in the opposite corner, touching his forehead in a polite salute. The stranger was out of place, in surroundings that provided only the simplest amenities, uncommonly elegant in a velvet trimmed Prince Albert and frilled shirt. "Do you see him, Reese?" he whispered. He didn't wait for an answer. "A member of England's royal family, with a Sodomite's fondness for small boys." There was something more than disdain in Bridger's face; more even than contempt. "The blood of kings, thinned by inbreeding, to produce a perverse filth!" Bridger's dark eyes turned ebony. "*Filth*," he hissed.

"But you let him stay," Sullivan observed dryly.

"Only until his inheritance is gone, and his family tires of paying for his indiscretions," Bridger snorted. "And then...?" He made a quick, slicing motion at his own neck. And all the while, he still smiled at the man.

"Wes Underwood," Sullivan prompted.

Bridger's face changed, the malice replaced by a benign smile. He sighed and shrugged his shoulders. "Rumors, Reese. Just..." he hesitated, as if trying to recall, "...sparse and fanciful rumors."

Sullivan's eyes narrowed. He'd spent a full day with his ear to the ground, and heard nothing. Playing the game, he asked, "What kind of rumors?"

Bridger was a master at sensing what another man wanted to hear, and equally adept in the telling. He leaned forward, keeping the words private. "That Wes Underwood fell under the spell of the oldest fairy tale in the world," he began. "That he had somehow become privy to the secret of the Inca, the Mayans, and the Aztecs, and those who plundered their wealth." He shook his head, one eyebrow rising as he contemplated the man's folly. "Cortez, and later the French."

"And?" Sullivan prodded.

Bridger finished his drink before answering. "It seems that Wes found a client as naive to the ways of the world as he was himself," he continued. "He duped the man into providing the money necessary to buy something he was seeking for himself, and then claimed it had been stolen in an attempt to cover his own thievery." He made the final announcement as if he had found it written in stone.

Sullivan poured himself a drink. He knew this much already from the papers Royal Torrance sent him, along with the letter from the senior partner in Underwood's firm denying any responsibility for Wes' wrongdoing, or any knowledge of the man's alleged client. "And you believe that?" He lifted the glass to his lips, watching Bridger's face as the man pondered his answer.

"It has happened before, Reese. One man willing to betray another, keeping something for himself that he has no right to have." Bridger's hand trembled slightly as he filled his own tumbler.

Sullivan lowered his glass. He saw the subtle movement as Bridger poured the whiskey, the faint chattering of crystal sounding as the neck of the ornate flagon danced against the rim of the man's glass. *Betray*, he mused, remembering the expression on Bridger's face when the man said the word, his shaking fingers. *Anger*. The word wasn't strong enough. *Rage*. Sullivan came forward in his chair, elbows resting on the table as he held the glass in both hands. "I don't give a damn about the rumors, Ansel. The fact is, Wes is dead, and I was hired to find the men who killed him."

Absently—as if he hadn't heard—Bridger nodded his head. "And beyond that?"

"The papers that were stolen from him in Yuma," Sullivan answered quietly.

Ansel's expression remained the same, but his eyes were instantly bright with the shock of sudden surprise. Just as quickly, the fire faded, and for the first time since taking his seat, he turned his head and met Sullivan's gaze head on. "Why you, Reese?"

Sullivan dispatched his drink before answering. "Because..." He was interrupted before he could finish speaking.

"Because Diamond canned him, and he needs the money. And my mother and I are paying him ten thousand dollars to do the job."

Bridger stared up at the young man who had just joined them. It was obvious Trey had been drinking. His face was flushed, the high cheekbones bearing a whiskey-red sheen. *Save for the scar*. "Ten thousand," Bridger echoed. There was a hint of ridicule in the words and he smiled again.

Abruptly, the man rose from his chair. "I want to talk to you, Reese." His eyes rested momentarily on the younger man. "Alone." He beckoned for the older man to follow him. Sullivan stood up, purposely ignoring his son as he fell in behind.

Trey pulled out a chair and sat down. He stared hard at his sire's back, watching as the man disappeared into the dark hallway on the other side of the arched doorway leading to Bridger's office. "Piss on him," he breathed. *Piss on them both*.

* - * - * - * - *

Bridger was waiting. He remained seated when Reese entered the room, nodding toward the empty chair and waiting until the man settled in before he spoke. He shut the door and crossed the room to his desk. "I suppose it's time to stop the farce," he volunteered.

"Past time," Sullivan agreed. He moved his feet, watching as the dog made a series of brief circles and lay down beside the chair.

There was an awkward silence as Bridger debated his next move. "I propose a bargain, Reese," he began. He still avoided the man's eyes. "The truth as I know it, for what you know."

Sullivan shifted in his chair, half-turning so he could observe the door as well as the man at the desk. The thin shaft of yellow-white light at the bottom of the door drew an even line above the threshold. He saw that light break at the same time he saw the dog's ears come forward, and knew someone was outside, listening. "The truth," he repeated. The growing tangle of deceit he had discovered made him wonder if the complete truth could be found, let alone told. He decided to give it a try. "You were a fool to let Wes die, Ansel," he said softly. It was a guess, a supposition based on the same instinct that told him there were two men beyond the closed door. But bit-by-bit the pieces were beginning to fall together.

The pencil Bridger held snapped. The suddenness of Sullivan's accusation—his certainty when he said the words—was alarming. He turned, the high backed chair he sat in screeching in protest as he swung around to face Sullivan fully. "Just how much do you know, Reese?"

Sullivan remained markedly calm. He took out his tobacco and began building a cigarette, studiously wetting the paper with his tongue, and then rolling it closed. He twisted the ends and lit up, exhaling through his nose as he spoke. "I know that you were Wes' anonymous client, and it was your twenty-five thousand dollars he used to buy the documents from that lunatic in San Francisco." Another presumption, this time based on facts he gleaned from the files and information Royal Torrance and Cade Devereau sent him; as well as the conversation he overheard between Bridger and Trey the night before. His eyes closed briefly, as if deep in thought. "As for the rest..."

Bridger's elbows rested on the desk, both hands clearly visible. There was no panic in the man's voice; but the words were cold, with a distinct edge indicating his profound and growing displeasure. "Does there need to be more, Reese?" he demanded. The fact that a hireling deceived him should have been enough.

He regained his composure, the color returning to his cheeks. "You're bluffing, Reese. You came here for the same reason you always come, to buy information, and maybe some time. The fact that Wes may have been working for me when he died...?" He waved the accusation aside, and poured himself a drink.

Sullivan leaned forward in his chair, his voice whisper soft. "Where's Mendoza?"

The question was totally unexpected, and Bridger could not hide the surprise. "Chato?" he breathed.

Sullivan hid the smile. "We've know each other a long time, Ansel," he grinned. "Long enough for me to know that—while I run with one hound—" he pointed to the dog at his feet, "you run with a pack. But I haven't seen any of them," he continued. "Not the 'breed', not one of the other mongrels you keep at heel." His tone changed, the words taking on a sharp edge. "They're hiding, Ansel. It doesn't take much hard thinking to figure out why they don't want to be seen, or who it is that might see them."

Bridger stood up and came out from behind the desk. He was sweating, but he stood at the small wood-burning stove in the corner rubbing his hands as if they were cold. They were playing a man's game of cat-and-mouse, and right now he wasn't sure which animal he had become. He didn't like the feeling of uncertainty, and made up his mind to become the cat. "Tell me, Reese," he murmured. "How much hard thinking does it take to comprehend that the boy has played you for a fool?"

It was Sullivan's turn to be annoyed. "Meaning?" His eyes were the color of slate.

There was no point in continuing the charade, and Bridger found himself strangely relieved. Sullivan was not an easy man to lie to or toy with. "Contrary to whatever lies the boy may have told you," his eyes narrowed as he contemplated the puzzle, "there are no papers, at least not here. Wes didn't have the documents with him in Yuma," he confessed. "As for how he died..." Bridger pulled himself erect. "I'm guilty of many transgressions, Reese, but few major sins north of the border." The smile was almost real.

"Unlike my friends with the *ruales*, your lawmen tend to be less corrupt, and more adverse to accepting a bribe."

Reese stood up. He stepped over the dog and helped himself to the bottle of whiskey. "And you can't buy yourself out of a murder in Arizona Territory," he observed. He poured the drink and downed it in one swallow. He faced Bridger, aware he was still being monitored by the two men beyond the door, and kept his words soft. "Wes *is* dead, Ansel. And the Arizona Rangers and the Territorial Governor are calling it murder, regardless of the circumstance."

Bridger was careful to keep his voice under control. "What happened to Underwood was an accident," he insisted. The smile turned snakelike. "Your son," he intoned. "Why don't you ask your son how his stepfather died?" The words were a challenge.

Sullivan felt the sting in the other man's words and was determined to ignore it. "I don't need to ask Trey," he returned. "I saw the report from the surgeon at Fort Yuma. The birds did a good job, Ansel, but there was enough left to make it clear Wes had been beaten, and twelve inches of steel had been shoved into his gut." In one smooth move, he bent slightly at the waist, and lifted his pant leg. He pulled the knife from his boot, and made an underhanded toss that buried the blade deep in the front of Bridger's desk only inches from the man's thigh.

Bridger worked the blade free. The leather bound haft was stiff, dark brown with dried blood. But the intricate carvings across the face of the leather were still intact. *Sullivan had known all along he was involved.* He toyed with the knife, contemplating his next words. "All right, Reese," he said finally. "I was there." The skin beneath his left eye twitched. "So was your son, and *he* is the reason Wes is dead. Chato was working his customary magic," he offered, remembering. He made a short, slicing motion with the knife as he talked.

"You've seen him work, Reese. You know how gifted he is in loosening a man's tongue, and in keeping him alive while he's doing it. The boy panicked, Reese," he continued. "He lost his head, made an impulsive attempt at heroics, and Wes died—before he could tell us anything." He paused. "We found nothing on him."

Short, concise, and—Reese Sullivan recognized—the truth. He relaxed, but only slightly. Everything else began to fall into place. "He's had Wes' papers all along," he reckoned, thinking aloud.

Bridger nodded. "And, it would seem, chose to tell the woman—and you—otherwise."

Sullivan's laughter was filled with bitter irony. "He knew Vanessa wouldn't pay me just to come looking for the killers."

Bridger's stance changed also. There was the feeling that he and Reese were again on common ground, and not adversaries. At least for now. "The papers belong to me, Reese," he began. "I paid for them, and I want them back." He tried again. "*I'll pay a second time to get them back.*"

Sullivan took his time before responding. He picked the words carefully; purposely choosing the ones Bridger would want to hear. "I'll make a trade," he declared. A lie, but it didn't matter. He knew from Bridger's face that it was believed. "The documents Wes stole," he paused, making the man wait, "for a share of what you find." Greed was something Bridger understood, and a viable way of dealing with the man.

Bridger's mouth opened, and just as quickly shut. There was a long moment of silence, broken by the muted rustle of heavy fabric as he paced the room one end to the other. He paused momentarily beside the shut door, stifling a series of dry coughs with his fist. Reese saw the dog's head come up suddenly, the animal's sides shuddering as a soft growl rumbled from deep inside the beast's throat. The yellow-grey ribbon of light streaming from beneath the door separated and then glowed in a bright, unwavering line. Bridger finally spoke; instinctively knowing that Sullivan wanted something more. "And?"

Even with Bridger's men gone, Reese knew he had to be careful. "Trey survived Yuma, Ansel. He obviously didn't see you, but he did see the men responsible for Wes' torture and death, and it's clear now just how bad he wants them. I'm going to give him what he wants, and keep him alive while I'm doing it."

The mulatto was nodding his head. "And of course it doesn't hurt that there's a bounty on those men," he reckoned. The governor of Arizona Territory was an unforgiving man. "All of them." He sighed. "How much, Reese? If I give you Chato and the others."

"One fourth," Sullivan bargained. "And I keep you out of it."

There was an audible rush of air as Ansel Bridger inhaled. "One tenth," he countered.

Sullivan was already shaking his head. "One fourth," he repeated.

Bridger stood up. He cast a wary eye at the dog, and then moved away from the stove. He began pacing, working the thing over in his mind. "The boy," he said finally. "Trey. I knew the first moment I saw him who he was."

He paused, watching Sullivan's face. "I hadn't considered that he would be there, and once Wes was dead," he persisted, "there was little point in leaving anyone else alive." The smile was empty. "Chato and the others," one eyebrow arched as he remembered. "They wanted to kill him. Don't make me regret my one act of fraternal compassion, Reese," he finished. "I wouldn't want to think I made a mistake in letting your son live."

Reese yawned and stretched. "The mistake would have been to kill him," Sullivan's voice was soft, almost a whisper. "Trey gave a good description of the man who beat Wes, and the two men who held him, as well as the other one who cheered them on," he intoned. "But he couldn't put a face on the fifth man with them, the one giving the orders; who made sure to stay behind him. Chato's knife told me all I needed to know about the *who*. I needed you to tell me the *why*."

He watched Bridger's reflection in the mirrored panels of the sideboard stretched along the opposite wall. Bridger's hands were clasped behind his back, and he kept flexing his fingers, making fists so tight the knuckles turned yellow-white beneath his dark skin.

"No more games, Ansel."

Bridger considered the other man's words, turning them over again and again in his agile mind as he weighed their merit. The idea of letting Sullivan have Chato in exchange for the papers concerned him far less than the thought that he might have to share what he had waited so long to obtain. "What makes you so certain you can get the documents," he queried. "That the boy will give them up?"

Sullivan grinned. "He claims he doesn't have them. How can I take what he doesn't have?"

The stoical expression on Bridger's face gave way to one of sly appreciation. This time the man's laughter was real, and the feeling of camaraderie fully restored. The idea of Reese stealing what the boy had stolen appealed to him. "I'll arrange a diversion," he offered. "Something to keep the boy occupied while you make your search."

Reese sensed that the sport had been anticipated long before Bridger made the suggestion. He didn't care. He had walked into more than he bargained for because of his son's lies, and he needed a way out before Bridger realized he'd been deceived. "I don't want to see him before sunrise," he grinned.

Bridger nodded. Then, the smile slipping, he grabbed Reese's arm, and just as quickly let go. He had forgotten the damned dog. "Chato," he breathed. "When you take him, Reese, and the others," he met the man's gaze head on, "it can't be here."

Sullivan understood the man's reasoning. Bridger was the only law in Limbo. If a man—any man—was taken within the compound it would happen only with his approval. *Approval only given when it suited Bridger's need or gained him favor with the men who governed the world beyond the mountains.*

"All right," he concurred. "You pick the place, Ansel, and you stay clear."

Again, Bridger nodded in agreement. "Until tomorrow, Reese." He offered the man his hand in farewell.

They shook, neither man totally comfortable in the parting. There were no more words.

Chapter Nine

The young woman moved across the room with the feral grace of a Bohemian gypsy, the long skirt somehow more provocative than the short dresses the saloon harlots wore. Entranced, Trey watched her, mesmerized by the wildness he saw in her eyes and heard in her laughter. Coyly, she avoided the men at the bar as she passed, pirouetting away from their clutching fingers and unwanted caresses.

Sullivan was at the archway leading from Bridger's private office. He stood, one arm above his head, leaning against the stucco wall as he watched his son watching the woman. Somehow, Trey didn't look so young now. If anything, he had ripened considerably from the first moment the young lady entered the room.

Pushing himself away from the wall, Sullivan joined his son. He slipped into the chair facing the front door, signaling the barkeep for another bottle and settling in to watch the show.

There was a sudden burst of raucous laughter from the men at the bar as the young woman poured a beer over the head of a too ardent and slightly drunk admirer. The girl's laughter mingled with the laughter of the men; soft, sensual. Then, tired of their attention, she spun away from them, the soft skirt swirling away from her ankles to expose the smooth curves of her slim calves. Trey joined the others as they whistled and called out to her. The cat calls increased, the floor vibrating as booted feet began to thump against the wide planking, the primeval cadence increasing as the piano player picked up the rhythm and began to play.

The loud stomping ceased. One by one, the men stilled their feet and put down their full glasses. Subdued, they watched as the young woman began to sway to the soft strains of a Strauss waltz.

She was a natural. The music flowed from the piano into her soul, transforming her body into something more than flesh. There was no separateness to her arms, her legs; her torso. Her movements were serpentine, hypnotic. Somehow, she seemed to draw the men to her, yet held herself aloof. Untouchable.

Sullivan watched her with a knowing eye. She was aware of everything she was doing, and who she was doing it to. He guessed her true age at eighteen, but her dark eyes bespoke a knowledge which transcended time as it was measured by man. She was as old as Eve herself, filled with centuries of wisdom, and eons older than the men who admired her. He tapped his son's arm, nodding at the girl as he spoke. "She's going to be expensive," he observed.

Trey's stare never wavered, his attention focused on the woman. A wicked fire burned far back in his eyes, stoked by a hunger too long ignored. "Not if I play my cards right," he grinned.

It was Sullivan's turn to smile. "This isn't a Sunday evening social, boy, on your mother's front lawn." He nodded at the woman. "You take *that* little girl for a walk in the moonlight you're going to pay for the privilege." As if suddenly inspired to indulge in a bit of belated paternal benevolence, he dug into his shirt pocket and pulled out a Bull Durham sack filled with coins and dumped them on the table.

Trey's eyes danced. It had become a different kind of contest now, as much between himself and his old man as between himself and the girl. "You want to make a little wager?" He nodded at the stack of coins Sullivan was piling at his elbow. "That I can get her in bed, and never pay her a dime?"

It was, Sullivan knew, the cursed blessing of the Irish. The love of gambling was as strong as the love of a good running horse, or a drink of fine whiskey. "How much?"

The corners of Trey's mouth lifted in a wide smile. "Five thousand," he answered, without so much as blinking an eye.

"You have five thousand?" Sullivan's voice was full of a mocking disbelief. "Last time I looked, you didn't have enough money to buy a decent pair of boots, let along a two dollar whore."

Trey ignored the dig. "I have a draft for the five thousand Vanessa agreed to pay you when you finish this job." It was a glib lie, told with the skill of a dormitory card shark. He lived well in his short stay at Harvard, and it hadn't cost his parents a cent.

Sullivan inhaled. "Let me see if I understand this." He played with his glass, drawing circles on the table with the condensation formed on the bottom edge. "You're going to bet me *my* five thousand dollars that you can convince the little lady," he made an ambiguous wave in her direction, "to do some charity work. And if you succeed, you keep my money and I—"

"Do the job for the five thousand she gave you in Chicago," Trey interrupted. The tempo of the music changed, the slow waltz becoming a wild *tarantella* as the young woman began to make a series of breath-robbing spins.

The crimson skirt flared out and away from the young woman's ankles, the bright red contrasting vividly with her fawn-colored skin. The fabric clung to her, then lifted away from her calves, her thighs. Her legs were completely bare, unfettered by the cloth, white lace showing at the soft curves of her small bottom. The crowd roared its approval.

Trey was on his feet. He reached down and picked up a twenty dollar gold piece from the stack of coins in front of Sullivan. "This one doesn't count," he shouted.

He held the coin between his fingers, waiting until the girl had completed her final spin. She faced Trey when the music stopped, her long black hair settling across her face like strands of black silk. With one hand, she swept the hair from her face, her firm left breast lifting alluringly as she crooked her arm and raked her fingers through her hair and piled it on top of her head.

The gleam of gold caught her eye, the gold and the young, blue-eyed *Norte Americano* who held it between his fingers. She smiled, canting her head and forming a kiss with moist lips the color of red wine. The gold piece shimmered through the air and she caught it with eager fingers.

Trey started away from the table, and found himself held back. Sullivan held another gold coin. He flipped it into the air, and when it landed on the table beside his son's right hand, pinned it to the tabletop with the blade of the knife that sprang from his left sleeve. He pried the stiletto free, raising the blade with the coin still impaled on the bright steel. He offered the pierced golden eagle to his son. "You bring this back come morning," he challenged, "and you keep the five thousand.

"You don't bring it back..." the wry smile reached his eyes, "...you give me the draft, and the next three years in El Paso."

Trey laughed. The whiskey and a bad case of the wants filled him with a bravado that defied reason. Deftly, he plucked the gold piece from the tip of the blade. "And if I bring back the other one, too?"

Sullivan couldn't believe the young man's gall. "You do that, son," he drawled, "I'll kiss your bare ass on your mother's front porch." Vanessa's home—the late Senator Danforth's pillared mansion with the Tiffany stained glass windows—sat on the main boulevard in midtown Boston.

Trey backed away from his father; his step jaunty. Just the thought of the high and mighty Reese Sullivan having to actually kiss his ass in the middle of Boston was enough to inspire him to new heights of carnal glory. "I'll mark the spot," he bragged.

Reese watched as Trey shouldered his way through the crowd that surrounded the young dancer. Then, content the young man would be occupied for the rest of the night, he turned and headed out the door.

* _ * _ * _ * _ *

Trey followed the young woman through the maze of back streets behind Bridger's *cantina*, his hand closing in a tight fist as he fought the urge to touch her. He had held her, for a too brief moment just before they left the saloon, his long fingers spanning her small waist and meeting at her spine. He had sensed fire beneath his fingers; fire and a great passion primed by wine and the music.

The girl hesitated at the end of the passageway, and reached back to take Trey's hand. "There," she whispered. She was pointing to a small house apart from the others that lined the dark alleyway; a twelve foot square cottage smaller than any room in Bridger's *hacienda*.

Trey was at her side now. Her hand felt incredibly small, and he lifted it to his lips. "And the light in the window?" he murmured.

Her laughter was at once little girl and woman. A small, mischievous giggle at first became the low, pleasure-loving laughter of a lustful creature skilled in the arts of need and desire. She rose up on her tip-toes, her breasts seeming to crawl up his chest. "*Mi esposo*," she teased. And then, in softly accented English, "Or perhaps, my mother."

Trey leaned forward, trapping the girl between his outstretched arms as he backed her against the wall of the adjoining building. "Is she beautiful?" Pressing close, he laughed.

"Is she friendly?" The pale light of the rising moon bathed his face and touched his eyes, the blue orbs the color of a morning sky.

The young woman inhaled sharply, one hand lifting to touch his cheek. She brushed her fingers across his eyelids, amazed at the contrast between his skin and her own. "Not as beautiful as I," she whispered. She kissed him then, full on the mouth, the fingers of her right hand trailing down his spine. "And she has forgotten how to be friendly."

Trey swept the woman into his arms, lifting her off her feet as if she were nothing more than a rag doll. Carrying her, he sprinted across the street, not giving a damn if there was a husband, or a mother, or the village priest beyond the door.

* _ * _ * _ * _ *

Vanessa Underwood sat stiffly erect in the straight backed chair, picking at her food in a manner that indicated her displeasure. She did not intend to enjoy her meal, no matter how good the food or immaculate the table. In spite of her stomach's noisy protests, she laid the fork aside, and concentrated on the wine. Finally breaking the long silence, she sighed. "I can't believe he allowed Trey to go with him."

Eva Delgado hid her smile behind the linen napkin she held in her right hand. She knew that Vanessa's words were nothing more than thoughts spoken aloud, and certainly no attempt or invitation to have a civil conversation. Just as quickly, she decided she didn't care. "And why not, Vanessa?" she smiled. Without waiting for an answer, she stood up and began clearing away the dishes.

Startled that there was a response to her out loud musings, Vanessa faced the other woman. The wine was working, coloring her cheeks and loosening her tongue. "He's a *boy*," she said finally. "His father," she corrected herself immediately, "Wes and I made every effort to keep him away from..."

Eva finished for her. "From Reese? From the real world and the things that happen when you strip away the polite facade of civil behavior?" She turned back to the sink, sorry that she was losing control of her temper. Briefly, she closed her eyes, counting to ten in three languages before she was able to turn around. "Trey managed to stay alive in spite of everything that happened in Arizona, Vanessa, just as he managed to come here on his own. And he worked very hard to prove to Reese he was man enough to go with him into Mexico." The last was, she felt, a justifiable half-lie. Trey had worked hard, but it had nothing to do with impressing his father.

"And that's supposed to make it all right." Suddenly, Vanessa stood up. Filled with a need to keep her hands busy, she began scraping plates with a vengeance, her fork clattering against the china. "How many times have you waited for Reese to come back from God knows where, sick with the fear that he's never going to walk through the door? Or worse, that he's going to be brought back, more dead than alive, shackled to some vile," she was trembling, her entire body shaking, "creature swearing revenge not on Diamond, but on Reese and everyone close to him!?" She carried the plates to the sink, dumped them into the pan of hot water, and then rolled up her sleeves.

"I lived with that fear," she uttered, the steam bringing sweat to mingle with tears she had suppressed for more years than she cared to remember. "First here, and then in Chicago. That was enough. More than enough!"

Without thinking, Eva Delgado began wiping the clean plates, as if this were a thing they had done together a hundred times in the past. "And Wes Underwood?" she asked gently.

"He loved me. Enough to offer me a life considerably more secure than the one I was living, with advantages and privileges Reese scorned as frivolous and unnecessary." Vanessa's head dropped and she averted her eyes. "For me, and for Trey."

Eva studied the woman's profile, measuring a beauty that had been enhanced by time, and would continue to improve with age. Like fine marble, or a bronze sculpture. And just as cold. Not once, she realized, had the woman expressed anything akin to a shared love. Only a distant concern, and that—in spite of her words—more for herself than any other. Her needs, her fears, her wants.

They finished their work in silence, each locked in their own thoughts. Then, needing free of the house, Eva went out onto the porch. She stood there, alone, until long after the sun went down and she was sure Vanessa had gone to bed; staring into the southern horizon and whispering the words as if the man could hear them. *Come home, Reese. Come home and let me love the emptiness away. For both of us.*

* - * - * - * - *

Trey felt the girl stir against his belly, a playful invitation in the way she moved her hips and pressed her buttocks into his groin. He felt himself responding, wanting her more than when he first saw her.

She turned over, her long hair whispering across his shoulders as she bent forward to kiss his forehead. *He was a good lover*, she mused. Much more of a man than Bridger told her, he was beyond the age where only his own enjoyment mattered, and willing—no, eager—to see to her needs while sating his own.

Gently, she caressed his shoulders, the fingers of her right hand kneading the muscles of his upper arm as she massaged his flesh and worked her way up to his neck. Her fingers closed finally around the chain Trey wore about his neck, the feel of gold warming her as she cupped her hand and allowed the links to slip through her fingers. She let the medallion rest against her palm for a long moment before she opened her hand. "For luck?" she asked, one eyebrow arching as she traced the profile of a goddess surrounded by six-pointed stars. The talisman was unflawed, burnished to a high sheen and glowing with a light of its own.

Trey's fingers closed around the young woman's hand. He considered her words before answering. "Yes," he said.

"Can I have it?" There was nothing timid in the girl's request, and she sweetened it with a gentle probing. "For luck?"

"It was a gift," Trey countered. "From my father." He saw the pout. "I'll buy you another," he promised. The young woman's exploration beneath the sheets stopped, then began again, more earnestly.

"Gold?" she demanded, laughing. "And of my own choosing?"

Trey felt his toes knot as the girl's hand closed around a familiar hardness. "Pure gold," he answered. The girl cupped her free hand around her right breast, and brushed it across his cheek.

Eyes closed, Trey kissed her, his tongue trailing from her lips to the hollow between her breasts. He held her, her scent reaching out to him; a blending of the rich musk of their coupling and the sweeter smell of her cologne. Light, like the aroma of spring flowers late in the evening.

A familiar fragrance, he realized. *It was Eva Delgado's scent.*

His arousal was sudden, intense. There was no gentleness in him this time, only the unsated lust he felt that day in the barn when he was alone with Eva and she had spurned his advances. Anger drove him, and he thrust himself into the girl, but it was Eva's face he saw. She tormented him with yet another *no*, damming his seed, and bringing the pain of one more refusal. He felt the ache deep in his groin and swore. "Damn you! *Damn you!*" Release came, but there was no satisfaction.

The girl sensed her failure. Angry, she sat up, turning her back on the man, and gathered the sheet around her. He reached out to touch her, to rub her back, and she pulled away. "A drink," she suggested.

It seemed like a good idea. Trey reached back and piled the pillows high against the headboard. Watching the girl, he was sorry he had thought of Eva. Still, she looked like the woman. The coloring was the same, the fawn-colored smoothness of the skin. She turned back to the bed, and he shook the thought away.

Her playful mood returned. She let the sheet fall away from her body, one foot on the floor, her weight resting on the other leg as she knelt on the bed beside Trey and handed him a glass.

He was flattered. She had given him the only glass, her own drink still on the dresser in the chipped coffee cup with the faded blue flowers. Teasing him, she ran her tongue around the rim of the proffered goblet, kissing the edge before pressing it to his lips.

The liquor was potent; different than the whiskey he had been drinking. There was a sharp bite, a burning against his lips that reminded him of his first taste of *salsa*, and he exhaled sharply through pursed lips. Then, seeing the girl's smile, the laughter in her eyes, he downed the *pulque* in a single swallow.

The effect was almost instantaneous. Trey's eyes narrowed as he tried to focus. The girl's laughter was all around him, yet somehow far away. He shook his head, vainly attempting to clear away the cobwebs being spun around inside his head. He felt the glass he had been holding slip from his dead fingers, the panic growing as the feeling of suffocation overwhelmed him and he clawed at the sheets that pressed like lead against his chest. His hands and fingers refused to work, and his legs...

He felt his feet slam against the floor, the impact so hard and so sudden that his spine compacted against the base of his skull. There was an explosion of white light that divided into spheres of wildly spiraling fireballs. Instinctively, Trey dodged the bursts of blue-white fire. He felt himself falling, and reached out to the bed to catch himself. His fingers clutched at the brass bedpost, failing to close around the metal in time, and he collapsed onto the floor.

The girl worked quickly. She swore softly, his head heavier than she anticipated. No longer caring, her long fingernails raked across his shoulder as she tugged the gold chain away from his neck. The links tangled in his long hair as she pulled it over his head. Wasting no time, she placed it around her own neck, careful to arrange the chain so that the medallion hung down her back.

The blouse was next. There was no time for the layers of underclothing she had worn, and she didn't care. The skirt and blouse were all she needed now; that and her shawl. She folded the wrap in a triangle and arranged it across her shoulders, carefully pinning it in place at her neck.

She was dressed and going through Trey's pockets when Bridger and Chato Mendoza came through the door. He was smiling, the same benign smile that he always wore when he was pleased with her. "*Niña,*"

Obediently, the girl stood up. She held out her hands. The two gold coins Trey had taken from Reese were in the palm of her right hand. Her left hand was empty.

"And nothing else?" Bridger asked.

The girl answered without hesitation, aware that Mendoza was watching her. "The money belt." She stepped over Trey's outstretched arm and lifted the corner of the mattress. "I was undressing," she nodded at the tri-fold screen that stood in one corner. "He didn't think I saw him put it here."

Mendoza retrieved the belt. He handed it to Bridger without saying anything, his eyes on the girl. There was a time, before this night, when he had wanted her. But not anymore.

Bridger's thick fingers dug into the three narrow pouches that made up Trey Underwood's concealed wallet. His dark eyes showed the emotion his face did not betray. Anger. Mistrust. There were no notebooks; no expected charts or maps. Only a few greenback dollars of small denomination, a business card bearing George Pullman's likeness, and a letter from the man giving Trey free use of his private car. "You were with our young friend for a long time," he began softly. "Perhaps, too long."

The young woman backed up a full pace. Chato was behind her now; had moved behind her without her sensing what he was doing. She tried to sidestep, but it was too late. "Please, *Patrón.*"

She felt the half-breed's arm close around her waist. "There was nothing!" Her voice rose. "I swear, *there was nothing!*"

Bridger opened the third pouch. A single sheaf of yellow paper was sweat-damp and compacted against the side of the small packet. He pried it loose and carefully unfolded it. "El Paso," he breathed. The smile was instant, full of humor and hope. "We'll find what we want in El Paso!"

Scrupulously, he refolded the piece of paper and placed it back in the pouch. Just as diligently, he rehid the money belt beneath the corner of the girl's mattress. He sighed, one foot lifting as he raised Trey's arm with his toe and let it drop to the floor. "The young *soldado*, Chato. The clean-shaven *capitán* sent by the governor-general. Is he still here?" He was toying with the girl.

Mendoza was still holding the young woman. "He and the others," he answered.

Bridger scratched his beard. Everyone, he reasoned, paid tribute in one form or another. Even he was not impervious to the encroaching proprieties of a government intent on imposing the restraints of civilization on all its people. His ransom was the occasional surrender of an outlaw to the authorities; always a man with a price on his head, or some inconsequential *gringo* with the means to buy his way out of a Mexican jail. *A trade, for a trade, for a trade.*

"Find the captain, Chato. Tell him," he smiled at the man, "there has been a murder. A most unfortunate murder."

There was a sound as the girl inhaled. For a brief moment, she felt a twinge of guilt. In any case, she did not want to see Trey die. "Please," she begged. She tried to pull away from Mendoza. "Don't make me watch..."

Bridger's smile was paternal. "Of course not, *niña*." His eyes swept her face and then lifted to meet Mendoza's.

Chato Mendoza's hand closed around the girl's mouth. In less time than it took to take a single breath, he cut her throat.

* - * - * - * - *

Sullivan's second floor room was unlit and seemingly empty. Only the curtains stirred, the lacy pattern repeated in a drawn out silhouette on the floor, the muted moonlight intensifying the blackness beyond the narrow rectangle of soft yellow.

The dog lay beside the bed, its massive head resting on its paws. Only its eyes moved, darting from the door to the window.

Then, its great head lifting, the animal concentrated on the wood encased portal.

There was a subtle noise outside the window, the soft shuffle of moccasin encased feet across the narrow balcony. The sound ceased, and the dog cocked its head, its nose working as it searched the air for a scent. The smell was beyond the glass, too faint for the animal to place. Whining, the dog inched forward on its belly, stopping dead as the soft footsteps resumed. Again, the black canted its head, anticipation making the onyx eyes come alive.

Outside the room, Benito Chavez leaned momentarily against the heavy shutters. He had seen Sullivan leave the hotel, watching until the man was well down the street. The bounty hunter had been alone, apparently in no great hurry as he disappeared briefly behind the batwing doors of one *cantina*, staying, Chavez assumed, just long enough for one drink before continuing on his way.

The Mexican inhaled. Sullivan's dog remained the only obstacle. The man had seemed almost naked without the animal, a grim phantom without a shadow, and somehow vulnerable.

Gingerly, Chavez eased on his gloves and pulled a packet of raw meat from his inside pocket. He had taken a particular delight in dosing the chunk of brisket with his own blend of poison, concentrating on the odorless yellow-white powder he favored above the others. Wearing gloves, he had cut a pocket in the beef, lacing the morsel with the raw drug, then killing his own scent with a filling of liver and kidney. Even now, the meat carried the peculiar aroma of a fresh kill, a mingling of blood and organ smell meant to appeal to the dog's primitive lust.

Chavez laid the piece of meat on the window sill. Using his knife, he pried at the sash, grimacing as the dry wood screeched against the warped frame. He could hear the noise as the sash weights thunked impotently within the casing, swearing as the window lifted only a scant two inches before jamming. Hesitant, he stepped before the glass, peering inside the room before using both hands to work the window free.

The room appeared empty, and Chavez knew a fleeting sense of relief. Common sense dispelled the brief reprieve. The dog had not been with Sullivan, and the man did not allow the animal to run loose. The big mongrel was there, inside the room. The question was where?

Chavez picked up the piece of meat, balancing it on his gloved palm as he debated his next move. His own shadow loomed across the floor, veiled by the lace curtain, cutting into the elongated square of light and dividing it in half. The interior light diminished accordingly, adding to the blackness. He stepped aside, making a flat-handed toss as he moved.

The chunk of meat slapped against the bare floor, dead center of the square of light, the pungent odor heightened by the limited ventilation. Chavez watched impatiently, waiting for some sign that the animal picked up the scent. There was nothing, no movement at all in the darkness beyond the yellow-grey luminescence; no sound.

Chavez' dark brow furrowed, his eyes narrowing as he puzzled out the thing in his mind. Bridger ordered him to search the room, in spite of Reese's pledge to cooperate in their hunt for Wes Underwood's missing documents. He also warned him about the dog. But now...

Once more, the Mexican peered inside the room. *Maybe*, he reasoned, *Sullivan's son came back and took the dog on a late night prowl.* Granted, he had left the saloon with Bridger's whore, but the young man had been drinking. Chavez thought perhaps the boy couldn't hold up to the woman's demands. It had been almost four hours, he calculated. He laughed, softly. The very young had a way of accomplishing in minutes what a grown man could enjoy for an entire night.

Certain the dog could not have resisted the offering of fresh meat, Chavez opened the window wider, and slipped inside the room.

As if propelled by an unseen force, the big dog catapulted up out of the darkness, the animal's teeth flashing white as its front paws struck the man's shoulder. Chavez screamed, the weight of the animal slamming against his chest and knocking him off balance. The Mexican fell hard, the back of his head striking the lower-most pane and shattering the glass. The brittle shards tore into his neck and face as his arms flew up instinctively to protect his eyes as he tumbled backwards through the opening and sprawled, flat-backed, on the rough balcony flooring.

The dog landed on top of him, a feral viciousness in the animal as he tore at the man's face and shoulders in a series of short, flesh-tearing snaps. Still on his back, Chavez used his feet to push himself away from the dog, desperately scooting across the narrow veranda in a vain attempt to free himself from the animal's attack. Sheer will kept him fighting, his screams giving way to a series of high-pitched shouts for help.

The dog was relentless, its teeth tearing into flesh and fabric as it savaged the man. There was no defense from the black's fury, the scent of fresh blood provoking a series of renewed attacks. Chavez kept punching at the dog's head, at the same time dragging himself closer and closer to the balcony rail.

Sullivan kicked open the door to the room, his pistol drawn. In the dim moonlight, he could see the torn curtains and the shattered pane of glass, a grim smile coming as he heard the dog's low snarls and Chavez' cries for help. Cocking the Remington, Sullivan called out, whispering the dog's name, "¡*Palas!*" The noise outside the window subsided instantly, a new sound coming as he heard the animal's claws scrappling across the unpainted wood.

The dog bounded through the window, coming to heel at the man's side, its great tail wagging as though it had been playing a game. He danced impatiently at Sullivan's knee and then darted back to the window, agitated when the man did not follow him. Twice, the animal barked, as if scolding Sullivan for his carelessness, and then returned to the man's side.

Reese watched as a hand groped at the windowsill, dropping back into the shadows as Chavez pulled himself to his feet. The pale light of a waning moon washed across the man's torn face, crimson streaming from a half-dozen open gashes across his forehead and cheeks. The blood made it difficult to see, and Chavez lifted his arm to wipe it away.

The man was swearing, babbling a stream of near incoherent curses meant for the dog. *As if the beast could understand him.* His voice changed then, a low singsong replacing the anger as he called out softly, bidding the dog to come to him.

Chavez had drawn his pistol. The dog was going to pay. Already, the Mexican was fantasizing about the animal's death. A gut shot, he mused coldly, a bullet through the kidneys, another severing the spine. Again, he called out to the black, smiling when the animal seemed to respond.

Nose in the air, Sullivan's hound strutted toward the window. Chavez took aim.

Reese stepped out of the shadows. "You should have used the door, Chavez," he rebuked. "And you should have knocked."

Chavez backed up a full pace, his mouth agape as he stared into the barrel of Sullivan's Remington. Certain he was already dead, he thumbed back the hammer on his own weapon, and swung it away from the dog in a direct line with Sullivan's belly. He squeezed the trigger.

Sullivan dropped to the floor, watching as the dog hurtled through the window to slam against Chavez' chest. The animal's teeth closed around the soft flesh at the Mexican's throat. The man's pistol tumbled from his fingers, clattering against the wood planking as he raised his arms to protect his face. In his panic, Chavez retreated even farther, almost running as he backed away from the dog's renewed attack.

Chavez' back slammed into the balcony railing, the man half-turning as he felt himself losing balance, a fresh flow of blood flooding across his eyes and blinding him. In his panic, he reached out for the corner post.

There was a long, terrifying feeling of being suspended in mid air, the sensation lasting no more than a heartbeat, yet seeming to encompass the whole of the man's past. His arms worked as if treading water, the railing at his back giving way, the wood splintering as the uprights were torn loose from their bracings.

Chavez hit the ground without uttering a single cry.

Chapter Ten

The building was old, a relic from the time when Limbo had served as a frontier garrison and way stop for Spanish *conquistadores* crawling their way north into the territories beyond the *Rio Bravo*. It had served its purpose well. The stink of age and human confinement lingering in the three-foot thick adobe walls, a mute testament to the men who had served and those who had perished in the four-by-six, windowless cells. There had been generations of them. The Spanish adventurers first, and then the Irish mercenaries who came unwillingly in the middle eighteen hundreds. And—finally—the French and Austrian troops who put Maximillian on the throne, and who, in the end, deserted him.

And now it belonged to Bridger.

He accepted the young captain's invitation to sit and eased into the chair behind the desk. Mendoza took his customary place at the man's back. The accepted protocol, the officer recognized it without being outwardly offended. Theirs was an uneasy truce, forged by a mutual feeling of distrust, but politically necessary.

Bridger trimmed a cigar and lit up before speaking. The words came between puffs of grey smoke that hid his eyes. "One of my young ladies is missing," he began, watching the other man's face.

The captain nodded. He cast a quick look at Chato Mendoza, and saw something akin to a smirk touch the man's lips, then swung his gaze to the dark night beyond the barred window beside the door. It was late, close to midnight, he reckoned. Too late to prolong the tedium by playing Bridger's insipid games. "One would assume, *Patrón*, that your young lady has often been...delayed...while pursuing her chosen avocation. Perhaps even to the point of staying away for days." Ignoring Bridger's frown, he took a brown-papered *cigarillo* from the covered humidor on the desk.

Bridger surveyed the young officer through narrowed lids. "No," he breathed softly, shaking his head. "Not this young woman. I would suggest, Captain Padilla," it was clear from Bridger's tone that he meant business, "you attend to your duties and deal with this matter with the same alacrity you would exercise in Juarez or Mexico City." His voice lowered, his tone conveying more threat then his words. "Unless you would like me to advise your superiors that you find your work here in the provinces too trivial, and my people too unimportant to merit your full attention."

Padilla weighed each word as the man said them, the words *your superiors* and *my people* heard and clearly understood. With some men of power beyond this mountain fortress, Bridger was still a force to be reckoned with, and he was as much the feudal lord as he believed. Padilla sighed. His chances for advancement in the military were already handicapped by the circumstances of his birth—he cursed his mother for her foolish indiscretions—and he could ill afford even the smallest blemish on an otherwise impeccable record. Ignoring the mulatto's smug grin, he surrendered. He took out the small pad he used for keeping notes. "If you could tell me, sir, when you last saw the young lady?"

Bridger sensed his small victory and savored it. "She left my cantina with a young man an acquaintance of mine brought with him from El Paso," he intoned. "In spite of my warning that the boy had been drinking quite heavily, she foolishly asked him to escort her to her home after her performance. She didn't come back to the *cantina*." He shrugged. "We checked her room, of course, but she was not there." A frown creased his forehead. "I want her found," he finished.

It was Padilla's turn to smile, the irony fully comprehended. Bridger intended for him to serve—*yes, that was the right word*—as some actor in his charade, a diversion that had, for some reason, become necessary to the man's intrigues. Despite his earlier passivity, he could not resist the urge to play with the man. "You've talked to Sullivan, of course? Asked him about where his son might be?" The reference to Reese Sullivan and his boy was intentional.

Bridger's jaws tensed, his thick beard looking even more like a lion's great mane, and he smashed his cigar out on the desk. He was surprised the officer—just recently arrived in Limbo—knew Sullivan's name. "We've talked," he snarled. He read something in the younger man's face he'd not seen before, a brief flash of defiance that sparked and just as suddenly ebbed. Impatient, no longer sure of what he'd seen, he shoved back his chair and stood up; his moves awkward as Mendoza failed to anticipate his intention and move out of the way. "Chato will show you where the woman lives," he announced.

Mendoza watched as Bridger stormed out of the office, torn by the desire to follow or to do what the man ordered. It was clear that the young *federale* angered Bridger with his impudence, but there was no time to deal with Padilla's breach of manners. *There was only the girl, and the need to place the blame for her death on Sullivan's son.* He grabbed the young soldier's arm, no consideration in him as his fingernails dug into the soft flesh above the man's elbow. "I'll show you the way," he droned.

* - * - * - * - *

Sullivan followed the dog through the maze of alleys behind the cantina. The animal moved back and forth at a trot, his nose a scant inch above the ground as he ferreted out Trey's scent and broke into a lope.

There was no light, the narrow passageways forming deep tunnels that merged into walls of blackness. Sullivan navigated the alleys by touch, his fingers skimming along the walls as he jogged behind the dog, the noise of his breath and footsteps magnified by the night-time silence.

He cursed, watching as the dog disappeared into another cramped passageway. Then, hearing the sound of the black's paws clawing wood, he slowed and called the dog to him.

The scratching noise stopped. Sullivan hesitated, his eyes narrowing as he waited. It didn't take long. The big dog reappeared at the entrance to the alley, one foot poised as his dark eyes searched out his master. Responding to Sullivan's summons, the animal trotted forward. As soon as the big man stepped out of the darkness, the dog paused, looked back over his shoulder, and then turned to hunt again.

Once more, Sullivan followed in the dog's wake. The scratching sound came again, this time more urgently than before, the animal's high pitched whimpering increasing as he dug at the wood. Sullivan caught up with the dog and pulled him away from the door. Canting his head, he pressed his ear against the thick planking, and—hearing nothing—tried the latch.

The door swung open easily, and then thunked against something solid. There was no light, and Sullivan worked the door again, pulling it to him then swinging it back until he felt the same resistance as before. Inhaling, he sucked in his belly and slid inside the room.

Sullivan felt the black worm between his legs, his fingers brushing across the animal's back in a vain attempt to hold the dog back. He could feel the animal's neck hairs grow stiff, and heard the dog growl, the sound coming as one with a soft moan.

He shut the door, afraid to risk a light with the door open. Even then, he did not bother to search out a candle or a lantern, choosing instead to rely on a single match. He cupped the stick with his hand, and stepped forward.

Sullivan felt a cold fist in the pit of his belly when the sole of his boot suddenly slipped across the wide planking. He knew instinctively what caused the wetness that spread beneath his foot, an old memory coming back to tear at his mind. It was like trying to walk the cold floors in a slaughterhouse, in the room where the cattle were hung to bleed out; the same sense of wet stickiness coming as he righted himself and took a second step. Nothing compared with the memory; not ice, not water.

The first match went out, and Sullivan struck another. He waited until his eyes adjusted to the dim flame, and then hunkered down on his heels.

The girl lay at his feet, no longer beautiful, a pool of congealed blood holding her flat against the floor. Her dark hair was already stiff at her ears and forehead. Sullivan reached out, a coldness in him as he probed the wound at her throat. The jugular was torn, the cut ending below the young woman's ear. *An inch more*, Sullivan mused darkly, *and her head would have been severed.* His somber musings were interrupted by a sudden pain in his thumb and forefinger, and he shook out the second match.

The darkness prompted another soft groan, and Sullivan heard the dog's anxious whine. He felt his way around the girl's body, moving toward the sound, and lit another match.

Trey's eyelids fluttered, the bright flash of light exploding before him as intense as the sun, and he turned his head in an effort to escape the pain. He was immediately sorry, his brain suddenly compacting against his skull. The spasm brought with it a wave of nausea, and he was sick.

Sullivan waited. Already, he was pulling Treys clothes from the bed and floor. There was no gentleness in him, only a sense of urgency. "Get dressed," he ordered.

Trey pulled himself up on one elbow, his eyes still refusing to focus. His tongue felt thick, as dead as his arms and legs. "I can't," he croaked. He was too sick and too disoriented to be contrary, and there was no antagonism in his words or his manner.

"Like hell," Sullivan whispered. Shielding the flickering match with the palm of his hand, he fumbled for the lantern on the table beside the bed. He discarded the globe, turning the wick down as far as he could and touched the dying match to the kerosene-soaked cotton. Mindful of the light, he placed the lamp on the floor and slid it beneath the corner of the high bed.

Trey had not moved. He still lay on his back, resting on his elbows. Sullivan reached out, shaking the youth. "I told you to get dressed!"

Dumbly, the younger man attempted to do as he was told. Nothing seemed to work, and he was aware of every sound. The noise was unbearable, unusually loud; from the stiff rattle of his own breath, to the dull scrape that came as he slipped a numb leg into his Levis. He waved away Sullivan's offer to help him with his shirt, the sickness clawing at his gut again. Gingerly, he rubbed at the pain with one hand. "Christ," he murmured. "I..." He turned to face Sullivan, and saw the girl.

Too late, Sullivan tried to block the younger man's view. He was not moved by any sense of compassion, only the need to keep the younger man moving. He shoved a boot into Trey's hand. "You were seen leaving with her. When they find her body, you're the one they're going to come looking for," he warned.

Trey was shaking his head, as much in denial of his father's words, as in what he had seen. "She was alive," he argued. "*She was alive!*"

Sullivan pulled the younger man to his feet. "Try telling that to Bridger," he countered, "or the local law."

They started for the door. Unsteady on his feet, Trey stumbled, his feet tangled in the rumpled sheets on the floor at the foot of the bed. Righting himself, he yielded to his temper and kicked the sheets out of his way, the toe of his right boot catching the lantern and sending it skimming across the floor. The glass-based lamp spiraled in a wide arc beneath the bed, glancing off one leg before smashing against the wall. The glass shattered. Kerosene spilled from the broken lantern, soaking into the dry adobe wall and across the plank flooring, quick fingers of blue flame following each trail of oily wetness.

Fleeing the smell of the fire, the dog bolted past Reese, slipping into the shadows and disappearing into the darkness. Reese was right behind the animal. He was well into the alleyway when he realized he was alone.

Angry, Sullivan made an immediate about face. He dog-trotted back to the small dwelling, cursing his son's obvious lack of intelligence, and his own sanity.

He stopped at the doorway, abruptly, one foot on the threshold as he realized what the younger man was doing. Unseen, he melted back into the shadows, a grim set to his lips as he watched his son, the pale glow of the kerosene-fed fire casting a blue-white haze that filled the small room and outlined the things within.

Trey was beside the girl's body, his weight resting on one knee as he searched the pockets of her full skirt. The money belt he'd hidden beneath her mattress was already slung across his shoulder. There was a cold-blooded determination in him as he probed about the girl's corpse, and—Sullivan sensed—an anger. Callously, the young man continued his search, until—finally—he found what he'd been seeking.

From the shadows, Sullivan watched as his son used one hand to lift the girl's head from the floor. His blue eyes turned the color of flint as Trey pulled the heavy gold chain from her bloodied neck and stood up.

There was a commotion in the street, the sharp sound of a man's voice barking commands in Spanish as booted feet stamped to attention. Trey heard the sounds, and turned.

Again, Sullivan drew back into the shadows. Unseen, he watched as the younger man sprinted into the darkness, waited, and fell in behind. Ahead of him, he heard the dog bark a single time, and the soft sound of his son's laughter. *As if they were simply playing a child's game of tag.*

*_*_*_*_*

Padilla's jaws tensed, his dark eyes mirroring the carnage on the barren floor of the dimly lit *casita*. The stench of the scorched adobe and the spilled kerosene still lingered, and he was grateful that the fire had burned itself out quickly. The girl, at least, had been spared the final indignity of being denied the customary public wake and a proper burial.

In his mid-thirties, Padilla was no stranger to death. His early years as a recruit had been spent in the harsh desert where Geronimo and his band of renegades had practiced their vile skills on the poor *pastores* and peasants who struggled to subsist in a land almost as cruel as the Apache. The savages had butchered their prey, just as someone had slaughtered the young whore. *It was not,* he knew, *a white man's kill.*

From the doorway, Chato Mendoza watched as the young officer made his slow inspection. Padilla moved like a leech, inspecting the girl's wound and then carefully covering her exposed body with a sheet before continuing his investigation. The delay worried the half-breed. Bridger had planned a quick inquiry, and an even quicker arrest. It was, he realized, important that there be no more postponements, and that Reese Sullivan and his son were detained as soon as possible.

Ignoring the trooper who barred his way, Mendoza pushed his way inside the room. "Padilla!" The annoying delays intensified the man's growing anger.

Padilla was making notations in his thick tablet. He paused only long enough to wet the tip of his pencil with his tongue, and then resumed writing. "Yes?" The feigned distraction was meant as a dismissal.

Mendoza was having none of it. "The *Patrón* told you, Padilla," he began. "It was the *gringo*," the word sounded vulgar, "who took her home, who was the last one to be with her."

Padilla closed his notebook, his movements exaggerated. "Then perhaps we should find the young man," he smiled. "And, of course, Mr. Sullivan." There was no warmth in his face, or his eyes. He bowed slightly at the waist, snapped his heels together, and gestured toward the door.

Mendoza hesitated, his mouth a tight line as he tried to read the captain's mocking smile. Uneasy, he turned, leading the way out the door. Padilla fell in behind him, so close he could feel the man's breath on his shoulder. *Someday,* Mendoza seethed, *you will pay for your insolence.*

* - * - * - * - *

From his perch in the loft above the livery stable, Sullivan watched the activity in the street below, a wry smile touching his lips as he saw Padilla's green recruits pairing up to begin their search. The captain was doing his job well. He stood at the open door of his office, framed by the small circle of light at his back, sending the men off in all four directions of the compass. Alone in the doorway, he watched as they disappeared. In time, Sullivan knew, the man would begin his own solitary search.

There was a noise behind Sullivan, the harsh scratch of a match against a rusty nail, and he turned to face his son. In the time they had been together, he had only seen the younger man smoke on one other occasion. Disgusted that Trey was as careless now as before, he tramped across the hay, and jerked the butt out of his son's hand. "I told you at the ranch," he scowled, "not in the barns. *Any barn.*" He crushed out the cigarette between his thumb and forefinger and pocketed the ash.

Trey's hands were shaking. He leaned against a stack of twine-bound bales of hay, still weak and requiring the support. "I need a drink."

Sullivan's frown deepened. "You had one. Remember? One long one in the *cantina*, and more when you were with the girl." He made no attempt to hide the sarcasm. *Or the accusation.*

The younger man's left hand disappeared inside his shirt. Nervously, his fingers rubbed at the medallion that hung around his neck. He had washed the talisman, twice, and it still felt unclean. He avoided his father's eyes. "She was alive," he whispered. The cobwebs still shrouded his mind, and he made the pronouncement like a man trying to convince himself it was true. He remembered very little now about what had happened inside the girl's house, and what he did recall was a jumble of images that had no real beginning or end, with no distinction between what was real and what had been fantasy. He repeated the words, with even less conviction than before. "*She was alive.*"

Sullivan snorted in disbelief. "And I have your word on that," he grimaced. He was back at the open hatch, staring down into the street.

Trey stared hard at his father's dim silhouette. *Bastard*, he swore silently. In spite of the numbness in his legs, he pushed himself away from the straw pillar and moved toward the man.

Sullivan's gaze was still riveted on the street below. He turned sideways, just slightly, enough that he could watch the doorway to

Padilla's office and still see his son. Then, his left shoulder lifting slightly, he moved.

Trey's mouth opened, but the words failed to come. His eyes opened wide in astonishment, the gloved fist catching him solidly on the side of his head, just above his right ear.

Reese moved with the swing, coming forward in a slight crouch as he braced himself to catch the younger man. He felt his son's warm breath on his cheek, a soft *poof* sounding as Trey collapsed across his shoulder. It was going to be a long haul, he reckoned, getting Trey out of the barn and into the jail. He didn't care.

* - * - * - * - *

Bridger stood in the narrow corridor outside the locked cell, his cigar smoke lying heavy on air already ripe with the stink of mold and damp adobe. Even in the dim light, he could see that the unconscious man sprawled on the straw pallet on the floor was Trey Underwood. "And Sullivan?" he asked.

Padilla took a long drink of his coffee before he answered. It had been a long night. "In his room at the hotel," he said finally.

Surprised, Bridger pondered the man's answer. "You've sent for him?"

There was another brief silence as the captain emptied his cup. "I sent a man," he answered. "Sullivan was shaving. He said he would be here when he was through." It was clear that Bridger presumed the captain and his men made the arrest, and Padilla did nothing to discourage the man's assumptions.

Uncomfortable and strangely subdued, Bridger nodded toward the door leading to the outer office. He didn't wait for Padilla, choosing instead to lead the way out of the cold passageway. "Shaving," he murmured, his eyes narrowing. He stroked his long beard. Then, turning his head, he addressed the officer. "He knows? About the girl?"

Padilla shook his head. "Only that the boy is in jail," the man answered. He stepped across the threshold and crossed the floor to the small potbellied stove. The wooden handle on the enamel coffee pot was hot, and chips of white paint flaked off in his fingers. He knew from the weight that the pot was empty and slammed it down against the grid. The noise roused the young corporal sleeping in the chair in the far corner, and he scrambled to fetch more water. Once the man was gone, he continued his conversation. "For all Sullivan knows, the boy has just been arrested for being drunk and disorderly, nothing more."

Bridger's eyes scanned the street. Sullivan's seeming lack of interest puzzled him. *Unless*, as Padilla explained, *the man really didn't know about the dead whore.*

"*Patrón?*" Mendoza was in the doorway, half in and half out. Even in the daylight, his aversion to small rooms with barred windows was evident, the look of a caged animal firing his dark eyes. The flame burned even brighter when a smiling Padilla pulled the door open and beckoned for him to enter. He declined, filing this affront with the one from the night before. "Sullivan," he announced, jerking his head a single time in the direction of the boarding house.

Bridger's eyes swung toward the street. Sullivan was coming, walking down the boardwalk on the opposite side of the street, the black dog following in his shadow. "I'm going to talk to him," he declared. "Alone." He put out his arm, effectively blocking Padilla's way when the man attempted to pass through the opening. Padilla said nothing. For now, he would play the part of the docile civil servant.

With Mendoza at heel, Bridger strode across the wide main street. He traversed the roadway without interruption, unmindful of the early morning traffic. The farmers and peddlers—the occasional mounted outlaw—paused to let him pass, yielding to the man out of habit.

"Reese." As if it had been planned, the two men met midway in the busy causeway. Bridger was the first to extend a hand.

Sullivan was lighting a cigarette. He kept both hands busy for a time, shielding the match as his eyes swept the roadway on both sides. "Ansel." The word came with a stream of pale smoke that dissipated immediately.

A single wave of Bridger's massive hand dismissed the man at his back. He waited until Mendoza withdrew to make his speech. "There's been some trouble, old friend," he began amicably. There was just the proper amount of hesitancy in his manner, and it matched the obvious remorse that softened his words.

Reese smiled. He resumed walking, snapping his fingers and calling the dog to heel on his left side. Bridger fell in on his right. "Full moon last night, Ansel," he observed. "Brought out the night crawlers, made the world a little crazy."

The walk back to the jail seemed longer than before, Bridger mused. "My men found Chavez," he volunteered. "I saw no reason to involve Padilla in something that does not concern him, so we simply disposed of the problem ourselves." There was a long silence as he chewed on his cigar, as if he were waiting for Sullivan to thank him for his efforts. When the other remained quiet, he tried again. "I didn't send him to your room, Reese," he lied.

Sullivan only nodded. "You said there was trouble." He stepped up onto the boardwalk in front of the jail. "If you're talking about the *chamaco*," his memory of how Trey happened to be in jail brought a smile that Bridger misread as ignorance. "If he got out of hand at your place, did any damage, I'll make it good."

Thoroughly convinced now that Sullivan did not know, Bridger said "The girl is dead." He reached out, his fingers closing around Sullivan's right wrist in a gesture of comfort. "They found her in her cottage, her throat cut. Trey was...gone.

"I'm not saying the boy did it, but..."

Sullivan's face darkened. "But what, Ansel?"

Bridger lowered his head, carefully considering his next words. "The young woman was greatly admired," he began, whispering. "If it were known that she was murdered, and that Trey was the last one to be seen with her..." He shrugged.

Sullivan was aware of the people passing by them on either side. He shook his head when Bridger began to speak again. "Inside," he breathed.

They went in together, Sullivan shutting the door before Mendoza could join them. "I want him out, Ansel." He looked past Padilla as if the man were not there. "Now."

Bridger was by the window beside the barred door. He nodded at the street beyond. "Out there," he began, "I control everything for as far as you can see." The benign smile was almost real. "In here," the smile grew, "Padilla is the *Patrón*." He swung his gaze from Sullivan to the young officer, enjoying the ruse. "I believe the charge is murder, Reese."

Padilla handed Sullivan a cup of coffee. "You'll want to see the boy," he offered.

As if debating his next move, Sullivan stood firm. "Our arrangement, Ansel," he said finally. "It's going to take me a little time to clear this up."

Bridger's hand rested on the doorknob. "I've waited this long, Reese. I can wait a bit longer." He hesitated, his voice lowering. "You must watch your son," he cautioned. "The girl had many admirers, and it would be tragic if—through some foolish sense of honor—they elected to avenge her death." Finished, he opened the door and stepped into the sun.

Sullivan waited for the door to close before speaking. "Is he still out?" Already, he was heading for the passageway leading to the small cells.

Padilla followed after him. "You must have hit him pretty hard," he noted. The corners of his mouth twitched as he made a vain attempt not to smile.

"Not hard enough," Sullivan retorted. Expectantly, he held out his hand. The keys were old, ornately decorated in the identical fashion as the weapons that had been produced in the same era. *As if the beauty justified the horror each represented.* Death and confinement, Reese mused. *Three hundred years of death and confinement.*

He inserted the largest key in the brass-bound lock, and felt the resistance as the mechanism worked, and the latch turned.

The young man was conscious. He was sitting up, his back pressed against the cool brick, his face expressionless as he surveyed the boundaries of the small, four-by-six cage. There was no window, the only light coming from three narrow ventilating shafts cut in the wall a good ten feet above the floor. The thin rectangles of sunlight thrust through the cold damp, bringing no warmth. Gnats swarmed beneath the light, circling above the dirt floor in a frenzy, like moths drawn to a candle. Trey watched the insects, a soft, self-mocking laughter coming as he realized that the winged mites were as much a prisoner as he, held by their own instincts in a wall of light that was driving them mad.

"You're in a pretty good mood, considering." Sullivan's voice tore into the silence. He stood in the corridor, as omnipresent and as unyielding as ever. "Of course, maybe you're used to this. You look pretty much at home."

Trey laughed again, his head rocking back and forth against the rough adobe. As before, there was no real humor in the sound. Suddenly, the laughter stopped. He faced the older man, a rigidity in him in spite of his relaxed posture. "Just who the hell are you working for," he demanded. The words were barely above a whisper; cold, distant. "Bridger?" His gaze swung to the man standing at his father's back. *One more corrupt greaser*, he mused, *selling out for a handful of Yankee gold.* "Or maybe, with a little help from your new—*compadre*—" the word sound dirty, "for yourself?"

With one finger, Sullivan traced an invisible line on the horizontal steel bar that spanned the narrow door to the cell, his fingertip making a muted *ta-tum, ta-tum* as it skimmed across the inch-thick uprights. He remained silent, and that silence offended his son more than any expected denial.

Trey bolted upright, the rage propelling him forward. He crossed the floor in two long strides coming face to face with his father.

Padilla gasped, the sound unusually loud. The resemblance between father and son was unnerving, something more than a physical sameness evoking the feeling that he was gazing at Sullivan and the man's mirrored reflection. The eyes, he realized. If it was true that the pale orbs mirrored the soul, then he was seeing the spirits of two men linked by something more than blood. *And they do not even know.*

Before either man could speak, Padilla stepped forward. "My name is Padilla," he began, his gaze locked squarely on Trey. "Emilio Padilla.

"Your father and I," he glanced briefly at the still silent Reese, "are working together for our respective governments." He paused, letting the words sink in.

Trey stared at the man. He was still—as much as the barred door would permit—nose to nose with Reese, and he had not yielded one inch. His eyes narrowed, his face showing neither belief nor disbelief as he swept Padilla's long frame from head to toe.

It was his first good look at the Mexican. He guessed the man's age as somewhere in his mid or early thirties, but something in Padilla's eyes made him look much older. *Haunted.* There was weariness there, that and a veiled resignation contrary to the man's bearing.

He was, Trey realized, an extraordinarily handsome man, neither as dark as he first thought nor as brown-eyed. The captain's coloring and features were different than the *mestizos* Trey had seen in the streets of Limbo; and distinctly more refined than the half-breeds who peopled Bridger's saloon. Padilla's dark hair was smooth, not much different in texture than his own, and markedly less curly. As for the man's bearing...

The word *regal* came instantly to mind, Trey's mouth agape as he was surprised by his own thoughts. He shook the thought away. "You're a liar," he breathed. He dismissed Padilla and faced his father. "And you are a dirty son-of..."

Sullivan's jaws tensed. He reached through the bars, grabbing at the young man's shirt, and cursing when Trey broke away.

Once more, Padilla intervened. "There are those of us, *chamaco*," he whispered, the words carrying just as far as he intended, "who believe that—if we do not honor the glory and traditions of our past—we can take no pride or place in the present, or the future.

"The treasure you seek, the treasure Wes Underwood meant to steal and Ansel Bridger covets so badly, belongs to the people. *My* people."

Trey was back against the far wall. He stared at both men for a long time before he finally spoke. "You set me up," he accused. The anger was back, more intense than before, and he slammed the wall with a balled fist. "The whole damned time!" he raged. "It was just a way of getting what my *father*," purposely, he emphasized the word, "died for!"

It struck Trey then, just how complex it had all become. He had been the bait, the piece of meat thrown out to draw the wolves from their den; in all likelihood from the very beginning. "You bastard," he seethed, his eyes boring into Reese Sullivan's stoic countenance. "You lousy, rotten bastard!"

Sullivan said nothing. He turned, his steps as precise as a soldier marching off to war.

Chapter Eleven

Padilla poured Sullivan a cup of coffee, saying nothing when the man dosed the strong brew with a large shot of whiskey. He'd only known Sullivan a relatively short time, slightly more than a year, and had not yet learned to read his moods. Neither, he thought ruefully—remembering his surprise when Sullivan appeared at his back door with Trey slung across his shoulder—did he fully comprehend the Irishman's unique way of doing his job. Nor had he been aware of the man's uncanny ability to adapt to any change which deviated from what had been planned.

The Mexican took his seat at the cluttered desk, savoring the warmth of the coffee and its aroma as he studied Sullivan's face. He watched as the man withdrew within himself, and it was almost possible to see his mind working as he weighed the facts carefully catalogued in his head. His eyes would narrow, a change occurring that Padilla mentally likened to the sudden shifting of the colored beads within a child's kaleidoscope, the summer blue warming or turning cold and dark.

Finally, Sullivan came forward in his chair. "The money belt," he said.

Padilla dug into the deep drawer on the right hand side of the desk, withdrew the belt, and placed it on the table between them. "It doesn't appear that anything was taken," he observed.

Reese was already examining the series of small pouches. There was nothing of interest, and certainly nothing to indicate that Trey had been carrying anything akin to what he expected. The sweat-dampened belt had molded to the few objects within, and there were no indentations or outlines that suggested that anything might be missing. No bulky maps, no bound notebooks. "You ask him if everything is here?"

The younger man smiled. He had expected the question. "He was still out when you brought him here, and for a considerable length of time afterwards. Certainly in no shape to answer any questions. What you see, is what there was. The telegram from his mother, a small amount of cash, and a card and correspondence from a man named Pullman. Nothing more."

Sullivan returned the belt, laying it across the desk, and stood up. Padilla had been thorough in his search, and right in his assessment of what he had found. *Nothing. Absolutely nothing.* He stretched, working the kinks out of a body that had been more than twenty-four hours without sleep. When he turned to face Padilla, he looked strangely refreshed. "We know Bridger set the boy up," he began. "Which means he had the girl drug Trey so that he could get into the house and go through everything the kid had with him.

"*Everything*," he repeated, emphasizing the word.

Padilla was nodding. "But nothing was taken," he argued. "And the girl..."

"...is dead," Sullivan finished. "A murder, and no robbery."

This, Padilla understood. If Trey's things had been taken, there would have been some questions as to what occurred in the young whore's cabin, and just who was guilty of what. It still, however, didn't make any sense. He shook his head, the frustration cutting deep lines across his forehead. He rubbed at them with the back of one hand. "*Maldito sea!*" he cursed. "For more than a year now, all of us—you, Devereau, my own people—we've followed one false trail after another, all because of the rantings of a madman...!" He quit rubbing his head and slammed his fist against the table.

Sullivan began pacing, his mind working. This time, he spoke his thoughts aloud. "Suppose," he began, "before Trey passed out, he told the girl something that Bridger wanted to know, something..."

"Wes Underwood would have revealed to his son," Padilla interrupted. He realized his mistake immediately, but continued without making any apology. "Something important enough that the girl would die for it, in the hope Trey didn't remember telling her." Sullivan's approving nod encouraged him, and he continued. "And with Trey in jail, accused of her murder," he chuckled, "...a *gringo* at the mercy of an unfriendly and unsympathetic government, *you* would be out of the way, and too involved in helping the boy to attend to business."

Again, Sullivan agreed. He hesitated for a time, thinking of everything that transpired the night before. The next was more difficult for him. His voice barely rose above a whisper, but the words were exact. "In all the time we were together, the kid told me nothing. Not about what happened at Yuma, and even less about what had happened before, in San Francisco. I assumed that what he wanted, what he came to me for was," he frowned, wanting to express his thoughts in a context Padilla would understand, "just to get even for what happened to his stepfather."

Padilla's right eyebrow raised. He went to the stove and refilled both their cups with hot coffee, careful to leave room in each for a healthy shot of liquor. "And now you think otherwise?" He returned to the desk, added the whiskey, paused, and added more.

Sullivan stared at the door leading to the cells. "He's a thief," he said softly, "and if he hadn't been kicked out of college, he would have become as big a shyster as Underwood, who was also a thief.'

There was an awkward stillness between the two men, Sullivan obviously embarrassed that he uncharacteristically put his most private thoughts into words. He cleared his throat and crossed the room to stand at the window, silently grateful when Padilla was gracious enough not to ask any more questions. "Bridger is holding the trump card right now, whatever it is, and he knows it," he observed. He was in control now, of his thoughts and his words. "If he did find out anything, he's going to make a move, and soon."

Padilla pushed back his chair. He leaned back, considering the other's words. "Tonight," he reckoned.

"Today," Reese corrected. He tapped on the window with his knuckles, his finger extending as he used the tip to draw a circle against the soot-caked glass.

The Mexican stood up. He joined Reese, his gaze following Sullivan's pointing finger and coming to rest on a group of men outlined within the sphere the man inscribed on the thick windowpane. They stood together near the shaded front porch of Bridger's *cantina*, each man clutching a half-empty bottle of whiskey; six men in a street where—only moments before— dozens more had trafficked.

Padilla had seen men like these before, more times than he cared to remember, in situations where emotions ruled and common sense no longer existed. The pattern was always the same. Drink. Whispered threats. False bravado primed by an unreasonable anger that increased in direct proportion to the abundant amounts of corn liquor consumed. These were men who had been turned loose and were encouraged by the people who now hid behind their shuttered windows and locked doors. "How soon?" he asked.

Sullivan answered the question without thinking. "About five seconds after those bottles are empty," he breathed. He swore.

* _ * _ * _ * _ *

Bridger left the saloon by the back door. Mendoza was with him. Four more of his men—the hired mercenaries Mendoza had hand picked—were already on their way south. They would leave the trail Bridger wanted found; a warm trail, not too easy to find, and looking as though some attempt had been made to conceal his destination.

Mendoza tapped Bridger's shoulder, a slow grin coming as he heard the single report of a hand gun. A second shot followed, accompanied by the noise of shattering glass. "They go for Sullivan's son,' he laughed.

Bridger's face radiated a similar joy. This was the diversion he needed to cover his own departure. He mounted the big gelding Mendoza brought from the *estancia* and pointed the animal north. "El Paso,' he shouted, kicking the horse into a run. "And the keys to the new El Dorado!" His laughter was that of a man much younger, filled with a renewed lust for life. He would find the treasure this time, with no interference from others, and he would claim it for his own.

* _ * _ * _ * _ *

Padilla was enraged. He pulled the rifles from the rack, cursing himself for his own vindictiveness. Angry at the young sergeant, Castillo, assigned as his aide, he sent the man and the recruits on an early morning patrol well into the mountains. It had been intended as a punishment, a humiliation for the noncom's posturing and arrogant behavior.

It had been a mistake. "I am a fool," he breathed. "A bigger fool than Castillo."

Sullivan shook his head. "We don't need your troopers," he announced. "At least, not now." A bullet thwacked impotently against the heavy, barred door, and Sullivan grinned. Similar *thwacks* sounded as the soft lead began to dig into the heavy adobe brick.

The noise roused Trey, and Sullivan heard him shouting. The words were garbled, made indistinguishable by the same heavy oak that comprised the jailhouse's front door. In spite of himself, Reese responded. "Shut up!" he bellowed.

Padilla laughed. He knew now that Sullivan was right about the troopers. The men outside the door launched a pitiful attack against a building once part of a great fortification. His laughter grew.

And then he sobered. "Bridger?" he murmured.

"Already gone," Sullivan answered. He said the words as if he had seen the man leave.

"But where?" Padilla demanded. The old frustration tore at him; the feeling of failure that had been a heavy cross on his shoulders for the past year.

"We aren't going to find out," Sullivan nodded at the men beyond the walls, knowing how long it could take before they tired of the game, or drank themselves sober, "until we get out of here."

The Mexican raked his long fingers through his dark hair, clutching a fistful and pulling it, as if he were trying to wake himself up from a bad dream. The bullets were still digging into the ancient brick and pinging against the ironwork on the windows and the door in an irritating cadence that had become annoyingly regular. And from behind him, he could still hear Trey's shouted obscenities. "And just how, *Señor* Sullivan, do you propose we achieve our freedom?" It was the right word, considering that the fortress had become their prison.

Reese had been busy. An empty cartridge box lay on the floor at his feet, and two repeating rifles were propped up against the wall. He was working on a double-barreled shotgun now, filling the breech with the shells he brought with him from El Paso.

Padilla had seen him load the cartridges. Bird shot, layered with grains of rock salt and thin shards of razor-sharp steel shavings. "Sullivan?"

Reese resented the man's tone. "You know how to stop a snake from crawling up your leg and biting you, Captain?" He didn't wait for the man's answer. "You cut off its head."

Padilla watched as Sullivan picked up a rifle. "Where are you...?"

"I'm going out the back door," Sullivan answered. He put the rifle over his shoulder. The shotgun was already concealed beneath the bulky serape. He had strapped it to his left leg, barrels pointing down; the stock resting comfortably against his thigh.

A dark shadow rose up from beneath Padilla's desk. The big dog came forward, stretching, its great mouth opening in a wide yawn; its gaze locked on Sullivan's face. It was as if the animal had been roused from its slumber by some secret communion with the man, and knew he was about to go on the hunt. Panting, the black padded across the floor and nuzzled Sullivan's hand.

Reese shook his head. "Not this time," he whispered. He scratched the dog's head. "Sit," he commanded. Then, "Stay." Immediately, the dog obeyed. Sullivan backed away, his tone almost the same when he addressed the man. "Give me five minutes," he ordered. He nodded toward the windows and the two Henrys. "You can buy me the time."

Padilla debated the man's words. "How much time?" he asked.

Sullivan's patience had reached its limits. "I told you," he intoned. "Five minutes." He turned, unlocked the door leading to the cells, and disappeared.

* _ * _ * _ * _ *

Trey watched as the door opened, his eyes narrowing as the light from the front office spilled into the dark passageway. He knew from the size and bulk that the man silhouetted in the doorway was his father, and he called out to him. "And now, old man?"

Sullivan passed the younger man without saying anything. He slipped through the back door and slammed it shut. Behind him, he heard the clatter of steel against steel as Trey raged and rattled the door to his cage. *It was a good feeling,* he mused, *knowing where the kid was, and that—for once—he was going to stay where he had been put.*

* _ * _ * _ * _ *

Padilla picked his targets carefully. He had little chance of making a killing shot, but there was still a sense of satisfaction in knowing he was able to retaliate. A head poked up from behind a rotting rain barrel and Padilla took deliberate aim. He aimed high and to the left, and squeezed the trigger.

The man's aim was true. He watched as the dry wood splintered, the bullet striking the wooden keg parallel of the wide iron band securing the staves at its middle, the lead slug following the curve like a train 'rounding a bend. A man screamed, the high-pitched yelp followed by a series of shouted profanities. Padilla smiled, watching as the man bolted upright, his thigh furrowed and bleeding from his knee to his hip. The sight of blood and the pain dampened the gunman's enthusiasm, and he retreated into the alleyway.

There was a brief lull in the shooting, and then a renewed barrage resounded. The shots were wild, the lead flattening against the dry adobe beside and above the window where Padilla held court. He shook his head, no longer angry at the bravados who tormented him. They were boys, primed with free liquor and beguiled by Bridger into playing at being men. *At what they thought were men.*

Five minutes, Padilla reminded himself. He thought of Sullivan, and picked another random target, this time firing above the man's head, and then into the dirt at his feet as he fled.

* - * - * - * - *

Sullivan watched the men in the street. There had been six when it started. Two of them were gone now, the one Padilla wounded, and a second man he scared off with a series of well-placed shots that nipped at his heels as he ran. The scarred earth told the story, the imprint of the mestizo's right boot cut deeper by a bullet hole almost dead center of where his heel had struck the dry earth as he ran. Sullivan was impressed.

He was also leery. The four men who remained had regrouped at the entrance to the alleyway beside the cantina. They stood, peering into the street, gesturing toward the jail; arguing, Reese sensed, one man clearly assuming the lead.

Unobserved, Sullivan eased around the corner of the building. He stayed in the shadows, watching the men as they watched the jail. He saw them huddle for another hurried conference, and saw them part.

He stepped out into the street, both arms raised as he held the Henry above his head. A white cloth fluttered from the rifle's barrel, tied with a single knot just below the front sight. He called out. "*Hola!*" As one, the four men turned, three of them to the right and slightly behind the dark-skinned youth; the one with long fingers and cat-like way of moving, Reese knew to be their self-appointed *jefe*.

Instinctively, the trio retreated back into the alleyway, grappling for weapons that hung up in their holsters. The forth man came forward a full pace, his right hand resting lightly on the grip of his pistol. He was smiling, a clarity in his eyes that was not obvious in the others, his whole demeanor more self-assured and knowing. He was also sober.

Reese kept his arms well above his head, the rifle in his right hand. He took a single step forward, the enigmatic smile of a fool pasted across his lips. When he spoke to the men, it was in softly accented Spanish. "*Vengo a negociar,*" (I come to bargain)", he began. He tipped his head, nodding toward the jail. "*Para el chico,*" (For the boy)."

Amused by the gringo's audacity, the younger man grinned. His teeth were even, a glint of gold showing as the smile widened. Just as quickly, the smile was gone. "*El mató a mi mujer,*" (He killed my woman), he whispered.

Sullivan's eyes narrowed. Somehow, he knew that the man had been the girl's pimp, and that greed prompted him; not any great love for the woman.

The other three men were drawing closer, bunching themselves around and behind their comrade. "*Es mi hijo,*" (He's my son,) Reese said finally. He made no reference to the girl.

There was laughter. From the young brigand first, and then in chorus, from his companions. He took off his hat, bending at the waist in an exaggerated bow. "Estevan Diaz", he announced, snapping his heels together. He straightened.

Sullivan shifted, his upraised arms getting tired. "*¿Mi hijo?*" (My son?)

"*Es un hombre muerto,*" (Is a dead man,) Diaz answered. There was nothing, he knew, this man could offer that Bridger would not increase ten fold. He drew his pistol. "The rifle," he ordered, this time in English. "And a clear look at your right hip." Expectant, he stepped back.

Sullivan's brow furrowed, and then smoothed. Diaz' English was surprisingly good. Knowing what was expected, he surrendered the rifle, and tossed it to the man standing directly behind Diaz. Smug, Diaz nodded, and then—using the pistol—pointed at Sullivan's right leg.

Reese backed up, slowly. Obediently, his left hand still at shoulder level, he lifted the wool serape away from his right hip.

Diaz shook his head. The laughter began softly, growing as the man assessed his position and determined that he held all the cards. Sullivan was unarmed, and stood directly between him and the jail. *Between him and Padilla's guns.* "Now," he said, the arrogance adding an edge to the words, "you and I will bargain with the other." He nodded toward the silent window where Padilla stood watching. "For the blue-eyed *bastardo* who killed my woman."

Sullivan's left hand seemed to tremble, the fingertips losing their color. "The arm," he said, wiggling his hand.

Diaz' smile was almost gracious. "It happens," he said. "When a man gets old, and careless." Again, he pointed at the jail, still using the barrel of the pistol as an extension of his fingers.

Sullivan's arm dropped with devastating speed. He swept the serape away from his left hip, his right hand disappearing to pull the strap that bound the shotgun to his leg. He fired without aiming, cradling the weapon against his side, and feeling the kick as the hammer dropped.

Diaz screamed, his chest erupting in a series of quarter-inched slits, the original bird shot load peppering his shoulder and face; the rock salt burning deep into his flesh. He was lifted up and back, his feet dangling above the ground as he hung suspended in midair. Sullivan watched him fall, swinging to his right as he leveled the sawed-off at the three men who stood at the man's back.

They froze, spattered with blood and bits of tissue, too stunned to move; terribly aware that Sullivan had only pulled one trigger. All three of them were sober now, the fight gone out of them.

The man holding Reese's rifle dropped the weapon and backed away. He kept backing away, staring hard at the dead man lying at his feet. And then he turned and ran. He was not alone. Reese raised the shotgun, aiming just above the heads of the fleeing men, and pulled the trigger a second time. When the smoke cleared, they were gone.

Padilla bolted into the street. He was out of breath when he reached Sullivan's side. "*Madre de Dios*," he breathed. There was a sudden burning in his ears and throat as the bile worked its way up his windpipe. He dropped down on one knee, feeling Diaz' limp wrist. A faint pulse fluttered beneath his fingers, and then ceased.

If Sullivan was troubled by the carnage, it didn't show. He'd already emptied the shotgun and was reloading it. Padilla stood up. "Was this," he gestured toward Diaz' body without looking, hearing the flies that had already begun to swarm, "necessary?" His throat was dry, and the words were brittle.

"It was if you intend on catching up with Bridger," Sullivan replied. He was already on his way towards Bridger's saloon.

Padilla started to follow. The sound of approaching horses came to him, and he changed his mind. Hands on his hips, he turned, and watched as the returning soldiers trotted into the village in an orderly column of twos. They would have just enough time to select fresh mounts, he mused, and to enjoy perhaps one hand-rolled cigarette. And then, by God, they would earn their month's pay. His gaze fell on Castillo and he smiled. *Every damned one of them.*

Grimly, his composure returned, he signaled to the man, holding up four fingers as he beckoned. Even Diaz deserved a Christian burial, he reckoned, and it would do Castillo—who had never served beyond a desk in his uncle's office—good to know that there were many ways for a man to die.

The young sergeant dismounted, his face betraying the stiffness in his joints. He hand-picked the four men who would help him, determined Padilla would not find fault with his selection. The long ride into the desert had humbled him, and he felt no desire to make the ride again.

Chapter Twelve

Sullivan watched Padilla through a thin haze of blue-grey smoke. The man stood beside his horse, militarily erect, and fully prepared for the trail. "We don't have any choice, Padilla," he reasoned. "Bridger has a four hour start, and we don't know for sure which way he went."

For a time, Padilla said nothing. Bridger's man at the cantina swore the *Patrón* had gone into the mountains to mediate a quarrel between two families who worked his land. Padilla's men, however, found the tracks of four horsemen riding southwest. He cleared his throat, measuring his words as he said them, and trying not to give in to his temper. "South," he declared stubbornly. "I believe they rode south."

Sullivan exhaled, his jaws working as he chose his words with the same care Padilla had just exhibited. "You have twenty men with you," he began. "Ten to follow a trail south, and ten more who could help me find just where the hell Bridger has really gone."

The young captain was already shaking his head. "No more, Sullivan," he said softly. Their fragile truce had survived longer than he had anticipated. But now, after what he had seen in the street...

Padilla had never considered himself a bigot. He had grown up aware of his own mixed heritage, painfully cognizant of a class-conscious society that penalized him for his mother's imprudence. Not only had she defied her father to marry an *Americano*, she married a Protestant. The man had been the embodiment of everything wrong about the country north of the big river. Brash. Arrogant. A plunderer certain that the only way was his way, and that whatever he took was his by some God-given superiority that placed him above the law.

Like Sullivan. Padilla's old prejudices returned, his inbred instincts telling him not to trust the man. Not anymore. "My men and I—all my men—will follow the trail south," he announced suddenly. His voice lowered. "You have known Bridger a long time. Perhaps, too long."

Sullivan's face hardened, his eyes the color of slate, the implication that he was in league with Bridger all but spoken. A flood of words played across his tongue, but he held them in check. He stepped back, well away from Padilla's horse, and watched as the man mounted.

They rode out, Padilla and his twenty recruits. Sullivan stared after them for a long time. He wondered what it was about the very young that made them so damned hardheaded and all-knowing, and decided he really didn't care.

* _ * _ * _ * _ *

Trey watched as Padilla's men rode by the window, a wry grin tugging at the corners of his mouth. It was, he felt, a sure sign that Bridger had taken his men south. Then, remembering that Padilla had been the one that had shackled him to the rusting grids of the office window, he called out. "Padilla!" There was no response. The tall Mexican rode on without stopping. Trey swore; vehemently. "Son-of-a-bitch!"

The door opened. Sullivan strode across the room, the big dog rising to greet him. He bypassed the animal, moving to the desk and rummaging in the top drawer, and then to his son. He stood just beyond the younger man's reach, the key to the heavy handcuffs in his upraised hand. "You've got two choices," he intoned. "You can rot here, or ride out."

Trey had the gut feeling there was more. He nodded at the key. "In exchange for what?"

Sullivan twirled the key on the end of his extended forefinger. "The truth," he answered. "For once, the whole damned truth."

Unconsciously, the young man's hands—both of them—knotted into fists, and then relaxed. He chose a spot on the wall directly above and behind his father's head and stared at it, hoping the man would think he was looking him in the eye. "I came here to get the men who killed Dad," he breathed. "There aren't any papers, and there isn't any treasure." His gaze dropped to the floor. As if he were ashamed for his original lies. "Never was any treasure."

Sullivan placed the key on the desk. It was in plain sight, and a good two feet out of the young man's reach. *But not so far that, with a little thought, he couldn't eventually manage to work himself free.* "Suit yourself." He turned, summoned the dog, and went out the door.

Stunned, Trey stared at the closed door, the disbelief washing the color from his face. Still unable to accept what was happening, he took a step forward, a wrenching pain in his right wrist as his steel tether drew him up short. He rubbed at the sudden tenderness just below the heavy manacle, feeling the heat of the abrasion beneath his fingers. A thin ribbon of blood appeared, encircling his wrist, and he raised his arm to his mouth. The disbelief turned to rage. "Bastard!" The fact that Sullivan was unable to hear didn't occur to him. "You bastard son-of-a-bitch!!"

* _ * _ * _ * _ *

Sullivan was inside the livery. He had spent a long hour clearing out his room at the hotel, and almost twice that time nosing around Bridger's saloon. And now he was ready to leave.

The pack horse watched him, standing inside its stall munching hay, its brown eyes patiently observing as the man sorted through the supplies. Packets of hardtack and jerked beef were laid aside along with several tins of canned milk. When he was through, Sullivan had packed into a single saddle bag all the provisions he would need for a week of hard travel. He saddled his bay, and tethered Trey's mount behind.

"¿El caballo? (The horse?)" he asked in Spanish, jerking a thumb in the direction of the pack animal. *"¿cuánto?" (How much?)*

The old hostler came forward, out of the shadows. He stood at the entrance to the stall for a long moment, and then went in. His arthritic fingers were surprisingly nimble as he skimmed the animal's flanks and legs. The boney digits traced the brand on the gelding's right shoulder, outlining Sullivan's mark. The horse trader knew the Celtic cross brand by reputation, just as he knew and remembered Reese Sullivan. There would be no haggling. Not with this man, and not over this horse. He picked the price he knew, under the circumstances, Sullivan would find agreeable. *"Cien."* (One hundred.) *"Americano,"* (American,) he offered. The horse would bring twice that in gold from a man on the run.

Sullivan nodded. *"En pesos,"* (In pesos,) he said; *"el cambio del banco, no Bridger's."* (Bank exchange, not Bridger's.) He held out his hand, a slow smile coming as he saw the old man's eyes widen.

The blow came from behind, a two-handed stunner that landed at the base of his skull. Sullivan fell forward on both knees, the quick pain bringing a flash of cold fireballs deep inside his head. Instinctively, he compacted himself into a tight ball. He rolled sideways, feeling a whoosh as a booted foot brushed his right ear. *The dog*, he wondered. *Where the hell was the dog?*

He reached up, both hands closing around the offending foot as he twisted it violently to his left. The other man was thrown off balance, a thunk coming as he tumbled onto the manure-littered floor. Sullivan let go of the boot and righted himself, rising up on his knees. He felt a need to take a breath, balancing on both knees and one hand as he shook the pain away. The brief reprieve was enough.

Bolting forward, Sullivan dove into the darkness, his fist colliding with bone and flesh. He swung again, only to have the blow blocked, and felt the sting of two quick punches against his mouth and his nose.

Blood trickled from Sullivan's snout, wetting his lips, and he licked it away. He struggled to stand, pulling the other man up with him, the wasp-like attack resuming as the swift tap-tap centered on his face and forehead. He ducked, his own fist plowing into the soft flesh at the man's middle, just below his ribs.

Sullivan felt the man sag forward, and hit him a second time in the same place. Then, grabbing his attacker, he pulled him close in a massive bear hug. They slammed against the wall, their feet tangling as they spun around; once, twice, the rough boards splintering and tearing into their clothes and skin.

They fell through the open barn door, both men blinded momentarily by the sunlight and breaking apart. Sullivan rolled away and was instantly on his feet. "You!" he roared.

Trey rose up out of the dirt, breathing hard as he balanced on one knee. He charged his father again, swearing aloud as Sullivan spun away. The fingers of his right hand clawed at Sullivan's pant leg, and he held on like a bulldog. This time, his fist collided with a more vulnerable portion of Reese's anatomy.

Sullivan doubled over, the pain in his groin shooting down his belly into his toes. When he righted himself, he struck out with his left foot. He caught Trey in the right leg, on the long muscle in the younger man's inner thigh. It was six inches shy of where the man had aimed.

The fight resumed in earnest, Trey light on his feet as he assumed the pose and prance of a bare-knuckle boxer. He danced around Sullivan, scoring coup with a series of sharp jabs; the muscles in his arms and shoulders hard and sharply defined. It had become sport for him, a game where he felt superior. Youth was on his side, youth and mobility. He was unarmed and unhampered by his clothing, clad in a chambray shirt and Levis, grim determination fueling an anger that had been ten years in the making.

Reese was on the defensive. There was no denying the kid was good. He watched his son bob and weave, secretly impressed with the younger man's natural ability and his tenacity. He backed away, quickly shucking the bulky serape, and unbuckled his gun belt.

It was true about the boy being good, but also true, Sullivan realized, that the kid was woefully ignorant in the not-so-noble art of street fighting.

Reese doubled over the heavy cartridge belt. It appeared, for a moment, that he intended to drop the gun and holster. Trey closed, protecting his face with his left as he scored two solid jabs to Reese's head with his right. Sullivan stood his ground, ducking the next blow, and swung out with the belt.

He caught Trey above the right ear, the barrel of his holstered pistol slapping solidly against the younger man's skull. Dropping the belt, he pulled Trey to him, his left hand closing around a fistful of hair. There was a brutal efficiency in the man as he finished the job; his right knee coming up to meet Trey's chin, the impact slamming the younger man's mouth shut.

Trey collapsed in a heap at Sullivan's feet, a soft sigh coming as he passed out. His entire body relaxed. He appeared to shrink, like a doll suddenly stripped of its stuffing. Reese stared down at the kid, feeling a twinge of remorse. Then, the glint of gold caught his eye, and he remembered the medallion Trey had taken from the young whore's body. Disgusted, he turned away, and went back to the barn. The old man met him in the doorway. He was leading Sullivan's horses.

Reese waved the man away. He paused at the watering trough, working the pump handle as he buried his head beneath a stream of cold water. The dog was beside him when he rose up, the gun belt clenched firmly between its teeth. The animal dropped the belt at Sullivan's feet, almost as if it were a peace offering for recent transgressions. Once, twice, the black tail wagged. Reese backed away, shaking a finger at the animal. "And just where the hell were you?" he demanded. The dog lay down on its belly and whined, inching forward in the dirt, its head turned sideways exposing the jugular in a gesture of total subjugation.

This time when the stableman led the horses forward, Reese accepted the gesture. He mounted, wincing as the pain touched him in a dozen places, and moved out. In spite of the hurt, he leaned sideways out of the saddle to pick up the discarded serape and then kicked the horse into a trot.

Trey sensed the departure, the earth under his ear magnifying the sound as the shod hooves passed close by his head. Fighting the sickness at the pit of his stomach, he pulled himself to his knees, paused, and then stood up. Tasting blood, he wiped his hand across his mouth, spitting into the dirt before he called out to the man. "That's right, old man!" he roared. "Run. Just like before!!" He was a child again, eight years old, and his father was leaving. *Forever.*

Sullivan heard the young man's shouts. He touched his heels to the gelding's sides, urging the animal into a run. He never looked back.

* - * - * - * - *

The high country north of Limbo was in full bloom. Spring streams ran cold and clear, fed by the mountain run-off from the last winter's snow, the water running white and wild across rock-filled beds.

Sullivan was watering the horses. He rested in the shade, a stream-chilled can of milk pressed against the bruises beneath his left eye. Trey had scored twice in the same place, finger-thick ridges marking the place where the boy's knuckles had pounded flesh into bone. Unattended, the welts had swollen considerably, and Sullivan's vision was already distorted.

A begrudging feeling of paternal pride tugged at Sullivan. First, because Trey had somehow managed to get himself out of the jailhouse much faster than he anticipated; and secondly, because he managed to get around the dog. Still a tad provoked, Sullivan gave the animal a sullen glance, and then repented. He tossed the dog a piece of jerky. He let Trey get too close, he admonished himself. Too familiar. The dog had been confused, his loyalty perverted. "It won't happen again," he said aloud; as much to himself as to the dog.

Renewed, he stood up and shoved the can of milk into his cavy sack. The sun was going down, marking the end to a day that had not been long enough, and Sullivan felt a sense of urgency. His gut told him he was not wrong, that his instincts about Bridger were right, but he had found no sign. Still he was as certain in his belief that Bridger had traveled north, as Padilla had been in his notion that the man's trail lay south.

He mounted, Trey's horse this time, still mulling the thing in his mind as he moved out. The enigma was still there, the why. He knew when Trey told him there was no treasure that the kid lied through his teeth. Just as he knew the young man was too unconcerned about Bridger or anything the man might have discovered. Or, for that matter, that Bridger was gone. Sullivan cursed; Bridger, Wes Underwood, but most of all, his son.

* - * - * - * - *

Trey stood up in the saddle, his head feeling as though his spine were being driven into his brain. The old cavalry-style saddle left a great deal to be desired, the split seat creasing his rear and leaving him tender. *When this is over*, he vowed, *I'm going to shoot the first jackass that even dares to suggest I ride.* A sobering thought struck him then. He had to make it back to the States first.

He dug into his shirt pocket, pulling out the sack of tobacco he had pilfered from the stores Reese abandoned in the livery. There hadn't been much to pick from, considering; the job having been made more difficult by the fact that—like a common nickel and dime thief—he had to do his plundering in broad daylight with one eye open for the old hostler. He rolled the cigarette, lighting up and inhaling. The nicotine stung against the raw cut on the inside of his lower lip, and he held the smoke without drawing it into his lungs. The pain began to fade, but not the memory of the fight.

Gingerly, with his right hand, he worked his jaw. The soreness reached behind his ears. He'd been kicked by one of the horses at the ranch, and the pain was the same. Deep, far down in the bone. As if the old man had drawn back and struck home with a hammer. He exhaled, releasing the smoke. *Bastard*, he breathed. *Someday...* He shook his head. There weren't any more somedays, at least not as far as Reese Sullivan was concerned.

The sun disappeared behind a cloud, and Trey felt a shiver course through his body. Panic hit him then, along with the realization he was ill prepared for a long night in the high country. And he couldn't turn back. To reassure himself, he patted the canvas *alforja* he had stolen. The hardtack was there, along with the packet of dried beef. And the bottle.

He took out the jug, working the cork free. It was *pulque*; warm and potent. Flicking the spent cigarette into the bush, he took a long drink, and then another. If he couldn't be warm on the outside, he'd sure in hell be warm on the inside!

* - * - * - * - *

Sullivan made camp. He picked the spot well, choosing the ruins of an ancient dwelling where the wind-eroded walls, now less than three feet high, seemed to grow out of the sides of a shallow cleft in the mountain's flank. He picketed the horses inside the enclosure, supplementing the sparse graze with measures of grain, taking care of the horses before tending to his own needs.

He debated the wisdom of building a fire, and then decided it was worth the risk. In the hours on the trail making his sweep, there had been no sign of Bridger and the others. Besides, he reasoned, he needed coffee; coffee, a cigarette, and a chance to do some mental reckoning.

The dog returned from his evening prowl, watching patiently as Sullivan gathered scraps and kindling for his fire. Only when the fire was built, and the coffee boiling did the animal settle in. The black chose a spot close enough to the fire to be warm, but still in the same corner against the wall where Reese had laid out his bedroll.

Sullivan built a simple supper, indulging his sweet tooth with the last of the dried apples and figs Eva had tucked in with his beef. The fruit sugar went well with the strong coffee, sharpening the man's senses, and he leaned back against his saddle to reflect on everything that had happened in the last several weeks.

He was certain now that at least part of what Trey told him was true; the need for revenge that pushed the young man to seek out the men who had killed Wes Underwood. As for the rest...

The treasure did exist, he was convinced of that. The where was still the big puzzle, and in what form.

He knew the legends. All about the solid gold disks that stood as tall as a man, the calendars and astrological charts that had adorned the walls of pyramided temples. And, of course, the obscene effigies. The golden icons to the many gods that the pious Spanish priests found so offensive. So much so, he mused, the majority were melted down to be remolded into the likenesses of the many saints that adorned the Catholic cathedrals; churches built above the remains of the pagan holy places that had been destroyed.

Sullivan took another long drink of coffee. Legends were one thing, he reasoned. Truth was another. The myths about Maximillian and Carlotta had been encouraged after the Empire collapsed, the stories about how the Austrian prince looted the remains of the Aztec treasure to fashion the jewelry that would bedeck his bride at her coronation as Empress of Mexico. Gold. Rubies. Emeralds of legendary size and brilliance.

Fairy-tales, he mused. A fiction created to obscure a sinister truth; an age-old conspiracy originating in Europe that had existed since the time of the Templar Knights. Sullivan pondered how all of this or any of it made any sense in a world of reality. Whatever treasure existed, the Vatican—or the secret societies throughout the world that operated with the blessings of the Vatican—would stop at nothing to find it.

He finished his coffee. Tomorrow he would make another search, this time heading north and east. Bridger and his men were out there. He could feel it. Come tomorrow he would find them.

* - * - * - * - *

Trey saw the fire from a quarter mile out. He was on foot, leading the horse; the animal minus its right front shoe. The nighttime cold kept him moving, the thin chambray shirt like ice against his skin. Still, he had the *pulque*. He pulled the horse to a stop, reaching back to take the bottle out of the pack.

The drink warmed him, setting his empty stomach afire. Still, it wasn't enough. He started walking again, heading toward the warm glow of the campfire. With any luck, he thought, there would only be one man. His pace quickened.

* - * - * - * - *

Sullivan heard the distant whicker, instantly awake as his bay whinnied in answer. The dog scrambled upright, its nose lifting to the wind. Reese laid his hand on the dog's side, and felt the animal's ribs quake, a low growl sounding in response to the restless snorting of the two horses. Again, the black lifted its head, the scent failing to come.

"Too far, old son," the man whispered. He patted the dog, keeping low as he pulled on his boots. The Henry was at his left, and he picked it up and levered a shell into the chamber. Then, leaning back, he waited. A slow grin creased the skin behind his ears as he stared out at his neat campsite. The fire was burning, stoked with the larger pieces of wood he had drug into the enclosure. And beside the fire pit...

A man-sized log, artfully draped with the damp saddle blankets. For all intents and purposes, the serene figure of a sleeping man.

* _ * _ * _ * _ *

Trey reconnoitered the campsite. It was like exploring a box canyon from without, or the dark interior of a Boston alley from the street entrance. He could see the dim silhouette beside the fire, and knew from the noise within the three-sided enclosure that there were but two horses. One riding animal, he reckoned, one pack horse. He wished there was more light.

He waited and watched as a cold wind blowing down from the mountains set his teeth chattering. It was only a matter of time, he knew, before the cold brought him to his knees. He needed food, and something to wear. And soon.

* _ * _ * _ * _ *

Sullivan kept a restraining hand on the dog's neck. He felt the animal raise its head, its ears coming forward, the black nose busy as the wind brought the scent. Reese's eyes narrowed, the dog rising up on all fours, and then settling back on its haunches; its head canted, the great tail lifting and thumping against the ground.

Trey! Silently, Sullivan swore. It never occurred to him the young man would have the audacity to follow after him, or for that matter, be smart enough to pick up his trail. *Unless*, he thought darkly, *the kid and Bridger were heading for the same place.*

Impatiently, he waited for the younger man to make his move. This time, when he took the boy, he would do the job right.

There was a sound, a subtle whisper of booted feet across the pebble littered terrain. The noise ceased, then began again, the step measured; cautious.

Sullivan waited until the younger man was inside the compound. He watched him for a time, a grim smile coming as Trey dropped down on one knee and reached for the blanket that covered the bogus "man". Silently, Reese came forward out of his hiding place, moving forward until he was close enough to reach out and lay his hand on his son's shoulder.

He used the Henry instead. Coldly, he tapped the kid's shoulder with the barrel, lifting the frigid steel a final time and resting it in the hollow behind the young man's ear.

Trey froze, his arms shooting skyward. *"Comida,"* (Food) he pleaded, the Spanish passable, if not perfect. *"Y aqua."* (And water.) His mouth was suddenly dry. *"¿Por favor?"* (Please.)

Sullivan withdrew the rifle. "And then what?" he asked. "My horse, and my money?"

Trey's eyes closed, his teeth clenched as he reflected on Lady Luck and her recent tendency to shit on him. He decided things had gotten about as bad as they could get, and it made him careless. "Hell, old man," he began. He turned. "It's just that I missed you so damned much." The sarcasm grew. "Why, these last few weeks..."

"Shut up!" It was clear from Sullivan's tone he'd had his fill. He turned suddenly, the rifle pointing at the opening in the wall. The uneven clip-clop of a single lame horse resounded, Trey's stolen mount trotting into the enclosure to join the others. "I sold that horse to the hostler in Limbo," Sullivan announced.

Too quickly, Trey answered. "And I bought him back!"

Sullivan's next words were whisper-soft. "With what?" he demanded. He braced his son, his left hand disappearing inside Trey's shirt at the neck. "The little trinket you lifted off the dead whore?" He yanked the medallion free, his hand closing in a tight fist. "You stole that horse!" he accused. He wondered what else the kid had done.

Trey didn't give a damn about the horse. He grabbed at Sullivan's hand. "I didn't steal anything from the girl!" His hand closed around his father's wrist. "The medallion is mine. She took it from me when I was out. I want it back. Now!"

The intensity of the younger man's request, his anger, piqued Sullivan's interest. He stepped away from the youth, moving toward the fire. Trey moved to block him. He extended his hand.

Again, Sullivan ignored his son. He hunkered down beside the fire, opening his hand.

The medallion lay in his flat palm, the gleam of gold intensified by the flickering flame. Reese had expected something more traditional, a St. Christopher, perhaps; a gift to Trey from his mother. But this...

It was legal tender, U.S. issue, more than a half-century old from its date, but with the appearance of a coin that had been newly minted. Sullivan held the gold piece between his thumb and forefinger, noting the care that had been taken to preserve its beauty. There was no hole in the coin, a gold alloy rim banding its circumference, a small latch provided for the gold chain. He stared at the piece, his eyes lifting to explore his son's face. The panic—no, the fear of discovery—drew grim lines across the younger man's face, his lips a tight line.

Sullivan decided the coin deserved more attention. He moved closer to the fire, examining the coin with greater deliberation; all the time aware of Trey watching him.

The gold piece was of small denomination; a half-eagle dated 1841, the mark indicating the coin had been issued through the New Orleans mint. An eagle with spread wings—arrows clutched in one claw, the symbolic branch of peace in the other—adorned the reverse side; the face of the coin bearing a profile of Lady Liberty, thirteen six-pointed stars surrounding her head. There was nothing, he thought, truly remarkable about the coin, and yet... He cast another long look at his son.

As if he'd lost interest, Sullivan backed away from the fire, the coin balanced in the palm of his hand. He hefted it, nonchalantly, and then tossed it into the dirt at his son's feet. He watched as Trey scrambled to retrieve the coin, noting the near-reverent way he polished the gold piece against the front of his shirt. "Hell of a fuss for a five-dollar gold piece," he observed.

Covetously, Trey clutched the coin in his closed fist. The chain was broken, and he struggled to fix it; silent until he replaced it around his neck. "Dad gave it to me." He regretted the words as soon as he said them, aware now of just how closely Reese had watched him. He realized he needed a better explanation. "It was minted the same year he was born."

Reese was on his feet. "That's a lie," he intoned. "Wes was born in '49, and you know it.

"I'm going to tell you this just once, boy," he warned. "For better or worse, you're here, and you're going to stay. Don't lie to me again." Still angry, Reese picked up a saddle blanket from the log and tossed it at his son. It was going to be a long night, and the kid was going to have to be watched. Just like any other two-bit horse thief.

Chapter Thirteen

A thousand demons danced inside the young man's head, each one livelier than the other. And they all wore leather-heeled boots and spurs.

He had drunk himself to sleep, the liquor the only way he could escape Sullivan's constant scrutiny. The man watched him the entire night, as enduring and silent as some damned monk keeping a vigil over an unwilling penitent awaiting his turn to enter the confessional. As if he were digging around inside Trey's head, ferreting out secrets not meant to be shared.

The smell of coffee overwhelmed the young man, and he pulled himself up onto his elbows. As much as he wanted the coffee, he wanted a drink more. He rolled over, looking for the saddlebags he laid next to his head when he turned in, swearing when he found them gone. When he looked up, Sullivan stood above him, a tin of coffee in each hand. He offered one to the younger man. "You look like you could use this."

Trey snorted. "What I could use is a drink." He looked up at the man, squinting against the early morning sun. "A little hair of the dog..."

Sullivan set the cup down in the dirt. "That's too damned bad," he sympathized. "The only thing we've got is coffee."

Trey bolted upright. The idea of not having anything to drink had never occurred to the young man. The liquor had always been readily available; in his mother's house, and anywhere else he had felt the need. "I had a bottle in my cavy sack," he groused.

Sullivan was back by the fire. He picked up the canvas saddle bags and gave them a shake. The tinkle of glass sounded, the fabric still wet. "Not anymore." He tossed the bags, watching as they landed at Trey's feet.

The young man sat up. He stared at the canvas bag, and then at the cup of coffee, his mouth feeling full of cotton balls. Deep down in his belly, the growling started, the liquor he consumed the night before trying to find its way out by crawling up his windpipe. Shaky, Trey stood up, and headed for the bush.

Under the right circumstances, Reese Sullivan could be a patient man. He waited beside the fire, the second pot of coffee brewing next to a pan of red gravy and sourdough dumplings. Good food, meant to tame a sore belly, and to entice a drunk in need of mending.

Trey came back, drawn as much by the smell of food as the need to get something to wash the taste of bile out of his mouth. This time, he took the proffered cup of coffee. Sullivan had mixed it with a healthy splash of canned milk, the liquid going down smooth, soothing his sore throat and stomach.

They ate in silence, Trey hungrier than he first realized. In spite of himself, he enjoyed the food, helping himself to the last of the gravy and biscuits, sharing them with the dog. Sullivan mopped the pan clean and stowed it with his gear. He poured his last cup of coffee and stood up, his eyes on his son. "We're going to talk," he said finally.

Trey rose up from his seat beside the fire. He saw right away where and how Reese was standing. The older man was between him and the horses and the opening to the enclosure. "About what?" He tried moving, widening the distance between himself and his father.

Reese moved with his son. "About this," he answered. The gold coin hung from the chain that was wrapped around his fingers. "And the telegram from your mother." The slip of yellow paper unfolded and fluttered between his thumb and forefinger.

Trey's right hand went immediately to his neck, his left probing beneath his shirt just above his belt buckle. Sullivan had taken it away from him, all of it, when he was passed out from the Mexican rotgut. "You took Vanessa's money," he accused. He was on the defensive. "Dammit! You let her pay you, and you were still working for Diamond!"

Sullivan poked a finger at his son. "And *you* let her think Wes had been robbed, that she needed to hire me to find what had been taken!" He held out the coin and paper again. "I asked you about these. I want an answer."

Trey grabbed at the chain. "Go to hell!"

The man's jaws tensed. "I don't have time for this bullshit," he breathed. He turned his back on his son and started toward the horses. Then, changing his mind, he turned around.

The blow was wicked, a back-handed slap driven home by all the power in Sullivan's broad shoulders. His right hand arced upward and down, striking the younger man's cheek, coming back to hit him a second time on the opposite side of his face. It was a calculated strike, meant to punish and humiliate the younger man.

Stunned, Trey retreated a full pace, touching his cheek. His eyes watered, the tears coming; and he was unable to stop them. The blow was totally unexpected, and more painful than anything he remembered from their fight. "You..."

Reese grabbed the younger man's arm and held on, his fingers digging deep into the tender flesh just above the elbow. "Bridger read that telegram," he whispered. He had memorized the message during the long night, and had cursed himself for not realizing sooner what Bridger had surmised. He repeated the words for his son. "*Your father's papers arrived this a.m. I know what you're planning to do. Wait for me El Paso. Mother.*" He let the words sink in. "Now, just where the hell do you think Bridger has gone?"

Trey's eyes opened wide. "No," he whispered. He shook his head. "He went south..." For the first time he met his father's gaze head on. "Padilla..."

"Found the trail Bridger wanted him to find." Sullivan still had hold of his son's arm. "The coin," he demanded. The half-eagle dangled less than an inch from Trey's nose.

Trey's mind was working. He stared at the gold, thinking of what it had cost; and what it still meant. "I told you," he said, his voice the same as the other's. "Dad gave it to me. A remembrance."

Reese slapped his son again, harder than before. "And I told *you* not to lie to me again."

They stood, nose to nose, breathing hard; their chests rising and falling in tempo. Trey was the first to speak, the words coming through clenched teeth. "We've got to catch up with Bridger." He had visions of the man, terrorizing Vanessa, trying to get information from the woman she didn't even know she had, didn't even know existed. "For God's sake!"

Sullivan seemed not to hear. "The gold piece," he prompted. The coin held between his thumb and forefinger again, he worked it back and forth. "You tell me about this," he nodded at the thing, "we'll go after Bridger." He did a good job of hiding the panic clawing at his own belly. Bridger would go to the ranch first, assuming Vanessa was there, and Eva... He shut El Paso out of his mind and concentrated on the coin, knowing there wasn't much time.

Mentally, Trey swore at the man. Torn between his concern for his mother and his dreams of what five million dollars could buy them. Nothing, if Sullivan took it all away. There was a sharp pain in his upper arm as Reese increased the pressure. "You're holding the treasure," he began. He saw the man's eyes narrow and continued. He reached out, taking the coin back, the same worship there as before. "There were fifty of them," he said softly. "That's all that were minted. And then they disappeared." He was quiet again. "Until Dad found this one." It was surprising, Trey realized, how easy it was to tell the truth. Half a truth. Wes Underwood *had* discovered the coin, along with the information that would lead him to the others. In San Francisco.

Reese turned loose of the younger man. "And?"

"It's worth a hundred thousand dollars," Trey answered.

Sullivan whistled. *A hundred thousand for a five dollar gold piece.* He came back to the here and now. "Bridger's money, and the documents Wes was supposed to have located in San Francisco?"

Trey was getting adept at bending the truth. "Dad used the money to buy this." It had been pure magic, he remembered, watching his stepfather con the original owner out of the coin. "As for the papers—the map—" There was just the right degree of disappointment and disenchantment in his voice. "There isn't any damned secret hoard," he lied; and then instantly turned the small fib into a palatable version of the truth. "No Aztec gold, no El Dorado; no Maximilian's plunder. There hasn't been, for a long, long time."

Reese was silent, mulling over the things his son told him. He realized now that Wes Underwood failed to understand the full measure of what he was seeking, or what Bridger sent him to find. And Trey... Trey was as big a fool as the man he still chose to call father.

Bridger, however, was another matter. Ansel Bridger knew that a treasure existed. Not a puny trove of trinkets or rare coins; but a store of immeasurable wealth accumulated across the centuries.

Sullivan began breaking camp. He saddled his horse, annoyed when Trey took too much time doing the same. "Are you coming or not?" he demanded. He mounted the bay.

Trey stared up at the man, extending his arm and catching Reese's leg. The coin hung around his neck, and he held it up. "It doesn't belong to Bridger," he announced. "I don't give a damn that it was his money that bought it. It doesn't belong to Bridger!" When Reese remained silent, he spoke again. "You took her money," he said, talking about his mother. "She hired you to find what..."

"...you already had," Sullivan answered. "What you and Wes had already mailed home! But then, I didn't know that, did I?"

"You were working for Diamond," Trey insisted. "Even before we left El Paso. And you still kept her money!" Trey moved with the horse when Reese urged it forward.

"If I had given it back, would you have gone home?" Reese reined in and waited for the answer.

"No!" Trey answered the question immediately. "I told you. I wanted the men who killed my father."

Again, Reese nudged the horse's sides, and moved out. "Then consider it pay for minding the baby," he called over his shoulder. The contempt in his voice cut even deeper than the words. "My chance to finally see how big a liar she raised, and just how involved you were in helping Wes steal something that never belonged to either one of you!"

Angry, Trey swung aboard his horse and kicked it into a run. The dog followed after him, yapping at the heels of the two horses Reese had turned loose. Both animals still followed them.

They rode east and south, moving at a full run. The panic increased with each passing mile.

* _ * _ * _ * _ *

Sullivan was afoot, leading his bay gelding through the narrow arroyo, Trey and the dog following single file behind. The younger man came abreast of him as soon as the dry ravine widened, the ankle-deep sand making it difficult to walk. Trey felt like he was taking two steps forward and one step back. "This—isn't—the—way we came," His words came in labored gasps.

Reese knew better than to talk. The horses were kicking up a considerable amount of grit as they plowed through the sand, and it was wise to keep the mouth shut. He kept moving, veering off to the right and starting to climb. A natural incline rose up from the floor of the small canyon, and Reese let the bay choose its own footing.

Trey's gripes started as soon as they were on flat ground. He mounted the horse, and fell in beside his father. "I want to know why the hell we're going this way!" He eyed the sun and did some mental navigation. They were moving southeast, away from El Paso.

"We're a half day behind Bridger," Sullivan answered. "I'm going to shorten the gap."

"By going south?" Trey pulled his own horse to a sudden stop. "Bullshit!"

Sullivan reined in, pulling the horse up short. The animal reared, spun around, and sprang forward. Reese bent sideways, grabbing the reins to Trey's horse. "We've got just shy of an hour to make fifteen miles," he declared. "Now get moving!"

"No!" This time, Trey's horse reared. He kept his seat, jerking the lines and pointing the animal's nose north. He kicked the gelding into a run.

Sullivan swore. He raced after the younger man, shaking out his rope as he bore down on his son. He made the toss, pulling Trey from the saddle and immediately taking up the slack. He reeled in, dragging the kid belly-down across the rough turf and then jerking him to his feet. He kept the rope tight. "Train," he said, as if talking to an imbecile. "Bridger and his men took a train."

Trey stopped struggling. He stared off into the flatlands, in the same direction Reese was pointing. A thin ribbon of smoke puffed along the horizon, moving north.

Reese let go of the rope, tossing it to the ground. "I've got a train to catch," he announced. The smile was vindictive and brief.

Trey watched as his father spurred his horse into a run. He had spent eight days of hell crossing the desert and the mountains with Sullivan on their trip south. *When they could have taken a damn train!*

He picked up the rope, his fingers agile as he shook out the loop and made the toss. He made the catch in a single try.

* - * - * - * - *

Bridger signaled to the man behind him, halting his horse and waiting to speak until the other came abreast of him. Mendoza took his customary place at the *Patrón's* right, remaining silent until Bridger addressed him. "You've seen to the hands?"

Mendoza nodded. "There were only two," he answered. He held up the appropriate digits. "An old man," he still didn't understand the ancient *vaquero's* function, "and the boy who tends the barn stock."

Bridger was visibly pleased. "And inside the house?"

Mendoza smiled. "The boy told me there are two. Sullivan's whore, and his wife." The 'breed' considered himself a good Catholic. He did not recognize divorce, and considered Reese's ex-wife the only Mrs. Sullivan.

"We'll go in together," Bridger announced, "just before dark. We are here to wait for Reese." He practiced the story aloud. "He sent for us, to help him find," the next brought a smile, "Wes Underwood's killers." He laughed, the sound rolling from deep within his chest. "Perhaps they will offer us dinner, Chato. Something warm, prepared as only a woman can prepare a meal."

Mendoza laughed. Perhaps, if the meal was worthy, he would not kill the women. *Perhaps*.

* - * - * - * - *

Trey watched as Sullivan argued with the Mexican engineer, the conversation ending abruptly when the telegrapher interrupted both men. The haggling ended, the tone and manner of the trainman drastically changing when the clerk was through. Sullivan thanked the man, and waved Trey forward.

"I had to clear things with the railroad," Reese announced. It helped, being able to call in favors from old acquaintances south of the border as readily as he did north of the big river.

He watched as the brakeman and the fireman opened the door to an half-empty boxcar. They rigged a makeshift ramp, and loaded the two horses. The dog was another matter. The black retreated against the wall of the small shack, growling and snapping at the two men when they approached him.

Trey called out to the animal. "Dog!" The beast hesitated, and then trotted across the platform.

Sullivan exhaled. "Get him aboard," he ordered. For once, Trey did as he was asked without arguing.

The big locomotive was building steam. A ten-wheeler, the old wood-burning engine was capable of great speed. Even standing still, the iron horse looked as though it were in motion, the great wheels spinning against the steel rails as the massive boiler was fired up.

Sullivan swung aboard. He stood at the open door to the boxcar, watching until the train began to move. Then, already feeling the car's closeness, he pulled the sliding doors shut.

Trey was perched on a stack of canvas-covered crates. He started to roll a cigarette, and then, seeing Sullivan's frown, put the makings back. "How long," he asked. He wished to God he had something to drink.

"Six hours," Sullivan answered, "maybe eight." It already felt like that many days.

Trey studied the man's face, not liking what he was seeing. "Did you wire El Paso?"

Sullivan's jaws tensed, adding a harshness to his already grim countenance, and his answer was terse. "The federal marshal; but there's no guarantee he's there." He didn't bother to tell the youth that the line went dead before the transmission to Devereau was completed.

* _ * _ * _ * _ *

Eva stood at the bottom of the steps leading to the front porch. She had been out to the barn, looking for the young boy that she had hired to handle the milking. The boy was usually so prompt; and so careful about doing as he had been told.

Then, feeling the warmth of a dying spring sun, she smiled. It was a good evening for fishing, she mused. And Toby Stevens was only twelve years old. She laughed, and headed for the barn. Tonight, she would take care of the milking.

* _ * _ * _ * _ *

Bridger saw the woman go into the outbuilding. Even from this distance—from the shelter of a grove of scrub oak a hundred yards from the house—he recognized Eva Delgado. She was as beautiful as he remembered. A bit older now—it had been five years—but just as attractive. She moved like a wild thing, a natural grace in the way she used her limbs. There was no wasted motion, none of the fanny-shaking moves meant to tease and entice. What he saw was a woman; unencumbered by laces and stays, her body a series of soft curves that flowed without interruption.

Mendoza waited beside Bridger, his gaze locked on the woman. Sullivan's woman. He scratched his crotch. "Now, *Patron*?" he asked.

The mulatto nodded. "Now," he answered.

* - * - * - * - *

Reese paced the length of the box car, his gait that of a man aboard ship. Trey watched him, inwardly amazed at the way the older man seemed able to adapt to any circumstance. In Limbo, he had become part of the crowd, looking more Mexican than Irish in his flat-crowned Stetson and heavy serape. And in Chicago...

Trey remembered what that first meeting had been like. Sullivan hadn't looked out of place there, either. He had dominated the room, looking more like the head of the agency than either Franklin Diamond or Royal Torrance. And when he left the building... Trey shook his head. He didn't give a damn about any of it. Reese Sullivan was a man. A flesh and blood man.

The scratch of a wood match interrupted the young man's daydream. He looked up to see his father lighting the small lantern that hung from a nail just above his head. Sullivan lifted the globe and touched the match to the wick. The soft light bathed the man's face, and he looked old.

Trey stood up. "You think they're already there."

Sullivan nodded. He stared across at his son, moved by what he saw in the younger man's face. "Your mother is a strong woman, Trey. A lot stronger than most people know." He was thinking of Wes Underwood, and how gullible the man had been, even in the beginning. "She'll know how to deal with Bridger."

Trey's mouth opened, and then shut. Those were the same words he would have used to describe Eva. But not Vanessa. *Never Vanessa*. The truth finally sunk in. "She'll try to buy her way out," he breathed. The worry added an edge to the words.

Sullivan laughed, softly. But not at his son. "It's hell, isn't it? To love a woman you don't even like." He turned away before the younger man could answer and went back to his pacing.

* - * - * - * - *

Vanessa Underwood was at the sink, washing her hands. She heard the soft tapping, and thought how curious it was that Eva would knock at her own door. She sighed. In the time they had been together, she found little about the woman she understood. Or approved. Wiping her hands, she went to the door. "Really, Eva..."

Ansel Bridger was smiling. He had taken great care to make himself presentable, his jacket carefully brushed, and the collar on his shirt properly buttoned. "Madame", he greeted. He bowed at the waist, and reached out to take her hand.

Startled, Vanessa responded more out of habit than politeness. She felt the man's lips brush against the back of her hand, clearly surprised at his manner. "Mssr.?"

Bridger straightened. "You don't remember," he smiled. His eyes warmed.

The woman's mind was racing. "Bridger," she said finally. The surprise was genuine. "Ansel Bridger."

He stepped across the threshold. "You look the same, Vanessa." Somehow, the words didn't hold the warmth of a compliment. None was intended. Vanessa had always struck him as a woman who held herself above others. Cold. Distant. Unfeeling. He went directly to the fire, and warmed himself.

Vanessa stared at the man, and then at the other who waited outside. She was relieved when she saw Eva.

The woman came out of the barn, the small milk tin in her right hand. She hesitated at the doorway, slowly appraising the two horses in front of the house, a small frown tugging at her mouth. The animals were well cared for, and well bred, but she recognized neither one of them. Still, it seemed harmless enough. Spring was here in earnest, and with the season, there always came the dozens of men who were looking for work.

Certain that there was no reason for concern she stepped into the barnyard. She had no work for them, but she could give them the hospitality of a good meal before sending them on their way.

* _ * _ * _ * _ *

Reese pulled the door open, cursing as the rollers hung up in the track, the heavy metal screeching in protest as he forced the door even wider. He heard the two horses snort and back up, their shod hooves slipping across the straw-littered floor. "Hold them!" he ordered.

Trey grabbed the reins of Sullivan's big gelding. He could see the whites of the animal's eyes, the bay's ears coming forward and then going flat as the door shrieked a second time. A gust of fresh air hit him then, and he felt the big horse bunch. "He's going to jump!" he yelled.

Immediately, Reese backed away from the door. The bay bolted forward, the animal's rear hoof catching his knee as it made the leap. "Damn!"

Sullivan was on the ground by the time Trey reached him. He had hold of his horse, and was busy examining its legs. There was a long cut on the right foreleg, and a tenderness in the shoulder.

"Can he be ridden?" Trey tried looking over Sullivan's shoulder, and found his way blocked.

"Get mounted."

Trey hesitated. "The horse."

Sullivan swung aboard. "I told you to get mounted. Now!" He kicked the horse into a run.

* - * - * - * - *

Eva poured Bridger another glass of wine. She watched him as he drank, wary. Something about the man's mood set her on edge. She had only met him on one other occasion, five years before; when Reese had summoned her to *Nuevo Laredo*. Bridger had been there, working with Reese on a case involving a man who had been trafficking in young women. The seemingly genteel mulatto had been the epitome of concern and outrage.

The next morning she had found him in a room with a twelve-year-old child.

It took a long time for her to forgive Reese for leaving Bridger with the little girl, but in the end she had understood. One child sacrificed for the good of many. Still, the memory sickened her.

She poured herself a glass of wine. "You said that Reese sent for you, Mr. Bridger." Her smile was gracious, but restrained. "I would have thought that, by now, he would have been in Limbo, and expecting to find you there."

Bridger lingered over the wine. He exchanged a long look with Mendoza. "My business often takes me away from Limbo, *señora*. I was in Laredo when I received word that Reese was in my village. It seemed more prudent—since he was on his way back—to meet him here."

For the first time, Vanessa Underwood appeared interested in the conversation. She leaned forward, her hand discreetly covering the separation between her breasts; the gown she chose to wear at dinner low-cut. "Are we to assume then that Reese found what he was looking for?"

Bridger smiled. "I have no way of knowing that, Mrs. Underwood." The smile grew. "Since I don't know what it was he was seeking. Perhaps if you told me what he hoped to find...?"

Eva's fingers closed around Vanessa's hand. She gave the woman's fingers a quick squeeze. "Reese doesn't discuss his work at home, Ansel," she smiled. "And Mrs. Underwood's real concern is for her son.

"You do know that Trey is with Reese?" she murmured.

The wine was working. Bridger held his glass out for more "Ah, yes," he said. "Trey. The very picture of his father." The man caught himself. "So I've heard," he finished. He saw from Eva's face that he had made a grave mistake. She knew.

Eva rose up from the table. "Pie," she said. "And perhaps some coffee?

Bridger's hand closed around the woman's wrist. "I think not, Eva."

Mendoza got up from his chair. He grabbed Eva, one arm around her waist; the other wrapping around her breasts. He applied a slow, grinding pressure, enjoying the way she arched her back in an effort to escape the pain. He held her, his lips brushing the back of her neck. "This one, *Patrón*." He laughed. "When we are through, I want this one."

Bridger was standing behind Vanessa's chair. "When we are through," he smiled, "you can have them both."

* - * - * - * - *

Trey saw the horse fall. The animal was in a full run when its front legs disappeared into a small berm of freshly turned topsoil, the bones snapping just above the fetlocks. Reese pitched forward in the saddle, falling head first onto the hard-packed ground. His weight, combined with the momentum of the fall, brought the horse up and over.

The younger man caught his breath; the gut-wrenching suddenness making what he was seeing even more horrifying. Sullivan disappeared beneath a swirl of dirt, the horse on its back, all four legs pawing at the air. The animal screamed, making a sound unlike anything Trey had ever heard.

He dismounted on the run, the dog catching up and racing along at his heels. There was a terrible feeling in the pit of his stomach. He could see the horse's agony, but he could not see Reese.

And then he found him.

Sullivan was on the ground, slightly to the right of, and below, the horse. He was still, laying face down on his belly, his arms akimbo. The gelding's upper body was lying across Sullivan's lower torso, its legs cutting the air dangerously close to Sullivan's head.

Trey pulled his pistol. He knew there was nothing he could do for the injured animal, the bay's front legs both broken. Carefully, he approached the lamed beast; aware of the way the animal's wide eyes followed his every move. Saliva spewed from the gelding's mouth, the white foam turning pink as the animal raised its head. Trey thumbed back the hammer of his pistol.

"No!" the voice rasped.

Trey hesitated. He moved around the horse, staying well away from the powerful hind legs. "I've got to get you out of there!" he shouted.

"Too close," the other grimaced. "Too close to the house." He reached out with both arms, stretching. "Pull," he ordered.

Trey holstered the pistol. He grabbed Sullivan's arms, one hand closing around each wrist. The loose gravel beneath Sullivan's belly rattled, Trey's shoulders ached as he struggled for footing. He tried again, falling backwards as Sullivan wriggled free.

Reese lay still again, his shoulders rising and falling as he inhaled. Closing his eyes, he tried moving his legs; grateful when he felt them work. He pushed himself up on his hands and knees and stood up. "We'll have to ride double the rest of the way," he said finally.

Trey nodded his head. He stared for a time at the injured horse, wanting to put the animal out of its misery. "The bay," he whispered.

Sullivan couldn't bear to look at the gelding. "We're less than a half mile from the house," he explained. "If Bridger's there," he took a single step toward Trey's horse, "he'll hear." His face hardened. "You'll have to ride behind." He mounted, the pain etching deep lines in his face and on his forehead.

There wasn't anything more to say, Trey realized. He swung up behind his father and held on.

Chapter Fourteen

They traveled by foot the last quarter mile to the ranch, following the small creek that lay south of the main house. The shallow stream wound through the scrub, the banks of the ten-foot wide arroyo steep enough to conceal both men and the horse they were leading.

Sullivan raised his arm, signaling his son to stop. Without speaking, he hobbled the bay gelding, choosing a place where the spring grass was long and tender. Immediately, the horse began to graze. Trey approached the animal without thinking, and began loosening the cinch.

"No time," Sullivan rasped. He said the words as if it hurt to speak.

Trey reached out, touching the man's arm. It was still difficult to address the man. "Are you all right?"

Sullivan nodded his head but did not answer. He pulled the rifle from the boot, working the mechanism. The Remington was next. He checked the piece, rotating the cylinder, and replaced the gun in its holster. Then, without asking, he took Trey's weapon and did the same.

The younger man watched as Sullivan rolled a cigarette. There was a deliberation in him, his hand steady as he curved the paper around his forefinger and tamped the flaked tobacco into a smooth, even line. He dampened the edge of the paper with his tongue, twisting the ends, and lit up.

Sullivan stood rock still, the blue smoke obscuring his expression as he stared off into the distance. He appeared to be looking through the dirt embankment and beyond the thick scrub, his eyes narrowing as he contemplated what was happening inside the house. He took a second long drag on the cigarette, a thin stream of smoke coming as he spoke to his son. "Now," he said finally. He flicked the still smoldering smoke into the shallows and moved out.

They began the slow climb up the high side of the ravine, Sullivan carrying the rifle as he led the way through the waist-high brush. It was rough going, the sides of the arroyo perpendicular to the creek, the loose gravel like marbles beneath their leather soled boots. Trey cursed, going down on one knee, and then scrambling to keep up.

Sullivan put out an arm, blocking the younger man's way as they topped the crest of the riverbank. He jabbed a finger in the direction of the barns, and then at the ground. At once, Trey dropped to his knees.

Both men kept low. Sullivan snaked through the brush, the heavy serape affording him more protection than Trey's thin chambray shirt. Trey snagged a sleeve on the broken branch of a stunted Osage orange, the sharp spines raking his arm. He could feel the blood growing cold against his skin, and bit his lip to keep from crying out. Ahead of him, Sullivan kept on the move. They were still two hundred yards from the barn.

Sullivan disappeared momentarily as Trey fell behind. The faint sound of his movements suddenly ceased, then resumed. He backed up, reappearing as suddenly as he had vanished. "Vasquez," he breathed. He held up a bloodied glove.

For a long moment, Trey did not understand. Then he remembered the old man who had mended the tack and tended the newborn foals. The Mexican had seemed ancient, more wraith than living man, a fragile shadow that moved and worked without speaking. He had just been there.

The panic gripped him then. "Eva?" He inhaled. "Mother?"

Sullivan didn't answer right away. In the darkness, he could not see his son's face clearly. "Vasquez has been dead a long time," he said. If he had harbored any hope that Bridger was not actually inside the house, it was now completely gone. "We're going to have to get inside," he breathed. "Soon."

* - * - * - * - *

Bridger stopped drinking. He stood beside Vanessa Underwood, his lips close to her ear, his voice much the same as a man speaking tender words to a lover. "You have Wes' papers, Vanessa." His left hand was on the back of the woman's neck, massaging the rigid muscles below her ears. "I want them."

The woman seemed remarkably calm. She stared into the fire, thinking of the last time she spoke to her husband. He had just come back from San Francisco, his second trip in as many months, filled with an excitement she neither expected nor understood. Nothing distressed him; not the news that Trey had been sent home in disgrace from college, not even the stack of unpaid bills. None of it mattered, he told her. They would be rich soon, rich beyond her wildest dreams.

She had believed him. After all the years of empty promises, she had really believed him.

And now this. Her mind worked as she tried to remember everything she had seen and read in the mass of papers Wes expressed to her before he and Trey left San Francisco. It took her a little time before she realized that Wes' papers were somehow incomplete, and that something was missing. Just like the extra money Wes had taken to San Francisco was missing.

She cleared her throat, angry that her mouth was so dry. "I have no idea what you're talking about, Ansel. And I don't have Wes' papers."

The soft sound of Bridger's laughter broke the cold silence, contrasting sharply with the woman's quiet declaration. "I read the telegram you sent your son," he breathed. His fingers dug into her neck. "You have his papers, Vanessa." The pressure increased. "He sent them to you."

The woman tensed under his fingers. "All right, Ansel," she said. "I have them." She felt his fingers relax. "But not here."

Bridger withdrew his hand from the woman's neck, his fingers flexing. "You will not toy with me, woman," he whispered. He nodded at Mendoza, his head bobbing a single time.

Mendoza understood. He was still holding Eva Delgado, his massive hand knotted in the thickness of her dark hair. He pulled the woman's head up and back, pushing her across the floor until she was directly in front of Vanessa Underwood's chair.

Vanessa's back stiffened. She tried to stand, and found herself held fast when Bridger laid both his hands on her shoulders. His fingers dug into the soft flesh above her collarbones, the pain radiating upward to the base of her skull.

Bridger spoke again. "It would be ludicrous for me to think that you would harbor any affection for this woman," he breathed. "Your ex-husband's whore." The pause was intentional. "Still, if she were to suffer, to serve as an example of what will happen to you..."

Mendoza's right hand cupped Eva's left breast. He fondled the softness, and then—viciously—dug his blunt fingers in and twisted. The woman cried out, the wail cut short as she clamped her jaws shut. Angry, Mendoza's fingers tore at her a second time. He spun her around, his hand dropping to her crotch. He used his thumb and forefinger this time, grinding away at the vulnerable softness between her legs. Unable to help herself, she collapsed against him, yielding to the pain.

Vanessa averted her eyes. Her hands were trembling when she lifted them to her mouth. She had never been a strong woman when it came to physical pain. Trey's birth had taught her that, and she determined then that she would never have another child. Neither could she stand to watch someone else's pain. "In my valise," she murmured. "Wes' papers are in my valise."

"Show me," Bridger ordered. His touch was paternal now, stern and paternal. He helped the woman out of her chair.

She led the way to her bedroom, terribly aware of Bridger behind her. He was so close she could feel his breath on her shoulders, and a very different kind of fear took her. She faltered, half-turning to face the man. "Please..."

Bridger's laughter was real. "You have nothing I want, Vanessa," he reached out to stroke her face with the back of his hand. "Except the papers Wes stole from me." His smile grew as he heard the sound of a struggle in the kitchen. The noise of tearing fabric cut through the silence, rising above the sound of scuffling feet and labored breathing; punctuated by the harsh crack of a flat-handed slap and silence. "I cannot, of course, speak for Mendoza..." He laughed again, pleased with his own joke.

Vanessa closed her eyes. She turned away from the man, and stepped through the doorway into her bedroom.

* _ * _ * _ * _ *

They reached the barn, Trey slipping through the door first and collapsing on a bale of hay. He was shivering, the night air colder now, the earth losing its warmth beneath the cold light of a rising half moon.

Sullivan dug out a saddle blanket and threw it over the young man's shoulders. Trey pulled the cover tight around his neck. "And now?"

Reese was at the door, staring out the narrow opening to the broad expanse of brush-free flat between the barn and the house. He had been adamant about clearing the land, stubbornly hacking away at the indigenous grasses and small shrubs that had dominated the clearing. At the time, it seemed wise, keeping the house clear on all four sides. Now his diligence mocked him. The few rock outcroppings that dotted the landscape provided only sparse cover, not nearly enough to give him easy access to the house from any direction. Even under the cover of dark, he mused. His hand curled into a tight fist, and he slammed it against the doorjamb.

Trey was on his feet. He stood at his father's shoulder. "We can't go in," he breathed. "Dammit! We aren't going to be able to get in!"

Sullivan ignored the outburst. There was a light on in the small bedroom at the front of the house, the room Eva reserved for their occasional guest. Through the curtains, he could see the pale, yellow-gray outline of two people, a man and a woman. He purposely moved in front of his son. "Then we'll have to figure a way to get them out."

*_*_*_*_*

Eva Delgado lay on the floor near the front door, her knees drawn up to her stomach. Her blouse was torn away from her shoulders, the light camisole she wore reduced to mere shreds and her skirt turned completely around. There was a great, wet stain just above the hem, and the pungent odor of the forced coupling.

And her face...

Vanessa bent down, cushioning her knees with her skirt as she knelt beside the woman. "Eva..." Her hand hovered above the other woman's face. "Eva?"

There was a soft rustle as the woman moved, her face betraying the physical pain. Her eyes bespoke a more intense spiritual wounding. "Please. Don't touch me," she whispered. A long cut at the corner of her mouth made speech difficult, but she continued. Purposely, she kept her voice low. "You've got to talk to Bridger, Vanessa." When the woman shook her head, she spoke again, urgency in her words. "You must convince him..." she paused, a renewed surge of pain tearing at her insides, "...that you don't have all of Wes' papers, that something is not there... They're going to kill us, Vanessa," she continued. "If he thinks he doesn't need us anymore, he'll kill us."

Vanessa sat down hard on the floor. She cast a wary look at Bridger, watching as the man sifted through her valise. Mendoza stood at his side, pawing through her clothing as the other man discarded it, and taking great amusement in the variety of lace underwear she'd taken great care to pack. "Reese," she whispered. "Surely, Reese will..."

Eva fought the need to cry, the pain worse now than before. "Reese was in Limbo," she murmured, "and Trey was with him." She kept remembering Bridger's comment about how much Trey looked like his father. "They could be dead, Vanessa," she finished. "Both of them. They could be dead."

It never occurred to Vanessa Underwood that she could lose her son. Not like this. Not in some god-forsaken hole far south of the border. Reese perhaps; she had always expected Reese to die this way. But not Trey. "Oh, God," she sobbed. She began to cry.

*_*_*_*_*

Trey paced the floor, the warmth returning to his body as he marched the length of the wide corridor between the rows of stalls. He hated the waiting; the impotent feeling that he could do nothing. And yet he knew Sullivan was right. Disgusted, he stopped, wishing for drink, a smoke...anything to break the tedium.

He was also hungry. Absently, he began digging into the stores of wheat and grain, looking for something to chew on. He settled on a handful of shelled corn.

Sensing the man's closeness, the red colt stuck its nose out between the slats of the big stall at the end of the corridor. The animal snorted, softly, its pink nostrils flaring at the smell of grain. Trey grinned, genuinely surprised at how much the little stud colt had grown in his absence. "You little beggar," he groused. He bent down, sticking his hand through the boards, the corn cupped in his flat palm. The foal nuzzled his hand, nibbling at the corn; the yellow kernels tumbling to the ground.

Trey reached down to pick up the loose grains, his hand digging into the straw. Instantly, he recoiled. "Oh, God," he breathed.

Sullivan joined his son. He stared down at the floor, watching as Trey dug into the thick bed of straw. A small, bare foot poked out from beneath the bedding, the rest of the boy's body completely hidden. Reese bent down, brushing the last of the straw away from the youngster's face. "Toby," he breathed. The child's throat had been cut. "Damn them," he swore. His entire body shook. "Damn them!" It did not escape him; how much this boy had resembled Trey when he was a child. The way, he mused—until that day in Diamond's office—he had remembered his son.

Gently, Sullivan lifted the boy up from the floor. With Trey following after him, he carried the youngster into the small tack room, and laid him down on the empty cot. The moonlight streaming from the small window above the bed bathed the youngster's face, and Sullivan saw the bruises he had not seen before.

Trey watched from the doorway, a twinge of jealousy filling his chest as he saw Sullivan's compassionate ministries. How many times he had longed for the same, for his real father to...

Sullivan pulled the blanket up across the little boy's face and stood up. He found himself face to face with his son, wishing he could read what was in the younger man's pale eyes. He shut the door to the tack room, and started to speak.

The pain took him then, deep in his chest, the same pain he had felt when he lifted the dead child's body from the floor. He began to cough, a loose rattle sounding as he inhaled deeply and tried to hold back the wetness in his lungs. The hacking began in earnest.

Trey stood back, the frown deepening as he watched his father turn away. Sullivan leaned against the top railing of the stall on this right and buried his head against his forearm, his shoulders convulsing as he stifled the noise. Trey reached out, his hand closing on the man's arm.

Sullivan pulled away, but not soon enough. There was blood at the corner of his mouth, bright red blood.

"Pa?" The word came from deep within the younger man, and he immediately corrected himself. "Old man?"

Stubbornly, his hands shaking, Sullivan dabbed at his chin with his handkerchief. The coughing had stopped, but not the pain. He chose to ignore the hurt. "I'm all right," he said finally.

Trey backed away from the man. There was no point in arguing. The question now was how long the man would be able to stay on his feet.

There was a subtle noise behind the younger man, and he turned to meet it. Instinctively, he drew his weapon, surprised at the ease with which his fingers closed around the grip and lifted the pistol from its holster. *As if, somehow, his father's abilities were now his.*

The dog dropped to its belly. Foot-weary from the long chase from the railroad siding, the animal's sides were heaving, its great tongue dripping saliva. The black had come home.

* _ * _ * _ * _ *

Mendoza's arm swept the supper dishes from the table, the china shattering against the uncarpeted floor. Crystal crunched beneath his feet as he completed the sweep, until the table was completely bare. "*Patrón*," he gestured toward the empty table, and watched as Bridger carefully laid out the collection of papers.

He arranged the documents in careful order, the frown deepening as he tried to make some sense out of Wes Underwood's scrawl. The lined note pads were filled with columns written in a neat and disciplined Spenserian script, hurried jottings in a different hand marring the wide margins. He turned to face the woman. "Madame."

Vanessa was still beside Eva Delgado. She stared down at the woman for a long moment, their eyes meeting, and then stood up. Without acknowledging the man's summons, she joined him at the table.

Bridger accepted her cold silence. *For now.* He selected a single sheet of yellow paper, and held it up for the woman's inspection. "You can, I assume, decipher what your husband has written."

The woman reached for the paper, fighting the wry smile when Bridger would not let go. "I need more light."

Bridger's eyes narrowed. He spoke to Mendoza without looking at the man. "A lantern," he ordered.

Mendoza did as he was told. He crossed the room, pausing to step over the still unconscious woman on the floor. On his trip back to the table, he kicked her; low, in the back, in the vulnerable softness above her kidneys. She whimpered, and her entire body went slack.

Vanessa was diligent but slow in her perusal of the papers, her mind working furiously. She knew, now, that Eva was right. They would remain alive only as long as Bridger needed them. She tapped a slim finger against the neat columns on the first page. "This isn't Wes' handwriting," she said finally. It was the truth, and she was grateful she did not have to lie. *Yet.* Her finger moved across the page to rest finally on the jumble of notes scrawled across the margins. "Wes wrote this," she said finally. That, too, was the truth.

Again, the single finger moved, tracing a series of numbers in the lower left-hand corner. The three lines were nothing more than an example of Wes' idle doodlings, but Vanessa knew she had to try. "He did this sometimes," she observed. "Marking some pages with Roman numerals, and others..." She bent closer to the table, studying the documents. Then, reaching out to a different stack, she picked up one of the parchment scrolls. Wes' marks were there as well, the peculiar form of shorthand he used when making notes. She had learned long ago to interpret his secret writings, a necessary part of her need to control him. *As she had never been able to control Reese.*

Bridger watched the woman's face. He prided himself on being able to see through the feeble facades women created to confuse the men who loved them, and the more devious fronts they perpetrated when conspiring to deceive those who did not. Vanessa's face intrigued him. She browsed the papers that were spread before her, one eyebrow rising slightly as she lifted one sheet and then another, nothing betraying what she saw, or what she might be thinking.

"I'm tiring of the game, Vanessa," he said finally. He raised a single finger and gestured for Mendoza. His move did not inspire the fear he had expected. The woman's face remained expressionless, even when Mendoza moved to her side.

"I told you. Something is missing," she said finally. When Mendoza reached out to touch her, she faced the man, stopping him with a single look that radiated ice. He recovered and grabbed her wrist. Bridger waved him away.

"I will not tolerate any lies, Vanessa," he threatened.

The woman's gaze drifted across the table again, and then lifted to meet the man's dark orbs. "Wes had a fondness for ciphers, Ansel. Anagrams in a foreign language; secret symbols," She lifted one of the scrolls and tapped a collection of Wes Underwood's meaningless doodles to the left of one column.

"Trey had access to all of Wes' papers," she began, "and he understood his father's little word games. It was a contest between them when Trey was a child, a game that did not include me." When she saw Bridger's head cant slightly in disbelief, she continued. "Consider what you are seeing, Ansel." She was horse trading now, as if bargaining with the man for something he was attempting to sell. "No maps," she was guessing, but saw from his face that she guessed right. "No written references to any geographical locations." She lifted one of the parchment scrolls, offering it for his inspection. "And this... It's in French, Ansel. As are Wes' notes."

Bridger still did not believe. "I know what the boy had with him," he countered.

Vanessa laughed. "He's Reese's son, Ansel. And mine. Do you really believe he would carry everything with him, to a place he didn't know?" She gestured with one arm, encompassing the entire house with a sweep of her hand. "He spent the first five years of his life in this house, Ansel. He was here alone, with no other children to entertain him.

"He could have hidden anything here." Purposely, she paused. "And if not here..." She shrugged her shoulders, leaving him to imagine the rest.

Bridger considered her words. "You are suggesting, Madame, that your son would lie to you, and keep what Wes intended for you to have?"

The woman's face hardened, the words carrying a sting that wounded her deeply. "I am suggesting that my son—who is, at times, still very much a boy—was thinking only of revenge. Against the men who killed his father, and even more against Reese for all the years and all the neglect..." She didn't finish.

This time, the man realized, her words made sense. Suddenly enraged, Bridger reached out and clutched a handful of documents, crumpling them within his shaking fists. The gods were toying with him again. They would pay. Before this was over, they would all pay.

* _ * _ * _ * _ *

Reese hunkered down at the doorway to the barn, grateful for the half moon. The ranch yard was bathed in the muted white light, shadows sharply defined against the landscape. It was, he reasoned, the better of two worlds. Enough darkness to allow them closer access to the house, and just enough light to let Bridger know, when the time was right, that they were there.

The dog slipped its head beneath Sullivan's crooked arm, joining him in his vigil. Reese scratched the dog's head, concentrating on the ears. Without looking up, he addressed his son. "You think you can steal another horse? Without getting caught?"

Trey's jaws tightened. He wondered if Sullivan would ever talk to him without reminding him of past sins. "I managed to do it in broad daylight," he boasted. "Middle of the night, it ought to be a damned cinch."

Sullivan nodded toward the house. "We're going to cut down the odds," he said. "I want you to take the dog, and turn Bridger's horse loose. And Mendoza's."

Trey could not fathom the man's reasoning. "And how the hell is that going to help us get into the house?"

Reese shifted, his legs getting numb, and dropped down on one knee. "If you were inside a house, and you heard your animals take off, just what the hell would you do?"

Silently, Trey cursed. *More damn tests*, he thought. *If you had two apples and I gave you two more...* He shook the thought away, but the antagonism was in his voice. "I'd take a look to see what was going on," he answered.

Using the Henry as a staff, Sullivan stood up. "Damned right you would." He pointed toward the house again, this time with the barrel of the rifle. "You'd stick your head out that door, and take a good look."

At last, the young man understood. "And get my head blown off," he reckoned.

Reese gave the dog a final pat. "Bridger will send Mendoza to take a look. One down, one to go." He turned to face his son. "We'll go out together," he said. "Bridger doesn't know we're here. We have that much to our advantage, but not much more."

Trey nodded. He thought about the inside of the house, as well as the exterior walls. The house had been built like a small fortress, at a time when both the Mexicans and Indians still raided back and forth across the border. Now, late at night, it looked as formidable as a small castle. He understood finally why Reese hadn't simply stormed the place; realizing how foolish such a move would have been. *How fatal.* With food, water, and ammunition—all of which were inside the house in abundance—a single man could hold off an army. And two... "I'll get the horses," he vowed.

Reese held him back for a moment. "Take the dog," he said. "Untie the horses, lead them well away from the house, and then turn the dog loose on them. I want Mendoza out of the door and onto the porch." His fingers tightened on Trey's arm. "Take off your boots," he ordered.

Trey did as he was told without arguing. "Now?" he asked.

Sullivan nodded. "I'll be there," he said, pointing to the low rock cairn a hundred yards from the house. He picked out several other places where the moon had drawn long shadows. A second scattering of rocks, the well house. A cluster of rose bushes Eva had nursed through a long winter. "Use whatever cover you can, and..." he paused. "Trey. Whatever you see when that door opens, I want you away from the house. You understand what I'm telling you?"

Trey didn't, not really. He would take the horses, drive them away from the house, and then... He shrugged. What the hell was there he could see that would make any difference?

Stealthily, both men slipped through the barn door, the dog trailing along behind them. Reese moved across the barnyard, moving in a direct line toward the stone pillar he had indicated. Trey joined him, waiting until the man was settled in before zigzagging across the yard toward his own objective.

Sullivan watched his son and the dog move, one eye on the young man, the other on the front door. He'd chosen his spot well. Hunkering down, he used a small slot in the rocks to steady the Henry, and began his wait.

Trey reached the well house. He stood, his back pressed against the bricked outer wall, the dog poised at his side. Bridger's big gelding snorted, picking up the dog's scent, and Trey flattened himself into the shadows. He waited, longer than necessary, and then—cautiously—peered out around the corner.

In spite of himself, Sullivan snickered. The kid was certainly no Will Bonney. He was, however, determined. Reese watched as Trey and the dog made a beeline for the two horses.

The dog was a willing accomplice. Trey patted the animal's back, appreciating the dog's silence as he untied the two horses. He led them away from the house at a walk. Then, satisfied he was far enough away, he knotted their reins and carefully pulled them up over their ears and looped them around the saddle horn. He whispered, calling the dog to him.

Sullivan's stance changed, a frown forming as he stared at his son and the dog. Trey was mere yards from the corner of the porch, and there was no indication that he was going any farther.

Sullivan cursed. "Damn him!" The kid was too close, much too close.

Angry, Reese moved out. The pain tore at him as he trotted toward the house, his gait awkward as his ribs jarred against his lungs. "Trey," he rasped. He knew now what the kid intended.

It was too late. Trey slapped the rump of the horse nearest him, his shrill whistle cutting into the nighttime quiet. "Go!" And then, to the dog, "Sic 'em!"

Reese dove for cover, bellying down in the shadows of the cluster of rose bushes, still a good hundred feet from the house. He cocked the rifle, leveling a shell into the chamber.

Bridger heard the uproar in the yard, the frantic barking, and loud throaty growls instilling an ancient fear. This was no lap dog, yapping at the heels of some passing carriage horse. The animal outside the door was big, wild, and wolf-like in its pursuit of the horses, the pair of geldings responding in kind. Their terrified whinnies tore into the man's soul, evoking a kindred fear, the shod hooves thundering across the yard and fading into the distance.

"Chato!"

Mendoza bolted for the door.

Trey was beside the front steps. He had heard his father's whispered summons and ignored it. "Just do your job, old man," he breathed. "You take the 'breed, and I'll take Bridger." He said the words as if Sullivan could hear them.

Once again, a need for revenge filled him. It was not so much the desire to avenge Wes Underwood's death, as the inner need to redeem his lost manhood. Left to die in the desert, too inconsequential to be considered a threat; too much a boy to be considered a man. *But not anymore.* He would settle both scores. Now.

The front door to the house opened part way. Mendoza's head and arm poked out the opening, his hand raised, his pistol cocked and at the ready. Trey stared up at the man, his eyes adjusting to the dim light as he studied the man's profile. The door opened wider, the light from inside the house washing across Mendoza's face and giving the young man a clear view.

The cry came from deep within Trey's soul, the rage and anguish of the last two months finally released. "You..." he screamed, finally recognizing the man Bridger had been so careful to keep hidden.

Gun drawn, Trey charged the door, his first shot wild. He lunged across the threshold, grabbing at the man's legs. Mendoza kicked at the young man's head, withdrawing back into the house in his attempt to break free.

Cursing, Sullivan fired. He aimed high, well above his son's head, intending now to drive Chavez back into the house and to give Trey the opportunity to get away. Mendoza dropped down on one knee, firing into the darkness and aiming at the flashes. Then, half turning, he fired at the dark shadow on his right.

Trey felt the sting as the bullet whined past his ear. He rolled across the porch, and righted himself, coming up on all fours. Springing forward, he charged the doorway a second time. His shoulder struck Mendoza's chest, knocking the man backwards into the kitchen.

Mendoza scrambled backwards across the floor, covering his face as Trey pursued him. The younger man pummeled his face again and again.

Horrified, Vanessa screamed. Bridger grabbed the woman, his hand closing around her mouth. He fumbled for his own weapon, dragging the woman away from the open door.

From his place in the front yard, Sullivan observed the pandemonium. He raised the rifle, taking aim, but changed his mind. Then, a figure loomed in the doorway, and he took aim again.

He caught himself, watching as Eva stumbled and fell; the woman struggling to regain her footing. She was hunched over, one arm cradling her belly as she pitched forward. Losing her balance, she then fell down the final three stairs. She landed on her feet, a final surge of adrenalin filling her as she regained her balance and dashed across the clearing.

Sullivan stood up, catching the woman as she raced by him. He pulled her to him, holding her close as he dragged her down. "Eva..."

Her arms tightened around his neck, the warmth of her tears washing against his cheek. "Oh, God, Reese," she murmured.

He held her, aware of every welt on her face as he caressed her cheek. "It's going to be all right," he promised. "I swear to God, Eva, it's going to be all right."

Chapter Fifteen

Trey came to slowly, aware that he was in an upright position, his hands bound behind his back and his ankles secured to the legs of his chair. Wisely, he chose to feign unconsciousness, using his ears to track movement within the room, his other senses heightened.

The subtle scent of his mother's French perfume reached out to him, growing more intense. Then he felt her fingers against his right cheek, conscious that her hand was trembling. The pain came then, a marrow-deep ache in the bone beneath his right eye, and he instinctively pulled away.

"Trey…" Vanessa's voice was whisper soft and filled with a barely controlled panic. When she repeated his name, it was with even more urgency. "*Trey!*" This time the fear was more evident.

The young man's eyelids fluttered. He was still attempting to continue the ruse, coming around slowly as he took his bearings and surveyed the room from half opened eyes. There was no pretense, however, when he attempted to speak. The single word "Mother…" came from a voice box that ached with the effort, and he cleared his throat. Before he could speak again, he felt a sudden tug as the cord around his neck pulled tight.

"Chato, there is no need to torture the lad." Bridger chided his *segundo*, as if he really gave a damn that Trey might be in pain. Reaching out, he pulled Vanessa away from her son and pushed her into a chair at the end of the table.

Grudgingly, Mendoza released the rope. He still, however, remained directly behind Trey's chair, his right hand on the younger man's shoulder.

Trey swallowed, the pain in his throat reaching his ears. He had no idea how long he'd been unconscious; in fact, he had very little memory beyond the time he saw Mendoza's face. When he spoke, his voice was hoarse. "It was you all along, wasn't it?" He didn't wait for an answer. "At the train-stop in Yuma…" He felt like such a fool for not having caught on right from the beginning.

Bridger was putting on his leather riding gloves, working the soft suede across his knuckles until it was smooth. There was a brief flash of white light as the intricate pattern of silver studs on the back of the gloves was caught in the bright glow of the overhead lanterns. "Wes Underwood was a thief," he said finally. "Wes Underwood was a *liar*!" He made no effort to hide the contempt. "The man *you* chose to revere as your father was an abomination, a man totally lacking in honor ..." His eyes narrowed, and he smiled as he saw the look on the younger man's face. He was enjoying the torment he was causing, to the young man, and to his mother.

"Honor?" Trey struggled against the ropes that bound him, his face contorted in rage. "Compared to what?" There was a scraping sound as the boy's chair inched forward. "A whoring quadroon and a litter of half-breed border scum!?"

The blow came without warning and no restraint, Bridger's fingers laced together to form a lethal weapon the size of a small ham. He swung his arms with such force that the blow, aimed at the younger man's head, knocked Trey sideways. There was a grinding pain in his left shoulder as his body collided with the floor, the side legs of the chair shattering beneath his weight on impact.

Vanessa screamed.

* - * - * - * - *

Instinctively, Sullivan knew the scream coming from inside the house was one of fear, not pain. It was also not his son. That single thought gave him a brief spate of momentary relief.

It was not the same for Eva. She grabbed Sullivan's arm and held on, her fingers digging into the tender flesh above his elbow. "Vanessa," she whispered. The torment was real.

Even in the muted moonlight that filtered into the barn it was hard for Sullivan to look at the woman and still control his growing rage. The marks on her face—the raw cut at the corner of her mouth and the other above her right eye—stoked a fury in him which tore at his very soul. It was an anger he knew he needed to control. *At least for now.* "I think we can get them out of the house," he said finally.

Eva's grip relaxed and her breathing returned to normal. "But how, Reese?" She worked the problem over in her mind, exploring the few possibilities that seemed even remotely likely. She knew Bridger would not fall for the same trick a second time.

Reese moved around in the barn, collecting a variety of objects. "We're going to drive them out," he answered. He held up the remnants of a burlap bag he dug out from behind a barrel of scrap leather.

Eva stood up, aware that the big dog had returned to the barn and now lay at her feet, the only noise the sound of his panting. "We," she gestured at the dog, "and what army, Reese?"

Reese crossed the small expanse of space separating him from the woman and the dog. "We aren't going to need an army," he answered. Forcing a smile, he touched her cheek, careful to avoid the bruises. Then, leaning on the woman's shoulder for support, he removed his boots.

Sullivan motioned for Eva to follow him, pausing momentarily at the door to grab a bucket and a length of rope. Single file and low to the ground, they sprinted across the dark clearing toward the back of the house. The dog scurried behind them, seemingly aware of the need for stealth.

It wasn't until they arrived at the fieldstone and concrete cistern that Eva began to understand. She was grateful Sullivan brought the bucket.

* _ * _ * _ * _ *

Mendoza secured Trey to a second chair; taking particular delight in the fact that the kid had regained consciousness and was aware. He took his time, twisting the torn remnants of a linen napkin to form a garrote before changing his mind. There was a perverse pleasure in him as he crossed the room to where the woman sat, and an even more carnal enjoyment as he groped at her throat.

Vanessa knew better than to protest. Stoically, she endured his touch, drawing herself even more erect. She regretted now that she had worn the triple strand of onyx beads, even more so when Mendoza knotted them around his fingers and pulled. Eyes closed, she remained determined not to cry out.

Satisfied, Mendoza lifted the beads over the woman's head. He tested them again, confirming the beads were strung with a fine yet sturdy wire. More than strong enough for what he intended. Almost as an afterthought, he leaned forward and whispered in the woman's ear. "I think, *Señora*—before I kill your son—I will let him watch you on your knees pleasuring me like any other whore." And then he laughed.

Sullivan worked diligently, grimacing as he struggled to lift the hinged lid to the buried holding tank. Even the slightest noise was cause for alarm, and Reese cursed himself for his legendary thrift. Instead of the usual hemp rope most men would have used (in spite of the fact it would have required replacement with annoying regularity), he had chosen to jerry-rig a tripod and chain mechanism for raising and lowering the cistern's cap.

Eva tapped Reese's shoulder. "I think it's high enough," she whispered.

Sullivan chucked a rock into the hole, counting under his breath until he heard the missile hit. Cleaning the large honey-pot was a chore he put off until late fall. "Room for the bucket?"

She stifled a nervous laugh. "Well, I don't plan on using my hands." The stench from the cistern was strong; stomach turning.

Sullivan hunkered down beside the woman, his tone serious. "I'm going to have to put you up on the roof of the house," he breathed.

The woman nodded. "I want you to kill them, Reese." There was no regret and absolutely no remorse in the words as she said them. "Both of them."

* _ * _ * _ * _ *

Ansel Bridger stood before the fire, rubbing his hands above the flames. Even though his stance was that of a man simply relaxing before his own hearth, his mind was working. He weighed all the facts as they paraded through his thoughts, his recent successes and failures. Vain, but not stupid, Bridger congratulated himself for what he had accomplished. He had the papers Wes Underwood stole from him. And he was certain he would soon possess the key to their secrets. It was only a matter of time before the woman or the boy gave him what he wanted. *And as for Reese...*

The smile crawled across the man's face, warming his dark eyes with a sinister fire. There had been no response to Vanessa's scream. None. But the boy; if Sullivan were to hear the boy cry out... The smile grew. "Chato."

Mendoza answered Bridger immediately. "*Patrón?*"

"Bring the boy's chair over here, by the fire." Half-turning, Bridger signaled the Mexican with a wave of his right hand. With his left, he picked up the ornate wrought iron poker.

Mendoza did as he was told. There was a sadistic anticipation in him as he shoved the chair before him. "Here, *Patrón*?" he asked, indicating a spot directly in front of the hearth.

Bridger toyed with the poker, stoking the embers before adding a log to the fire; and then another. Finally satisfied, he jammed the poker between the two logs, the tip buried deeply in the crimson ash. "Turn him toward the windows, Chato," he ordered.

Again, Mendoza immediately obeyed. He enjoyed the game, having played it many times before under similar circumstances; so much so that he felt himself growing erect in expectation. "And the woman?"

Bridger was shaking his head. "Patience, Chato, her turn will come." He nodded toward the table. "Underwood's notebook," he said.

Trey flashed his mother a quick look, hoping for something from her—anything—that would indicate she had a clue as to what Bridger wanted. What he saw was an emptiness that filled him with an odd sense of relief.

He knew they were going to die. He had no doubt Sullivan had taken Eva and headed for parts unknown. And why not? Considering their current relationship, he wouldn't have blamed the man; in all likelihood he would have done the same.

But as for Bridger... Bridger would rot in Hell before he told him anything about the coins. Anything.

"And now, boy?" Using his clenched right hand, Bridger lifted Trey's head away from his chest, forcing him to meet his gaze. "You have something to tell me?"

Trey jerked his head away but did not avert his eyes. "You're going to kill us," he whispered. "Why the hell would I want to tell you what my *father*," he purposely stressed the word, "was willing to die for?"

Bridger laughed, amused as much by the younger man's words as his bravado. "Your *father*," he mocked "is out there somewhere..." he gestured toward the door, "waiting for the opportunity to fix—once again—what you have managed to corrupt!"

It was Trey's turn to laugh. "Sullivan's long gone, Bridger. He's taken Eva and ridden out, just like he did when I was a kid!

And he never even bothered to look back; not then, and sure in hell not now!"

The laughter stopped when he heard Vanessa's murmured, "*Oh, Trey.*"

Bridger was smug in his certainty. "She knows, Trey," he announced arrogantly. "She knows that what Reese has wanted more than anything else was the chance to have you back in his life; no matter what the cost." He lifted his hand in an expansive wave meant to encompass the entire ranch. "Who do you think he built this for, *chamaco*, if not for you?"

Instantly, Bridger's mood changed, the need to philosophize gone. "The treasure, Trey. I want you to tell me *everything* you know about the treasure." When the young man remained mute, he reached out with his right hand. There was a sudden wrenching as he grabbed the front of Trey's shirt and pulled hard, the sound of tearing fabric filling the room. Still, the youth refused to respond.

Bridger straightened, his eyes narrowing as he studied Trey's features. It was like seeing Reese Sullivan as he must have been at the same age; the stubborn set of the young man's jaw, and the intense gaze of someone whose mind was working, plotting. *Seeking a way to escape.*

There was hope in the young man's eyes, as well. In spite of what he said before about his father, there was still a glimmer of expectation shining there; the thought that if he could somehow stall what was happening, delay telling, Reese would ride to the rescue and justice would prevail.

Bridger began to laugh, a soft, cynical laughter that was somehow mocking. He reached out, toying with the young man's torn shirtfront, pulling the cloth away from Trey's chest. The gleam of gold caught his eye then, the shimmer of firelight against the large medallion that rested against the young man's sternum. Intrigued, he touched the piece, his fingers warming as he realized it was a gold coin and not some token piece of religious protection. He also was aware that the young man immediately tensed when he weighed the piece in his palm. "Your *lucky* piece?" he whispered.

As much as he was able, Trey pulled away from the man's touch. His attempt was fruitless, the strips of linen that bound him holding him fast. "A gift, from my father," he lied.

Bridger pulled himself erect. He was still smiling, but there was no mirth in the expression. Turning slightly, he reached for the poker he had placed between the two logs now smoldering a bright crimson. The tip of the poker, when he withdrew it, showed the same vivid red. "How sad," he breathed, "that it must be sacrificed to teach you a lesson." He turned, and plunged the hot poker against the medallion, and held on.

There was an instant reaction from the young man; one with the sound of his flesh sizzling beneath the heated coin as it began to melt. He tried in vain not to cry out, but could not help himself. And then he was lost in a pool of blackness, the sound of his mother's high-pitched scream pulling him into a dark abyss where there was no more pain.

* _ * _ * _ * _ *

Sullivan stopped in his chore, his back going rigid as he recognized his son's outcry. "Trey..." The sudden silence following the boy's shout was even more fear provoking than the sound of his voice. He repeated his son's name, softly. "Trey."

Eva reached out, her hand on the man's shoulder. "We have to hurry, Reese."

Regaining his composure, Sullivan nodded his head, more determined than ever to succeed. Hand over hand; he pulled the bucket of sludge from the cistern. He used the piece of burlap he had been carrying to cover the thick liquid, using a stick to saturate the cloth. "They've stoked up a pretty good fire," he whispered. "If we can get this down the chimney..." He hesitated, searching out the woman's face in the darkness. "Wait until I get back to the front of the house," he ordered. "They'll be looking to get out, and I'll..." he reconsidered, nodding at the big dog, "we'll be waiting."

Eva reached out to him again, and then leaned forward to kiss him. "He's all right, Reese," she said softly. "Trey is going to be all right."

Together, Sullivan and the woman moved across the yard, heading toward the back porch. The dog followed them, his nose to the ground. The animal was still with them when they reached the place Reese intended.

When they reached the back of the house, Reese pulled the woman to him. He held her for a time, close to his chest, his lips warm against her left ear. "Stay clear until I come for you," he whispered. "I *will* come for you," he promised.

Gingerly, he lifted the woman up until her bare feet rested on his shoulders. He steadied her, marveling at her determination. She moved like a cat, her feet whispering against the brick wall, and then across the shingled roof. He knew that she was in pain, and yet she continued without making a sound, lying on her belly now as she reached down to take the bucket.

* _ * _ * _ * _ *

Mendoza stood at the sink, filling a large clay jug with water from the pump. He turned, waiting for a signal from Bridger, and then threw the entire contents of the jug at the unconscious form still strapped in the kitchen chair.

Trey bolted awake, the sudden splash of cold water rousing him from a place where there had been no pain and propelling him into a here and now filled with an intense throbbing deep inside his chest. He was aware of an excruciating soreness just above his heart, and a sensation of his flesh being torn. This time, he did not cry out, grimacing as he clenched his teeth and steeled himself for what he knew was to come.

Bridger was standing directly in front of Trey now, the poker he held in his right hand still warm. The medallion was a concave cap on the poker's tip, traces of Trey skin bright red against the softened gold. Bridger lifted the poker just a hair to his right; just enough to create a tension that pulled the chain around Trey's neck tight against the young man's throat.

"Your courage is commendable, *chico*; just what I would expect of Reese Sullivan's son." He was smiling now, but there was not one hint of humor in his dark eyes or his expression. "But what you need now is your father's intelligence; his ability to know when he's beaten." Using his gloved fingers, he pried the gold coin loose from the end of the poker and let it fall against the younger man's chest. "The treasure, Trey. I intend to have the treasure."

Trey could hear his mother weeping, the sobs coming from deep within her. There was anguish in her he had never heard before, something foreign to her usual control. He could feel himself feeding on her fear, and somehow it gave him a purpose he didn't really understand, but was determined to use. He began to laugh; a soft, mocking laughter that grew in volume until it filled the room.

The young man's sudden laughter—the almost maniacal sound—filled the room. "Treasure!" he roared. He wrestled against the straps binding him to the chair, actually scooting forward across the varnished floor and marring the finish. *Oh, shit; the old man will raise real hell over this!* he thought, aware of the scarred planking. The insanity of that one thought made him laugh again, even harder. "Treasure!"

Surprised and alarmed, Bridger retreated. Mendoza's response was different. He charged forward and the two men collided in the middle of the floor. Bridger was the first to regain his composure. His face ashen, the large vein in his temple throbbed a deep purple as his rage grew. He struck out at the woman this time, knocking her to the floor beside her son. And then, with one great sweep of his right arm he cleared the collection of documents from the table, and swept them onto the floor and into the smoldering fire.

* - * - * - * - *

Sullivan waited at the front of the house now, his gaze on the roof and the chimney. He could see the faint silhouette of the woman; see her struggle with the heavy bucket. Silently, he urged her on; so intent on what the woman was doing when the black dog unexpectedly nuzzled his elbow he felt a brief sense of panic.

And then Eva completed her task. Sullivan watched as she dumped the entire contents of the bucket down the chimney. She finished the job by stuffing the saturated burlap in the opening.

* - * - * - * - *

The acrid smell of human waste invaded the room as soon as the sludge began to spread across the burning logs. Trey could hear the sudden sizzle as the liquefied dung dripped to the floor of the fieldstone hearth, his eyes smarting as the smoke thickened. Helpless, he watched as his mother crawled across the floor, away from the stench. He called out to her, softly, "Mother!" and then more urgently, his voice angry, "*Vanessa!*"

Bridger desperately tried to put out the fire, yelling at Mendoza to bring water. Mendoza did as he was told, filling the clay pot to the brim, the water sloshing onto the floor as he tried to do his patron's bidding. Coughing, he moved to Bridger's side, the pungent odor of ammonia permeating the room and burning his eyes. Awkwardly, he struggled with the water jug, holding his breath as he approached the glowing hearth and dumped the entire contents of the pot onto the burning logs.

Bridger realized the mistake immediately. The water turned into a vile smelling steam combining with the thickening white smoke. At first, gravity pulled the caustic cloud toward and up the chimney flue, regurgitating the thick fog back into the room when the saturated burlap blocked the upward swirl. The entire room filled with the wet stink of condensed human waste, the air becoming unbreathable.

Vanessa stayed closed to the floor, groping for her son as he continued to call out to her. She fought the nausea as she reached out to him and whispered his name. "Trey…"

He kept his voice low. "Untie me."

The woman struggled with the torn linen that bound his wrists. It was difficult, her fingers numb, eyes watering. She freed his right hand first, and then his left, amazed at the speed the young man displayed as he loosened the bonds securing his legs.

Trey rolled away from the chair, staying low as he attempted to get his bearings. He could see Mendoza's lower torso beneath the heavy layer of smoke, see the man moving away from the hearth in an attempt to escape the foul smelling haze. The man was heading for the door.

Too late, Bridger realized his *segundo's* intentions. "Chato!" He yelled the man's name in a vain attempt to stop him, and failed. His failure only served to stoke his anger, and he took his frustration out on the window at his back. Using both hands, he smashed the leaded glass, moving close to the empty sash in pursuit of fresh air.

Chapter Sixteen

The sound of shattering glass came at the same time the exterior door burst open. Both noises spurred Sullivan into action. He rose up from his place in the darkness and bolted for the porch steps, his pistol drawn. The big dog ran ahead of him now, barreling up the stairs with a ferocity unlike anything Sullivan had seen before.

Mendoza struggled to breathe, his vision impaired by the effects of the pungent smoke filling the front rooms of the house. He stumbled across the threshold just as the dog came up the stairs.

The animal's attack was brutal and without warning. A frenzied growling came one with the shredding of coarse fabric as the dog lunged savagely against the man's belly just above his belt buckle. Mendoza was propelled backwards into the kitchen, the black using his teeth and front claws to drive the man further across the floor. Sullivan followed in the dog's wake, dropping to the floor as he came through the door.

Trey was on his hands and knees. The one thing on the curriculum he had excelled at during his brief stay at Harvard was the Friday afternoon football scrimmages. He scrambled across the kitchen floor, head down, aiming directly for Mendoza's legs. The hit was good. Mendoza collapsed backwards onto the floor, his head bouncing against the unforgiving planking with a dull '*thunk*' rendering him unconscious. Only then did the dog release its hold on the man's shirt.

Reese rose up on one knee, his eyes scanning the room in search of Bridger. The smoke, thinning now, funneled out the door and dissipated into the cold night air, but the stench remained. "Trey," he whispered the young man's name, grateful when the youth turned to face him. "Get her out of here!" he ordered, nodding at Vanessa.

For once, it appeared the youth was going to do as he was told. He reached out, taking his mother's arm, his face suddenly changing as he sensed a movement in the smoke-filled corner of the room, near the kitchen sink. "Bridger!" He shouted the word and stood up, shoving his mother behind him as he charged across the room.

Reese bolted after the younger man, using his shoulder to knock him aside. He was face to face with Bridger now, aware that the quadroon was armed; the man's pistol pointed directly at his son. "Ansel!" he shouted the man's name, seeing something in the desperado's eyes that reminded him of a shaman stoked up on sacred mushrooms.

They fired at the same time, Sullivan moving quickly to his left as he placed himself between Bridger and his son. Only then did Bridger's eyes regain a brief spark of clarity, the expression quickly fading as the man pitched forward and fell to the floor at Trey's feet. His last move was to claw at the young man's leg, his fingers closing around the stiff denim and refusing to let go.

Vanessa Underwood screamed. As one, father and son turned to face the sound. There was another noise, at the open doorway, and Reese swung in that direction, the pistol at waist level. Cade Devereau stepped through the opening just as Chato Mendoza stood up and lunged at Vanessa.

They fired in unison; Reese Sullivan and the marshal. Mendoza convulsed as the slugs tore into him; one in his chest, the other in his back, just between his shoulders. He stayed on his feet just long enough to half-turn in place, his face frozen in an expression of utter surprise. "*P-Patrón?*" The single word came as a plea, as if Bridger were capable of hearing and making him well.

"Reese," Devereau stepped over the dead outlaw's body. For a big man, he moved with considerable grace. He touched the brim of his Stetson in greeting with the barrel of his revolver, as if this kind of meeting with Reese was nothing out of the ordinary.

Sullivan smiled. "You're about a day late and a dollar short, *compadre.*" He holstered his pistol. "You come alone?"

Devereau surveyed the scene with a dispassionate eye. "Brought a clean-up crew," he answered. "And your lady," he nodded at the doorway.

Eva stood for a time at the threshold, her eyes sweeping the room before settling on Mendoza. She stepped into the kitchen— *her* kitchen—her movements fluid, as graceful as an apparition in an erotic dream, and strode straight to where the dead man lay. "*¡El dios me perdona, pero lo puede quema en el infierno!*" (May God forgive me, but I hope you burn in hell!)

Vanessa was less charitable. She joined the woman; the iron will so recently failing her now returning. "He was subhuman; a cretin!" Her eyes narrowed, she turned to face Sullivan. "Your usual companions, Reese. Just like before..."

Sullivan was having none of it. "Shut up, Vanessa. For once in your life, just *shut the hell up!*"

* _ * _ * _ * _ *

The three deputies that Devereau brought with him from El Paso worked with military precision cleaning up the carnage. The bodies were thoroughly searched and removed from the house, kept separate from the bodies of the old man, Vasquez, and the boy, Toby.

Eva worked with them, scrubbing the floor as they swept, ignoring Sullivan's suggestion for her to join Vanessa in the front room.

Trey knelt at the fireplace, taking his time as he cleaned out the hearth, something furtive in the way he poked through the charred remnants of the documents Bridger had thrown into the fire.

Devereau and Sullivan were at the table, sorting through the papers they retrieved from the floor. The marshal's eyes were busy elsewhere as well, watching the boy with keen interest. "Is it just me, Reese, or is he trying real hard to make sure that we don't see what he's seeing?" He whispered the words, keeping them private.

Sullivan seemed momentarily distracted. He cleared his throat, and called out to his son. "Trey." When the young man did not respond, he spoke again, louder. "Trey!"

The youth rose up suddenly, his head striking the capstone beneath the mantle. He swore under his breath, and then turned around, his hands behind his back. "What?!" Annoyed by the interruption, it showed in his voice as well as his eyes.

"The papers," Sullivan answered. "The ones behind your back. Put them here with the others." He tapped the table with a single finger.

Trey's eyes narrowed. "They're filthy," he said finally, shrugging his shoulders, "in fact, they're kind of full of shit." He laughed, as if he had made a joke.

Sullivan took a single step forward. "They're parchment," he observed. "They can be cleaned." He nodded to the man at his left. "Devereau can have them cleaned. Isn't that right, Cade?"

The lawman sensed the game, and decided to play. "That's why they pay me the big dollars, son," he volunteered, smiling. "To get things done."

"Put them on the table, Trey," Sullivan repeated the order and extended his hand.

Trey was already shaking his head. "They're mine," he said. "Bridger's dead, *and they're mine!*"

Sullivan's jaws tightened and he shook his head in disgust. There it was again; the same insatiable greed that turned Wes Underwood into a thief... He turned away from his son and addressed Devereau. "Arrest him."

Devereau considered the request and found it reasonable. "You'll testify?" The question was more for the younger Sullivan's benefit than the elder's.

Sullivan nodded his head. "You name the day and the place," he answered.

Dumbfounded, Trey watched the exchange between the two men. "No." He still shook his head. "No!"

Sullivan reached out, grabbing his son's arm. Rewarded with a sudden punch in the belly on his left side, just above his belt, the sucker punch only increased his resolve. This time when he took hold of his son, he slammed him against the edge of the table and held him in place. "Where do you think they'll want him first, Cade?" He did not wait for the man to answer. "California?" When he saw the puzzled expression on his son's face, he provided the answer. "The madman in San Francisco, Trey. Someone killed him, just about the time you and Wes left town." He hesitated for a moment, and then began again, a veritable litany of possibilities. "France? That's where the stolen documents came from. Maybe Mexico? *Again*. The dead girl?"

Trey began sweating, profusely. "It was just the coins Dad was looking for," he breathed. "Just the damn coins!"

Devereau was behind Trey now, facing Reese Sullivan. He nodded, just once; signaling his colleague that he was satisfied the kid told the truth. As he and Reese suspected, it was Bridger who had known the truth; there was a greater treasure than a measly five million in purposely corrupted coinage for sale to private collectors, and the documents Wes Underwood stole held the key.

Sullivan chose to continue the sham. "Then I guess we need to find those coins," he reasoned. He turned loose of his son. "The papers, Trey. Now."

Grudgingly, the young man surrendered the documents he'd been concealing. He laid them on the table beside the others, no longer able to hide the once hidden symbols rendered visible by the combination of fire and water.

Vanessa Underwood returned to the kitchen, silently watching the exchange between her son and her ex-husband. "Leave him alone," she commanded, her voice betraying something more than anger. There was still a small shred of hope within the woman; hope that her son would prevail and protect the secrets he shared with his step-father. *The fortune she now knew truly existed.*

"If he doesn't give up what he knows now—*right now*—Devereau will arrest him, and he will go to jail." Sullivan's voice matched the woman's in intensity. "Federal prison, Vanessa," he said the words like it was a solemn promise. "Not some city jail you can buy him out of with a smile to a friendly judge, or empty promises to a lawyer who doesn't know any better." He hoped his son was listening.

Trey faced his mother, watching her face; the myriad of emotions that swept across her features. He realized, possibly for the first time in his life, he was now no more to her than any man had ever been. A tool, simply a tool to be used to get what she wanted, what she needed. He turned back to face his father. "You'll be needing this," he said softly. He bent forward slightly, pulling up his right pant leg and reaching into the long vamp of his right boot. When he rose he held a cylinder six inches in length and as thick as a large man's thumb.

Sullivan reached out to take the decoding mechanism, turning it over and fingering the series of rotating rings which encompassed the entire circumference of the rod. For a time the only sound in the room was the soft *click, click, click* as Reese worked the piece, and then Trey became aware of another sound; closer and somehow ominous.

It was the black dog. He stood at Sullivan's left, his head down and his tongue lapping greedily at the thick pooling of a dark liquid beside Sullivan's left boot. Alarmed, the young man reached out, his eyes searching his father's face, not liking what he saw. "Pa?" Softly, and then louder, "Pa!"

Sullivan heard the boy calling to him, but could no longer see his face. He felt himself falling backwards, and was aware of a pair of strong arms keeping him from something dark and foreboding, but there was no escape from the pain.

* - * - * - * - *

Vanessa waited beside the buggy, her face showing the strain of her recent ordeal and her uncertain future. She reached out, touching her son's arm, and felt him tense. "You haven't brought your bags, Trey," she said softly.

Devereau watched the pair from the porch, lingering over his morning cigar and his final cup of coffee. The wind was with him, and he could hear their conversation without straining, anxious to hear what the boy had to say.

Trey faced his mother, turning so he could avoid Devereau's constant scrutiny. Living in his father's house before the trip to Mexico had been like a daily breaking of bread with the Pope, but living with the lawman's constant supervision was like existing under the very eye of God. "I'm not going back with you, Vanessa," he said finally. "I'm staying here."

She couldn't believe what he was saying; what he intended to do. "You owe him nothing, Trey. Absolutely nothing!"

He laughed, surprised—under the circumstances—that he could. "Just another five thousand dollars, Mother." She had kept the balance of the cash she promised Reese, and Trey knew she had no intention of ever paying. Not even for *his* life. His voice lowered until it was whisper soft. "He took a bullet intended for me, Mother. *For me.*" He hoped the words would make a difference.

"He almost succeeded in getting us both killed, and he took what your *father* intended for me to have!" She could no longer control the anger, and she made no effort to hide the bitterness she had nurtured for more than a decade.

Trey grabbed the woman, his fingers closing around her upper arms. "My *father* is laying inside that house more dead than alive!" The words were difficult to say, but he had to give them voice. Knowing it was fruitless, he let go, his hands hovering above her arms for a long moment until he finally backed away. He turned abruptly and marched back to the house, eyes straight ahead.

Devereau thrust his cup into the younger man's hand as he passed. Then, making no effort to hide the smile, he made his way down the stairs and across the yard. Firmly, he took the woman's arm and led her to the front of the carriage. "*Me permettre de vous aider, Madame.*" His French was impeccable. Her two word response was not. It was, he knew, going to be a very long ride.

Epilogue

Eighteen days into his recovery, Sullivan awoke to the loud incessant buzzing of a blue-tailed fly. The insect flitted around the room in an annoying pattern that defied nature's logic. He watched the insect for a time before he realized he felt hungry; incredibly hungry, and in serious need of some water. Struggling to sit up, he became aware of a dull ache in his left side, his senses sharpening as bits and pieces of his recent past came tumbling back.

He took a tenuous breath and swept the room with his eyes, surprised when—in the far corner in the dim light of a single lamp—he saw the dog. Beyond the animal, sprawled out in a Morris chair, his son, Trey, slept, his long legs stretched out and crossed at the ankles; his father's battered Stetson pulled down over his eyes.

Sullivan eyed the dog again, seeing its head come up, the black's tail beginning a slow *thump-thump* against the bare floor. The animal seemed to be smiling, the upper lips lifting away from its teeth in an apologetic grin. Sullivan was having none of it. He pulled the heavy down pillow out from behind his shoulders and made the toss. "Traitor," he breathed. The dog ducked and sprinted for the door.

Trey came awake suddenly, his right hand reaching for a pistol that was not there. He bolted upright in the chair, immediately looking for the dog and finding the pillow instead. He picked it up, staring at it for a long time then finally realizing its source. He stood up and crossed the room to the bed, carrying the kerosene lamp with him. Adjusting the wick, he put it on the table beside the bed and waited.

Sullivan looked up at the youth, inwardly pleased when he saw the deep tan and the day-old beginnings of a beard. "My dog, my hat," he began. "You steal anything else while I was out?" The words were tempered by a smile.

Trey shrugged. "Tried to take the woman," he answered, "but she wouldn't have me." The words were only half in jest, and he regretted them as soon as they were uttered.

"Again?" Sullivan's smile grew. "I thought you'd be in jail," he intoned.

Trey snorted. "Might as well be." This time he wasn't joking. "Devereau is still here; has been, ever since…"

"…Bridger," Sullivan finished. It was all coming back now; the assault on the ranch house, Eva and Vanessa taken hostage. "Eva? Your mother?"

Trey nodded toward the window. The first rays of a rising sun were just beginning to paint the far horizon a pale gold. "Eva's sleeping. Vanessa is gone." When he saw his father struggle to sit up straighter, he replaced the pillow Sullivan tossed at the dog. He was still bending over the man when he felt a tug on the medallion that escaped his open shirt front.

"What happened?" Sullivan held the misshapen coin in his palm; releasing it when his son straightened up.

Trey hesitated before answering, taking the time to roll himself a cigarette. He lit up before he spoke, the words coming with a stream of blue smoke. "Bridger." He used one hand to unfasten the last two buttons on his shirt, displaying the white scar where the coin had lain against his bare chest. He could still feel Eva's hands, the tenderness she displayed when tending his wounds. "Hot poker." He laughed, sardonically. "A hundred thousand up in smoke!"

"Win some, lose some," Sullivan observed. "I suppose that's my tobacco, too?" he asked.

Absently, Trey nodded his head. He surrendered the remainder of his smoke, and began to build another. Down the hallway, he heard the clatter of a stove grate, and the sound of water being pumped into a porcelain pot. "Eva," he breathed.

Sullivan threw back the blankets and swung his legs over the edge of the mattress in an attempt to sit up on the side of the bed. He made it, but changed his mind about trying to stand up. "Ask her to come back here, son." The next word came a littler harder. "Please." He raised his hand. "Tell Cade I'll talk to him later."

Trey nodded. Knowing the woman would scold him, he put out his cigarette, and then took his father's. He winced, grinding them both out between his fingers, and stuffed the dead butts into his shirt pocket just as he entered the kitchen. Sharing the early morning chores, Eva and Cade Devereau were both at the table. They seemed surprised to see him. "He's awake," he announced.

Eva didn't need to hear anything else. She rushed past Trey on winged feet, her face radiant with the first real smile he'd seen since the shooting.

In her wake, Trey heard Devereau's whispered, *"Remercier Dieu."*

"The old man said he'd talk to you later," Trey's tone was cavalier, bordering on the sarcastic. When saw the look on Devereau's face, he rephrased the sentence in a manner he knew would be more to the man's liking. "My father said he would be talking to you later."

Devereau's smile was slow in coming, but it was there. "We'll *all* be talking later," he said. "And I wager you'll be doing a fair amount of listening."

Tired of the sparring, Trey surrendered. *For now.* "Yes, sir," he agreed. He nodded toward the kitchen door. "Chores," he said, excusing himself and escaping the confines of a room that had suddenly become too small.

Out the door and down the stairs, he kicked a day-old horse apple in front of him as he made his way to the barn. Trey looked forward to listening; to hearing more about the mysterious horde of contraband cataloged in the documents he and Devereau had been decoding. Centuries of treasure collected by the Mother Church, all the way back to Rome and beyond. *And for what? Some mythical King and Queen, Emperor and Empress; loyal to the Pope, sitting on a non-existent throne in the Americas?*

He was whistling now. Like his old man said, *Win some, lose some.*

Next go-round, he intended to win.

About the Author

I'm Kit Prate. I grew up in a small town in the Midwest; a great place where people never locked their doors and where the neighbors watched out for each other and all the children. Consequently, we had to work very hard to get into mischief without getting caught.

In my case, it was pretty easy. I was a tomboy. I fished, I hiked; I explored acres of open fields, carrying my own Red Ryder BB Gun. My real playground was the stockyards.

It was a wonderful world. Horses, cattle; real cowboys who tended the livestock and who allowed me and my best friend—within reason—free run of the barns and the corrals.

You can learn a lot from cowboys. How to roll a cigarette, how to fashion a proper hangman's noose, how to ride bareback at a full run, and how to tuck and roll when you fall off. (And you do fall off.) You also learn to be respectful to your betters; to say *yes, ma'am,* and *yes, sir.* Oh. And to never get your thumb caught when you dally a rope.

Of course, there were some drawbacks. Until I started school, I actually thought the proper name for bovines was *goddamnmiserablesonsonsofbitches*; all one word.

And so began a life-long love affair with all things cowboy. History, fiction; great movies without computer enhanced special effects; in other words, open country.

Years later, when I was working as a subcontractor for the Bureau of Indian Affairs, I had the opportunity to rekindle that love. There was nothing better than a weekend on horseback riding through places like Monument Valley, the hill country in Texas, the deserts in Arizona, the vastness of the Sioux reservation; or the same country where Billy the Kid rode, and ultimately died.

I don't write history. I write western fiction; what could have been. Stories of strong men and women who survived the best and the worst the West had to offer.

All in all; it has been a great life. Especially with four kids tossed into the mix. Every day is a gift, and a surprise.

Visit me at: http://kitprate.blogspot.com/

If you enjoyed this story from Kit Prate, please try:

westerntrailblazer.yolasite.com/online-store.php